'Lucky, lucky.' Deevers hissed the words through his teeth as the window itself slid up. Some people were mad, Deevers reckoned. They deserved everything they got. Not that he was a thief. He didn't want anything that Martin Ashford had in this poky flat. What he wanted were the things the guy had in his head: his peace of mind, the people he cared about and the hopes he had for the future.

He slipped off his shoes and left them on the sill. No point in being obvious. He might leave a little present for Martin, something to cause him anxiety maybe, but nothing that would advertise the presence of the invisible man who was turning the pages of Martin's life.

Martin was the kind of guy who'd keep in touch with his mother. Probably gave her a call once a week, went up for a meal on Sundays. Deevers went to the tiny hall where the phone stood next to a local directory. There was only one Mrs Ashford so that must be her. He noted down the address and number on the message pad by the phone and tore off the sheet. On the next sheet he drew an X, digging the pencil into the paper. That would start Martin worrying. Where had it come from, had he done it himself? Maybe he'd think he was going mad. Or maybe he'd reckon someone was going to X him out . . .

CASUALTY

ONE DAY
AT A TIME

Mike Walker

*From the television series created by
Jeremy Brock and Paul Unwin*

WARNER BOOKS

A *Warner* Book

First published in Great Britain in 1994 by Warner Books

Copyright © Mike Walker 1994
Television Format and Series concept
copyright © Jeremy Brock and Paul Unwin 1985

A CIP catalogue record for this book
is available from the British Library.

ISBN 0 7515 0665 6

Typeset by M Rules
Printed and bound in Great Britain by
Clays Ltd, St. Ives plc

Warner Books
A Division of
Little, Brown and Company (UK) Limited
Brettenham House
Lancaster Place
London WC2 7EN

1

The operating theatre was silent except for the regular rasp of the ventilator and the electronic bleep of the heart monitor. The anaesthetist nodded: 'OK, we've got him, blood pressure and pulse are stable.'

There had been a momentary fluctuation and the operation had paused. Now they were back on course. You could almost hear the surgical team's collective sigh of relief.

Ash moved forward, between the hunched figure of the surgeon and the theatre sister. He reminded himself: it was a person on the table, a patient, someone who relied upon them utterly. He shook his head, trying to get rid of the tiredness. He was asleep on his feet. He should have been off duty hours ago and yet, due to staff shortages, he was still working.

The flesh had already been cut and peeled back to reveal the abdomen. The patient's aorta, normally an inch in diameter, had swollen until it was as big as Ash's arm. The danger was that the stretched artery would burst and cause serious internal bleeding. Had the swelling, the aneurism as it was known, been small, like a balloon, the surgeon would have tied it off at the neck and removed it with ease. In this case, however, the bulge extended along the artery and it would be necessary to clamp each end and insert a tube of synthetic fabric, which would knit into the flesh far better than plastic.

'Mr Ashford, I'm talking to you.' The surgeon's voice was sharp, angry. 'If you can't keep awake . . .'

'Sorry . . .' He shook his head. What had he been asked for? The surgeon barked out the request again: 'Clamps, if it's not too much trouble?'

The sarcasm hurt. He knew he had to succeed, show he could cope with the pressure, or he was finished at Holby. His career would be over for good.

'Scalpel . . .' The nurse passed it, slapping it confidently down into the surgeon's waiting hand.

'Thank you, nurse. Now, I'm going to clear a little ground here so we can see what we have to deal with. Observe the enlargement . . .' The scalpel blade paused, pointed, then cut into the tissue, around the artery. 'We're going to cut here,' the surgeon went on, talking himself through the procedures as much as instructing his junior, 'and insert a tube . . .'

The voice droned on against the steady pump of the ventilator. It was a hypnotic sound and once again Ash found himself slipping away, swaying on his feet. How long was it since he'd been off duty?

'Are you ready with those clamps?'

His face was slick with sweat, his throat dry. Why was he here, he wasn't trained for this . . .

'Mr Ashford!'

'Yes, whenever you want . . .'

'Now, please.'

His hand darted forward, twisting the first clamp to apply it above the swelling. Sweat dripped down his forehead into his eyes. He squinted, trying to position himself, missing, grazing the incredibly delicate tissue.

'Oh my God . . .!'

The swollen artery had ruptured, spurting blood in

every direction. The monitor went wild, the beeps becoming a screech.

'Suction!' the surgeon bellowed, 'get me suction in the abdomen . . .'

The nurse ran for the pump. The anaesthetist murmured: 'BP falling dangerously. We're going to lose him if we can't compensate.'

'Stop the bleeding, Mr Ashford.' The surgeon was glaring at him, eyes red above his spattered mask, 'or the patient is dead on the table.'

He looked at the opened abdomen, at the lake of blood in there. What should he do? He didn't know. He shouldn't be here. The patient was going to die because he didn't know what to do.

'Mr Ashford, we don't have much time!'

He reached in and tried to press the aorta closed above the tear but his fingers kept slipping. He couldn't hold on. He looked around desperately for someone, anyone, to help. The alarm bell began to shrill, boring into his head like a saw. He tasted the acid of panic in his throat and knew that the situation was out of his control.

Ray Deevers swung the wheel and turned sharp left into the crematorium car park. It was early, not six thirty yet, but he didn't sleep much now, not since she'd died. No, he corrected himself as he slammed the car door, not since they'd killed her.

He was a short man but well muscled, in his late twenties, hair cut close over his scalp, his eyes moving restlessly, as if looking for someone who might disagree with him or get in his way. And if they did, then it would be their bad luck and his pleasure to walk all over them. Because Ray was a hard man, even his friends said that, and as to what his enemies thought, if they thought anything at all after he'd finished with them, he didn't care.

3

He walked quickly up towards the crematorium itself and stood for a few moments in front of the ornate wooden doors. He remembered the scene only a week before when they'd buried Sherry: the undertaker's men in their long coats and black gloves, the priest ushering them in, Ray right at the front with no one else daring or caring to sit near him. He'd felt their eyes on his back during the service, angry accusing eyes but frightened too, not daring to risk his anger because there wasn't one of them who hadn't seen him at some time or another administering punishment.

'Let us remember those who are left behind,' the priest had droned, 'especially Sherry's dear husband Raymond.'

He'd wanted to get up and smash the priest in his fat self-satisfied face. What did he know, what did any of them know?

Afterwards, when Sherry's coffin had gone sliding on its squeaking rollers into the furnace, he'd left, not waiting to shake hands with the other mourners, knowing that they would not shake hands with him. Well, sod them all.

He'd come out here, into what they called the garden of remembrance, which was the nearest thing that Sherry had now to a resting place. Stupid bitch that she was. Oh, she'd kept her mouth shut, he'd give her that. She'd been loyal, even after the hot fat, when they'd taken her down to Casualty. It had been her fault, anyway. Always yapping out of turn. She knew well enough what it would mean if she hadn't got his supper ready when he got home. He put in good time, hard time, working for the house, working for both of them.

He looked up at the morning sky. It was bright blue with the white lines of a vapour trail drifting out behind a tiny jet. That's where he should be, up there, heading out, not stuck down here in this stupid town where a

4

man couldn't get the respect that was due to him.

He lit a fag and blew the smoke out in a savage stream, remembering how it had been that night when he'd got back, his head pounding with one of his headaches, so tight he felt it would explode any moment. Oh yes, she'd been looking for trouble, just like always. And don't tell him the bitch didn't ask for it, coming out with some lie about the car breaking down and her being late because of it. He knew what she was like. Probably with some other guy she'd been going with behind his back.

He could still feel how the rage had exploded inside him and how, suddenly, he'd known exactly what he had to do. And there on the stove had been the fat heating for his chips, and her stupid pleading face. It had all been so clear and obvious.

Then later, at the hospital, he'd begged them: 'Save her, save my Sherry. She means everything to me.' Because she'd forgive him, just like she always did. He knew that this time it would have come out all right. There would have been no more headaches, no more disobedience, no more punishment. It would have been perfect.

And they'd let her die.

And then tried to fob him off with their stupid lies: 'I'm so sorry, it was her heart, it just gave out. We could have coped with the burns but the shock was too much.' And their sympathy. It had made him want to puke. 'Would you like a cup of tea, Mr Deevers? Is there someone we could call?' Didn't they know who he was? Ray Deevers, a hard man in a hard world who'd never asked a favour nor taken one from anyone?

The lies and the sympathy and then the looks and the questions. 'How exactly did you say it happened? Are you sure about that, Mr Deevers?' The doctors had gone on and on about how unlikely the burns were, how they

5

were in the wrong places for the accident he'd described. As if they knew something. Their eyes had accused him, and one most of all. The black guy.

He'd been trying to get Sherry to talk, Deevers was sure of it, from the way he'd gone on and on, like a dog yapping until Deevers' head had begun to throb again. He was the one, bothering Sherry with his questions, pushing her too far, not allowing her the time she needed to heal. He was the one who would pay. Oh yes.

A smile crossed Ray Deevers' face; the smile of a man who suddenly knew the way forward. The black guy's name? It wouldn't take much to find out. He already knew where he lived. He'd follow him into the hospital this morning and ask someone. And once he knew, he could start to make the bastard pay for what had happened.

He dropped the fag and ground it under his heel. Time was getting on, if he wanted to catch the guy when he left for work he'd better move. As he went back down the slope towards the car, the memory of something he'd once heard had swum into his head. It was a saying: Revenge is a dish best eaten cold.

Ash reached out and flicked off the alarm. He didn't feel like he'd slept at all. His mouth was dry, the dream had been so real he could still taste the anxiety. He knew it was not uncommon for nurses to have nightmares in which they found they could not cope, but that didn't make them any easier to bear.

Groaning, he kicked off the duvet and stumbled through to the kitchen, filling and turning on the kettle before going into the tiny bathroom.

Medication first. His mum had drilled that into him during his childhood until it had become second nature. He could no more forget now than he could forget to breathe. He examined his face in the mirror. He didn't look good. Not even for this time of the morning did he look good. He reached through the plastic shower curtain and flicked on the water.

He'd put the shower in himself and he reckoned it was the best investment he'd ever made. Hot first, to bring you slowly out of sleep and then a quick twist of the controls for a few invigorating moments of icy cold water to wake you up fully. Only this morning it didn't seem to work. Pulling on his robe he still felt caught up in his dream. Even the sun that flooded through when he opened the curtains didn't make any difference. He just had too much on his plate right now. Too many decisions.

The kettle was boiling. He unplugged it and filled his mug. The smell of instant coffee suffused the kitchen. He wondered if a beautiful older woman might come and knock at his door to ask if she could borrow a spoonful or two. No such luck; maybe he used the wrong brand.

Letters thumped on the mat. Postmen, he thought, the only people who get up earlier than nurses. Except milkmen, of course. He grinned to himself but the smile went sour on his face when he saw the familiar windowed letter from the bank peeping out from under the *Nursing Times* and a couple of free offers which he just wouldn't be able to refuse.

He slipped a slice of wholemeal bread into the toaster and opened the letter. 'Dear Mr Ashford, I regret to inform you that since the standing order . . . etc. etc., overdrawn . . . more funds . . . can't pay your mortgage for this month . . . very sorry but must charge you £27 for this letter . . .'

The toast popped up. Somehow he didn't feel hungry any more. Just sick and angry. How could they bounce his mortgage payment and then charge him for the privilege? He'd do better borrowing from the Mafia – at least they didn't pretend to be nice. Still, he'd have to find this month's payment from somewhere and that made just one more problem.

He put low-fat spread on his toast, regretting that he didn't have any nice unhealthy butter to spread on good and thick.

Maybe he could borrow something from his cousin Benny. He always seemed to have his finances under control, though God knew what he actually did for a living. Import-export, he used to say, leaning out the window of his new Jaguar. Well, great for Benny, but right now, Ash felt that his own life was running away with him.

He slapped marmalade on the toast and began to chew. Too many problems. His mum for a start, and that stomach pain she'd been having for a couple of months now. Feeling full after even a small meal, too much wind, but of course she'd never admit to that. And the pain. She said it was nothing but he'd seen her wince and turn away to hide her face. And she wouldn't go to the doctor, in spite of everything he said. 'Mum, if it's nothing, then great, let's get the anxiety out of the way.'

She'd leaned forward, holding his wrist with her hand, just as she used to when he was a kid and ready to run off at any time. 'And what if it isn't, Martin?' Her accent, when she was worried, always become more Barbadian, reminding him once again of his childhood and the island stories she'd told him, of magic and pirates and duppies.

'Look, Mum, if it isn't, then the sooner you do something about it the better. Can't you see that?'

'That's what they said about your father.' She'd looked around her flat, crowded with mementos and photos of Ash's dad. 'They said it was just a little operation but once they got him in that hospital, why, they never did let him out again except to pass away.'

So that was that, she wouldn't go. But the pains were still there and he had a horror that one day the paramedics would arrive with her in Casualty and then it really would be too late.

Marmalade had dripped off his toast, all down his sleeve. Well, he needed to visit the launderette soon, he was running out of shirts. He grabbed the washing-up cloth and scrubbed at the cuff. The doorbell rang and, cloth in hand, he wandered through to answer it.

'What happened to you? Been awake playing poker all night?' Charlie grinned and caught the cloth Ash flung at him. 'Come on, we're going to be late.'

'Yeah. Sorry, Charlie, I forget. I mean I still thought I had a car that worked, a mortgage that was being paid, a job I could handle. Coffee?'

Charlie flicked a look at his watch. 'OK, a quick one. I'll do it, you change your shirt.'

'I don't think I've got a clean one. I told you my life is falling apart.'

'Missing Nikki?' Charlie scooped a couple of spoonfuls of instant into the mug. He liked his coffee strong. Ash had once drunk from his cup by mistake and had almost spat it straight out.

'Well . . . I guess you can't finish something like that, in that way, without a lot of pain all round. I mean the whole thing about the baby.'

Ash had lived with Nikki for over a year. They'd both felt that maybe there was something long-lasting about this relationship, perhaps even the possibility of marriage. Then Nikki had got pregnant. No, that was unfair, it made it sound as if it were her fault when nobody was to blame. To begin with, Ash hadn't been over the moon about the situation. He didn't feel he was ready to settle down. But even so, when Nikki had announced she'd had an abortion, he'd taken it badly. He believed in any woman's right to control her own body and terminate a pregnancy if she wanted to, but when it was his child he felt he should have been consulted. Nikki hadn't seen it that way and they'd parted.

'You're talking like it's still alive,' Charlie said.

'I don't know what I feel. It's not even the big things that hurt so much any more.' He went into the bedroom and found a thick winter shirt, the only one clean. Well, it would have to do. As he pulled it on he continued: 'It's just having somebody around so you can say what a tough day you had or let's go out for a pizza. I mean, we used to wonder, when we were at a restaurant, what it was like for those weird people who sat alone reading a book while they ate. Well, now that's me. Mr Lonely.'

He did the buttons up, finding one missing. Charlie threw him his coat. 'Come on, then, Mr Lonely, there's a department full of friends waiting for you out there.'

Ash grinned. 'Oh sure, Mark Calder for a start. He's really president of my fan club.'

'I think Mark just resents your union work. He thinks it's standing in the way of turning Casualty into a totally efficient unit which deals only with statistics. You got everything?'

On the hall table lay the book he'd promised to get for Lisa. He grabbed it and shoved it in his pocket. 'Ready when you are, Charlie.'

Outside it was a fine morning. Charlie had parked just behind Ash's old VW. Ash checked it over quickly. Everything still seemed to be in place and he breathed a small sigh of relief. There had been an increase in vandalism and robberies in the area recently. A flat in his block had been turned over and he'd seen the state it had been left in by the thieves. He'd fitted double locks on his own door soon afterwards and bought a new alarm system for the car. Not that he thought it would make much difference to anyone who seriously wanted to steal the thing. He almost wished someone would. It would be cheaper than getting it repaired.

He climbed in beside Charlie and squinted as they pulled out and the sun glared down on to the wind-screen.

'Going to be another hot one,' Charlie said. They'd had almost a month of unbroken sunshine and everyone was beginning to feel the tension of the heat. They certainly were in Casualty. The rate of fight injuries had almost doubled. Charlie, who could remember way back to the early days, was getting seriously worried about riots. They had happened before in Holby and the cost then, in injury and property, had been terrible. No one wanted to see it happen again.

On the inner distribution road the traffic was still light and Charlie was able to speed up so they could get some breeze. He glanced briefly across and said, 'So, have you come to any conclusion yet? Are you going for promotion?'

Ash thought about the letter from the bank lying there in his flat. 'I could use the extra money, Charlie. Only . . . where would I go?'

'Up,' Charlie laughed. 'That's generally what happens with promotion, isn't it?'

'You know what I mean. I like the department. I like what we do there, I think it makes a difference. It's front-line medicine. The problem is, there's only room for one clinical nurse manager in A and E and you're not think-ing of going, are you?'

'I like it here too. But why not move?. Don't get me wrong, Ash, I don't want to lose you, but you've got a lot to offer, a lot of talent and I know you're ambitious.'

'That's my mum's doing,' he laughed. 'After my dad died she was always pushing us to do better because there was no one except ourselves we could rely on.'

'Well, you should think about it seriously. Why not

move, if that's where the jobs are? What's keeping you here in Holby anyway?'

He thought about it. 'Nothing, I suppose. Ah, I dunno. I'll have to wait and see.'

'Hey, what the hell—' Charlie wrestled with the wheel as a car cut them up, almost forcing them into the concrete road divide. Ash had a fleeting impression of an angry staring face before the car, an old Vauxhall with a pair of furry dice in the rear window, slipped away into the traffic flow.

'Bloody lunatic,' Charlie muttered. 'He could see I was turning.'

'Well maybe we'll be meeting him again before too long – on a stretcher,' Ash said.

'He'll just be another RTA.'

Holby General came into sight, its bulk towering above the smaller buildings around it. Charlie leaned out and, as usual, found he was just too far away from the auto-barrier to slide his card through. He backed up a couple of feet. A car behind honked and they saw Mike Barratt grinning and making hurry up motions. Frankie zipped past them on his bike. 'Mornin' Charlie, mornin' Ash. Get a bike next time, you'll be fitter and faster!'

'Maybe you should take it into the department, Frankie,' Ash called back, 'so you could be a bit faster in there.'

'Cheeky bugger,' Frankie laughed and, standing on the pedals, powered away.

Charlie found a parking space and they got out. The cool of the early morning was beginning to dissipate. The sun was now heating the tarmac and beating back into their faces.

'You coming straight through?' Charlie asked.

'No. I have to deliver this.' He held up the book, a science fiction novel. 'I told Lisa I'd get it for her.'

Charlie reached out and took his shoulder, holding

him back. 'Look, I don't want to tell you how to do your job but . . . What I'm trying to say . . .'

Ash held up a hand, halting him. 'You're trying to say I'll get hurt if I identify too much with patients. Right?'

'Yeah. It happens.'

'So whoever said we shouldn't get hurt in this job, Charlie?'

There was no answer to that. Charlie shrugged and walked away. Around the car park others were arriving. Adele Beckford, Karen, Mie, a couple of agency nurses, Josh, also cycling. Another day, another shift.

2

Deevers sat watching the car park. He saw the tall black man get out of the car and stand for a moment talking to the other one, the lousy driver. He laughed. It had almost been too easy and too soon. A quick flip and they'd have been wreckage. But the black guy wouldn't have known who had done it and Deevers wanted that, to see it in his face as he went down. He needed to be able to say why and what it was for.

Anyway, he was beginning to enjoy the game. There was something satisfying about the way he was following the guy, prowling round his whole life, without anyone knowing he was there. It was like being the invisible man.

He climbed out and slammed the door behind him, not bothering to lock it. It didn't occur to him that anyone would dare to steal his wheels. Across the park a Japanese girl was getting out of her car, a Mazda, of course. He remembered her from before. She was some kind of receptionist, something like that. Deevers didn't like Japs. But he reminded himself that right now he had a purpose, he was on a mission and everything else would have to wait in line .

He stepped out in front of the girl as she came past the barrier. She caught her breath and looked up worriedly, her hand snaking into her bag, probably for her rape alarm. He almost laughed. Another stupid bitch. As if anyone would come if they heard a rape alarm.

'Excuse me . . .' He stepped back a couple of paces. No point in frightening her.

'Yes?'

'I wonder if you could help me?'

'Uh, I don't know. If you have an enquiry you should ask inside.'

'Yes, I know. It's just . . . well you see, a little while ago my wife was in Casualty and . . .' He saw her eyes widen in recognition.

'Of course, I remember now. It was . . . so sad.'

'Yes, so sad. But, you see, I wanted to write to one of the people who helped. Sort of to say thank you for what they did and I don't know, I'm not quite sure of the name. The black guy who just went through over there?'

'Oh yes,' She smiled, relaxed now. 'Martin Ashford. Ash. He's the senior charge nurse in Casualty.'

'Of course. Martin Ashford. Thank you so much.' Bowing slightly he backed off and let her go past, watching her as she walked away, a sardonic smile playing across his face.

'Martin Ashford. Martin Ashford.' He said the name a couple of times, getting used to it, fitting himself around it, making it familiar. After all, he and Martin were going to be very close before long.

The children's cancer ward was something between playschool and a modern laboratory, with hi-tech equipment and cuddly toys, picture books and feed lines occupying the same space. There were parents and nurses, hospital teachers and, of course, the patients.

Ash hurried through the public ward, nodding to a few of the kids with whom he'd built up a relationship during the weeks he'd been coming up here. They were

15

a pretty good lot on the whole, though there were often behaviour problems on the ward. Parents couldn't be blamed if they gave their children anything they wanted rather than saying wait for your birthday or for Christmas, because some of these kids wouldn't be around by then. However, it did lead to a lot of spoiling and the kids could become demanding, giving way to tantrums when they didn't get what they wanted. Lisa had never been like that.

Ash had met her first in Casualty, when she'd been brought in one night by her mother with severe cramps and stomach pains. She'd been having headaches for some time but her mother had assumed, as she was twelve, that her periods were starting and had given her an aspirin and told her to get on with her life.

Once in the department she'd developed breathing problems and it was soon clear that something serious was wrong. The mother had been distraught, guilty, blaming herself and so wrapped up in her own misery that Lisa had been virtually left alone. Ash, himself feeling cut up over parting with Nikki and the thought of the child that might have lived, had been shocked out of his self-pity by Lisa's courage when it became clear she wasn't going home but was going into children's ward for tests.

He'd kept in touch, going up to see her at odd times, and had been there when the tests confirmed everyone's worst fears: she had acute lymphoblastic leukaemia. The specialists had been able to explain that cure rates had risen dramatically in recent years, often going as high as sixty or seventy per cent, but the mother – there was no father and no family back-up – had been unable to cope. She sat and wept or tried to apologise, she was worse than useless. Between them, Ash and Angela Read, the Macmillan nurse, had taken over as Lisa's family.

Right now she was undergoing yet another treatment and was in isolation. Ash could only peer through her window and talk on the intercom. He thumbed the button and saw the tiny, wasted figure, no bigger than a seven-year-old, turn and grin at him through the forest of lines around her. On her head she wore a knitted Jamaican cap Ash had picked up for her to help with the baldness. It looked absurdly big now and kept slipping down over one eye as she thumbed her button.

'What's up, Doc?'

'Somebody's hunting wabbits,' he answered, and aimed a finger at her. 'I bought you this,' He held up the book, *The Crystal Singer* by Anne McCaffrey.

'Oh great, brilliant, Doc. Just tell me it's not too long so I'll be here to finish it. Her humour was black but that was just her way of coming to terms with the situation.

'Hey, Lisa, there's another fifteen in the series. You have to get through them all.'

'You better be right, Doc, or you'll never get those exams.'

'I'll never get them anyway.'

'Hey, you know I believe in you, Doc. You gotta go back to school, learn all that stuff.'

Lisa had told him once that she'd wanted to become either a science fiction writer or a doctor. She was certainly bright enough to be either and took a constant interest in what was going on around her, sometimes to the considerable embarrassment of the nurses when they tried to fob her off with a less than honest answer. But over the last few weeks, as her condition had deteriorated, she'd begun to weave a fantasy in which Ash somehow took over and became the doctor she would have been. It was a heartbreaking game because, Ash thought, it meant she was beginning to lose any hope of recovery.

'So how're you feeling today?'

'Well, I got a new joke.'

'That bad, huh?'

'Wait for it, Doc.' Her eyes glittered with mirth as she gathered her energy. 'OK, here it comes but you gotta be fast to catch it as it passes. What is brown and sticky?'

'Brown and . . .?'

'Well?'

'I don't know. I hope I don't know.'

'OK, stupid, it's a stick. That's brown and sticky.'

He laughed, he couldn't help it. He usually did at her jokes.

'Where do you get these things from, Lisa?'

'Ah, we must have our secrets, us medical types.' She smiled. Her face was grey now, from the effort of talking. The eyelids began to creep down and her breathing became regular.

'Enjoy the book,' he said. 'Signing off.'

'Signing off.' Her voice was a whisper, a tiny echo of his. He turned from the window.

'Hi.'

It was Angela, the Macmillan nurse. She had the sort of calm about her that Adele seemed to radiate. God knew where it came from since she was always giving other people hope and help to face the unfaceable.

He handed her the book and they walked out of the department together. 'She's looking thinner.'

'Well you know how it is, Ash. Chemotherapy is tough on anyone, children especially. It's like the First World War: hit the body with everything we've got and hope the cancers are destroyed while there's something left of the patient.'

'It sounds pretty crude when you put it like that.'

'It is pretty crude. But we keep trying and we're getting better all the time.'

'What about Lisa ?'

'She's in there and she's still fighting. And her friends are still fighting with her.'

'You'd better believe it,' he said.

They were passing the canteen and Angela asked if he wanted a coffee.

'No way. I haven't clocked on shift yet. I'm way behind. I'll catch you later, maybe.'

'That's what they all say.'

'We must watch the same TV shows.'

'Ash, where the hell have you bin?' It was Karen Goodliffe, bearing down on him, white coat flying.

'I see what you mean about being late.' Angela ducked into the canteen. Ash went to follow her but Karen grabbed him.

'No you don't, Mr Ashford. Mark bloody Calder has been turning the department upside down lookin' for you. So you just get your personage up to his office and maybe the rest of us can do what we're paid for.'

'Do the job for which we are paid.'

Karen always went wild when he corrected her grammar but he didn't give her time to explode, twisting out of her grasp and running off down the corridor.

Ted Bryant eased his belt out another notch. He was definitely putting it on a bit these days, but then why not? The business was doing well in spite of the recession and now he was getting older, not that fifty was exactly old, but it wasn't young, he didn't have to keep up with anyone. They kept up with him. Still, Brenda wouldn't be pleased. She was always on at him to cut down the cholesterol, eat more fibre, drink less.

He pulled on his jacket and hurried downstairs into the kitchen where his boiled egg was waiting with two small triangles of toast. He would've preferred a good fry-up like he'd had in the old days but those were long gone now.

'Come on, love, your egg'll be getting cold and you know you don't like a cold egg.'

'Well, not bitter. But this is fine.' It was, too. Brenda could cook an egg to the second.

He picked up the *Telegraph* and gave the front page a quick scan before turning to the cricket. Yorkshire were doing better. Well, thank God they'd had the sense to give up that daft notion of no overseas players. Richie Richardson was scoring up a storm for them, and good job, too.

'See, what did I tell you.' He showed the scores to Brenda, who nodded. She'd never taken to the game, which was odd, her being a Yorkshire lass. He remembered how once she'd actually gone shopping rather than watch Geoff Boycott reach another century. Daft. But then who could understand women? Not him, not even after thirty years.

'Are you going to finish that egg, Ted, or shall I throw it away?'

'Waste not, want not.'

'Well, then eat the thing, man, and stop mooning around over that silly game.'

A couple of scoops finished it and he downed the tiny triangles of toast in another few mouthfuls. He drank his tea and had another cup.

'I'll run you to the station, shall I?' Brenda asked.

'If you would, love.'

Back home in Yorkshire the office had been right next to the house but since moving down to Holby, and moving up in the world, he was no longer able to walk to work but went into town by train instead. He'd given up driving since the trouble with his eyes had started, but after seeing the optician a couple of times and getting the new ointment, things had begun to improve. He'd finished the first of the bottles the day before and Brenda had picked up another. She was always the one who remembered. If she hadn't reminded him, ninety-nine days out of a hundred he would have left the house without taking the drops.

'Drops, love, before you go,' she said.

'I'd be lost without you, I reckon.'

The bottle was in its usual place in the cabinet and while Brenda got the Rover out the garage he administered the three drops per eye, then blinked away the blurriness, wiped his cheeks (don't want the staff reckoning the boss has been weeping!) and went out to the front of the house.

It was another glorious morning, though to tell the truth Ted could have done with a decent bit of Yorkshire rain for the garden. They'd had a hosepipe ban for a couple of months and the situation was getting desperate. Underfoot the grass was brown and dry and the soil in the flowerbeds looked like something out of the desert.

As usual traffic was heavy. Once Ted would have gone in early, been at his desk by half past six, but now he never got in until nine; after all, the boss had to have some privileges. He tried to read the number plate of the car in front. It was a test he'd been setting himself to measure the improvement in his sight but this morning he couldn't see more than a blur. He rubbed his eyes.

'All right, love? No trouble?'

'I'm fine, I'm fine. Just a bit of soreness, that's all.'

They pulled up in the station forecourt and Ted got out. 'Right, I'll see you at six, love. Give you a call if I'm going to be late.'

Brenda leaned out of her window. 'Ted—' But he was gone, swept away by a crowd of commuters released from a bus, all rushing for their trains. She sighed. They hadn't missed a goodbye kiss in the morning for years, not for years, and now there he was rushing off. She shrugged and pulled away from the stop, sliding back into the endless flow of traffic.

3

'I won't, I bloody won't. I fought for my country and I won't do it, not for no bugger!'

A trolley clattered and skidded across the floor, spilling its mattress and blankets. Charlie was almost emasculated as it slammed into his groin when he hurried from his office to see what the noise was. Ash, coming through from Reception, arrived at the same time.

Sara Eeles, the new Project 2000 nurse, and Dr Goodliffe were being dragged bodily out of a cubicle by a ragged giant of a man.

'Scrubbs!' Charlie gazed up at the ceiling in exasperation, as if hoping it might fall down and get rid of this problem.

'Well, Karen, looks like you can't keep from grabbing people today,' Ash laughed.

'Will you stop making stupid comments and do something!' Karen fumed as she was dragged a few more paces by the roaring giant.

Sara, who had hold of his upper arm, was trying to talk calmly to reassure the patient, just as she'd been taught. As was often the case she was finding life in Casualty just didn't conform to the situations outlined in her textbooks. 'Now, please, Mr Scrubbs, there's nothing to be worried aboooouuuut!' Her calm tone became a shriek as her feet left the ground.

Mike Barratt popped his head out of another cubicle. 'Can we try and keep the noise down please, Karen? This *is* a hospital.'

For a moment the only sound was the grinding of Karen's teeth, then Scrubbs roared again. 'I have got my rights. I am not a number, I am a man. I'll twist your bloody heads off if any one of you comes near me.'

'Ah, right.' Mike murmured, 'Well, it's all yours then.' And he slipped back behind the curtains.

Ash and Charlie advanced. They knew all about Sergeant-Major Scrubbs. You could almost say they were old friends. As soon as the giant saw them, and saw the frown on Charlie's face, he grinned sheepishly and put Karen and Sara back on their feet.

'Well, what's it all about, then, Scrubbsy?'

'Aw, Mr Fairhead, sir. Mr Ashford, can't you tell these ladies here—'

'This doctor and this nurse,' Karen cut in angrily.

'That it just ain't on. No way. I mean a barracks, fine. I fought for my country in Korea. The Thirty-seventh Parallel, the hell of Hill Twenty-seven.'

'It was Hill Twenty-three last time, Scrubbsy,' Ash said dryly. 'Come on, cut the waffle, just tell us what the problem is. We've got a department to run here.'

Karen flushed at the reminder of her earlier remark. She said: 'He was brought in by the police. Drunk and incapable, except he managed to break a couple of ribs trying to stuff a young constable down a drain. We've bound him up but I'd really like to have a few tests done. If you look at the colour of his hands, the general skin condition . . .' Without being too obvious, she was pointing out the symptoms of kidney damage. 'I think there might also be the possibility of a duodenal ulcer which certainly has to be looked at.'

Left to themselves, Ash or Charlie might well have

23

discharged Scrubbs. He was a long-time drinker, he'd been around the town for years, as long as Charlie could remember and had abused just about every substance known to man, and quite a few unknowns, too. Once he must have been quite a figure, a real sergeant-major if his stories were true, but now the ability of even his massive frame to bear punishment was reaching a limit. To put it plainly, which of course neither of them ever would, the man was dying, and it seemed the kindest thing to let him go in his own way and in his own time.

Unfortunately, now that Karen was involved, the nod-and-wink approach to medicine was no longer practical. Procedures had to be followed. Procedures which depended to great degree on patient co-operation.

Ash took hold of Scrubbs' wrist and began to massage it gently with his thumb. 'Now, Sar'nt-Major, you heard what Dr Goodliffe said. She'd like you to take a few tests. OK? It just means a couple of days on the wards.'

The hand jerked from his grasp and Scrubbs' wild-eyed face was thrust into his. He opened his mouth and Ash flinched as the breath from hell washed over him. 'Wimmin!' Scrubbs bellowed. 'It's all them bloody wimmin!'

'What are you talking about?'

'He doesn't want to go into the mixed ward,' Karen said, referring to the new Holby policy of housing men and women in the same wards.

'I do not. And what's more, I won't. You've got no right. I want a decent barracks or nuthin'.'

'Have we got a place on an all-male ward?' Charlie asked.

'I called the reg. Nothing.'

'Well, look, Scrubbsy. It's up to you. I mean, you're an old soldier, aren't you ?'

Scrubbs swayed upright to something resembling attention.

'That's correct, sir. Third Lancers. RSM Scrubbs. DSO and . . .' his voice faltered and for just a moment a far-away look came into his eyes, as if he were remembering, then the old wild expression returned. 'King and country. Mud, muck and bullets. Psychological warfare, that's what they done out there beyond the Forty-second Parallel.'

'Then what about obeying the orders of your superior officer, eh? I'll bet you didn't say, "Don't fancy that, sir. Won't do that, sir." '

'Court-martial offence.' Scrubbs was standing to attention, his thumbs in line with where his trouser seams would have been had he been wearing any. 'A soldier must obey his orders.'

'Mixed wards, then. Undergo the tests?' Charlie asked.

'Very good, sir.' He saluted.

Charlie nodded. 'Carry on, Sergeant-Major. Follow the nurse, she'll show you the way.' He nodded at Sara, who set off, rather nervously, Scrubbs marching in her wake.

'That was pretty good,' Karen said. She was impressed, it was clear. So was Ash. Charlie had a way with difficult patients. He never pushed, he let them find their own way to the solution he wanted them to reach. It was a gift in part but it was also the result of a lot of experience and hard work.

'I don't know that I blame him, though,' Charlie said.

'You don't think it's a good idea?' Karen asked.

'Oh, it's a great idea. I can see why they came up with it. It'll look brilliant in the annual report. Holby up to date, another new technique, more efficient, better people management. Except I don't think it works.'

'You're beginning to sound sexist,' Karen said.

'Maybe. But I do know there are things, bodily functions, about which it's a damn sight easier to be

25

comfortable among your own sex. And that goes for women as well as men. People are at their most vulnerable in hospital and I don't feel that's the best time to try experiments that change the way most of them have lived for most of their lives.' He grinned. 'On the other hand, I could be wrong.'

Ash said: 'It has been known.'

'One thing's for certain, though,' Karen said. 'We've all had enough of being messed around.'

'Which reminds me, I haven't seen Mark Calder yet. I expect he's approaching melt-down by now.'

Charlie and Karen both pointed at Reception like disapproving Victorian parents. 'Go, and never darken our department again!'

The Holby train was late. There had been a cancellation due to lack of crew and the 8.32 would be picking up two loads. The platform was crowded and as Ted Bryant hurried down the steps from the bridge his heart sank. The journey was only twenty minutes but this was the last station on the line and by the time the train reached it there would be no room at all. He hated standing, crushed so it was impossible to open his newspaper or think about the problems of the day. He reached the platform and launched himself into the crowd, edging through towards the front. Might as well give himself the best chance.

'Morning, Ted. Not got a chauffeur yet?' John Higgs was a partner in a rival firm.

'Not for me, John, we don't charge those kind of fees. We work for people, not big business.'

'Go on, get out of it. Vultures never go hungry.'

It was a joking remark but there was enough truth in it to give Ted a twinge as he shoved and wriggled on through the crowd of commuters. The solicitors' firm in which he was a partner had done considerable work locally as bankruptcy commissioners, settling up the affairs of those companies and individuals who had been unable to keep their heads above water. It was a necessary job and somebody had to do it, but all the same . . .

'Watch out!' Somebody shoved him, a yuppie (did they still exist?), intent on his mobile phone, snapping out orders. Ted slipped past and found himself on the edge of the platform, just behind the yellow painted line that gave clearance for opening carriage doors.

He looked along the track to see if he could make out the train yet but couldn't seem to focus. He blinked a couple of times and looked again. This time he could hardly see to the end of the platform. It was as if there was a mist in front of his eyes, creeping in, bringing an insistent pain with it. He rubbed his eyes and blinked again but the pain wouldn't go and the mist got thicker until he couldn't even make out his hands in front of his face.

He was going blind.

'Hey, someone, hey, please, can you give me a hand!' His voice was thick with panic. He swung round, feeling people but unable to see them. There was a sound, a rushing storm of sound, and he realised the train was coming in. He felt a moment's horror as the bodies pressed against him, forcing him back towards the rails he couldn't see, and he pushed against them, his arms outstretched, clawing at nothing as he lost his balance.

'He's pissed as a newt,' he heard someone laugh.

'No, I think he's sick,' someone else said, 'Are you OK, mate?'

The noise of the train was huge now, drowning out his reply. His only thought was to get clear of the platform edge. Later he could worry about his eyes. Just get clear. He pushed free, feeling hands grabbing at him

27

and a voice shouting, 'No, hold him, he's trying to kill himself!'

Then there was a sound like someone had just burst the atmosphere, and all the air in the world was rushing out into space: a great dull clap of thunder as he was hit by something unimaginably hard and thrown into an endless black tunnel.

'Come in.' The summons was cold and when Ash let himself through into the office, Mark Calder's expression matched his tone perfectly.

'You're late, Mr Ashford.'

'I had someone to see.'

'Oh, really?'

'A patient.'

'I hope it was. After all, the Hospital Trust does pay your wages so it isn't, perhaps, unreasonable for us to expect a little of the time you can spare from union work.' Mark Calder hated the union. That was putting it mildly. And there was very little about Mark that was mild. He thrived on confrontation. In that, he was about as far away from someone like Charlie as it was possible to be, though Ash sometimes felt there was an uncomfortable similarity between himself and the abrasive group manager.

'My union work is done in my own time, Mark, you know that. Unless I'm representing one of my members at a hearing.' The last time the two had clashed had been over the dismissal of Norma. On that occasion Mark had come out on top, mainly because Norma had always refused to join the union and Ash had only been able to act as an observer. He was still convinced, however, that if Norma had had the strength of the union behind her, she would still have been working at Holby General.

Mark nodded, as if Ash had just confirmed his worst

judgement, and then said: 'But I haven't asked you up here to go over old business.'

Ash wasn't aware that he'd been 'asked' anywhere. As far as he knew it was a straight summons.

Mark went on: 'As you know, the Hospital Trust tries to stay in the forefront of patient awareness and to help us continue in this mode –' sometimes Mark began to sound like a caricature of himself '– the board has decided to conduct a Monitor exercise over the next few days.'

'What exactly is a monitor, Mark, when it's at home?'

There was a tap at the door and Mark smiled, a master of timing. 'Come in,' he called, and stood as a young woman entered the room. 'Ms Lowell, come in. I'm sorry to have kept you but Mr Ashford was held up and . . .' he spread his hands, as if washing them of any blame. To Ash he said: 'Ms Lowell will be conducting the exercise and while she's working in Casualty, I'd like you to act as her liaison.'

Ash nodded dumbly.

'Any questions? I mean surely you must have some objections?'

Normally he would have protested straight away but right now he couldn't think of a thing to say.

The young woman came across the room and extended her hand. Ash managed to croak out: 'Ms Lowell.'

'Please,' her voice was deep and musical, he tried to place her accent – Kenyan perhaps, certainly African – 'Let's not be formal if we've got to work together.' Her handshake was firm, the skin cool to the touch. 'Call me Josette.' She was, quite simply, the most beautiful woman he had ever seen. He felt like a child in her presence, tongue-tied and stupid.

'Uh, may I,' she began, 'have my hand back?'

He realised he was still holding it. 'Oh, sorry. I uh . . . uh . . .'

'Mr Ashford, is something wrong?'

'No, no. Please, call me Ash. Everyone does.'

'Well,' Mark cut in, 'if there's nothing else, perhaps I could leave you to it. Ms Lowell basically has permission to go where she wants at any time as long as there's no medical prohibitions. I know I can rely on you, Ash, to smooth Dr Lowell's path.'

You're a doctor?'

'Statistics.' She smiled. 'I thought it best not to use the title here, just in case somebody grabbed me to deal with an emergency. I have an office – well, it's more of a cupboard really, on the Admin floor, so perhaps we could go up there now.'

He nodded but remained rooted to the spot.

'Well?'

'Oh, of course.' He hurried across to the door, fumbled with the handle and at last managed to get it open. Mark Calder was already back at his desk, immersed in paperwork.

In the lift going up to the top floor Ash stood awkwardly looking into the mirror, his face turned into a pattern of planes and shadows by the milky light. He tried not to stare at Josette but wherever he looked she seemed to be reflected there. At last, as the lift finished its silent journey, she cleared her throat.

'Ash . . . um, look, it's very flattering but do you think you could stop treating me like the answer to all your prayers? Mark told me you were a bit of a firebrand. He said you'd object to me interfering in the department, that I'd have a bit of a struggle to establish my point of view. I mean, I wasn't expecting a walkover.'

The doors opened and they stepped out into the corridor. 'I'm sorry,' Ash said. 'I'll try to be more disagreeable in future.'

'Just try and be more communicative.'

'I don't normally get to meet beautiful women.'

She stopped and looked at him. 'Well, I asked for communication!'

'I'm sorry, I don't want to be . . . offensive, sexist, but you are beautiful. That doesn't mean that I don't wish you weren't here and that I don't think you're going to cause a real nuisance in the Department and who needs a monitor exercise anyway.'

'I've changed my mind. Can we go back to the way we were? I preferred the walkover,' she laughed.

'Only if you'll have lunch with me today.'

'Oh,' she said, 'I intend to be out asking questions, speaking to patients as much as possible while I'm here. I want to see all I can, so that's fine, I'd love to.'

'What about after the shift?'

'Do you get through your union business this quick?'

'We could have dinner together. There's a nice pizza restaurant . . .' The last time he'd been there had been with Nikki. He hoped he'd have enough cash to afford it.

'Look, we shouldn't rush our fences. I have a job to do here and some of my conclusions may not make comfortable reading for your department. Let's keep it friendly but let's keep it professional, too.'

Taking a key from her bag she opened an office door and went through. Inside was a desk, a couple of chairs, a computer terminal and not much of anything else, especially space.

'You weren't joking when you talked about a cupboard.'

'Small but my own.' She edged around the desk and Ash couldn't but notice the swell of her hips escaping the tight waist of her jacket. 'So, if you don't mind, shall we begin with you?'

Two piles of forms lay on the desk and she offered him one from the smaller heap, marked 'Personnel'. As he flipped through the pages he saw there were nearly two hundred questions to be answered and he began to wonder if he'd be doing any medicine at all today.

'OK, number one: your name and your qualifications . . .'

4

Scrubbs had followed the little nurse as he'd been ordered and now he sat in the cubicle they'd given him, listening to the chatter of old women, not daring to go out and face them. He'd followed his orders all right but enough was enough. There were some things you couldn't ask a man to do. It was strictly volunteers.

The curtain at the end of the bed shivered and a white-haired head looked round. 'Hello, luv. New, are you?'

He glared back and clamped his jaw shut.

'Like a cuppa, would you? Do with a nice cuppa?'

Tea? He hadn't drunk tea for twenty years or more.

'Go on, luv, make you feel twice the man you are now.'

Well, couldn't be any harm in it. He wasn't going to get anything decent to drink, that was for sure. He nodded.

The face smiled. 'That's right, luv. You just wait a minute and I'll get you one. They do a nice cuppa here, a bit of strength in it.' She sniffed. 'Hmm, it is a bit strong an' all. Back soon.'

The curtain closed.

Scrubbs sniffed. There was an odd smell in here. Sort of greasy and damp, like old wet clothes. Or old socks. Very old socks. His socks. They'd given him a hospital gown and dressing-gown, slippers as well, but he still had his socks on and he hadn't had a bath in how long?

Bloody hell, he couldn't remember. But there were so many things he couldn't get straight any more. Still, he couldn't have no lady coming in, not with that stink. For the first time in years he felt embarrassed.

He got up off the bed and shuffled to the curtains, where he put his head through. A porter passed him pushing an old chap on a trolley who winked and said, 'Bloody load of rubbish if you ask me, mate. Women's ward.'

That was true. Blokes could have a laugh and a grumble together but with ladies around – well, you had to keep up your standards.

A nurse passed and he called out, 'Oi!' The sound of his own voice, rough and angry, surprised him. 'Um, excuse me.'

'Yes?'

'I was wonderin' . . . er, if I, er, could have . . . a, um . . . if you might have . . .?'

'Yes?' She crossed her arms and cocked her head on one side. She seemed very young, but then they all did.

'A barf.'

'A bath?'

'Yeah. If you might have one handy.'

'You'd like a bath,' she looked at his notes on the end of the bed, 'Mr Scrubbs?'

'Sar'nt-Major Scrubbs.'

She grinned at him. 'All right, I'll see what I can do for you.'

He pulled his head back through and sat on the bed again. There was a nasty pain in his gut, a sort of burning. And he needed the latrines. He wondered if they were mixed, too, and felt an edge of panic worse than anything he'd ever experienced in Korea. Best not to even think about it.

'Here you go, luv.' A hand came through the curtains holding the cup. He reached out and took it.

'Thanks.' It was a long time since he'd said that to anyone.

'That's all right, luv. Just call out if you need a refill. The name's Barbara.' The hand vanished and she was gone. He was glad she hadn't come in with it. Thoughtful of her, you might say. Maybe after his bath he should go and ...

He shook his head. It was all a bit much. Best leave things a while and see how it went. He sipped the tea. It tasted vile and made him wish more than ever for a proper drink.

By the time Ash had filled in the form and introduced Josette around the department, it was getting on for half past nine and he was glad to slot himself back into the daily routine for a while.

As always there was a mix of patients: those who should have gone to their own doctors but hadn't and had let their symptoms get worse and worse; those with everyday sprains and cuts who sat patiently waiting their turn; mothers with toddlers who had drunk the disinfectant or swallowed a button or a needle; there were the nutcases who had nowhere else to go and thought they might as well sit inside, even on a day as hot as this: and then there were the emergencies, rushed into Crash by the paramedics, as was happening now. Josh was shouldering the swing doors aside, protecting the lines already put in with his hunched body.

Adele moved in smoothly beside him, followed by Ash and Karen, who was peering down at the still form on the stretcher.

'Edward Bryant. In his fifties. Hit by a train door,' Josh recited. 'Injuries to thorax, broken shoulder, ribs, internal bleeding. We intubated and gave a hundred cc of nubane. Also put a line in and he's had two units.'

'OK, fine, let's get him on the cot,' Karen snapped, as if Josh were taking too much valuable time. 'Mr Bryant, can you hear me? We're going to move you onto a cot and then we'll able to make you more comfortable. Right. So we'll just be a minute.'

They manoeuvred the ambulance trolley next to the cot and Josh and his companion slipped in beside the others as they lifted the considerable weight of Ted Bryant on to the A and E bed. Ash noticed that Sara Eeles had arrived and taken care of the lines, transferring the fluid bottle to the permanent support. He smiled briefly and she nodded back. This was obviously more like her idea of Casualty than dealing with Scrubbs had been.

Adele was cutting the patient's clothing free to reveal a chest which was mottled with huge bruises and contusions, the skin broken in one area where a splinter of bone protruded.

'Any deep structures damaged, d'you think?' Ash asked while he cleared the mouth and throat area. Immediately a pale raspberry foam began to appear on the patient's lips.

Karen flicked a glance, taking in the foam. 'Could be. Anyway I'm concerned about his airways. I think we should ask the anaesthetist to put a tube down for us. Sara, could you—' The young nurse had gone already.

'Are we going to want x-rays?' Adele asked. She knew they would but had phrased the statement delicately.

'Yeah, it looks like a pneumothorax.' This, the puncturing of the lung by a broken rib, which let the air out of the lung into the chest cavity, would cause considerable breathing problems and would mean inserting a line through the chest and into the lung to reinflate. 'Ash, before we move him, I think he should have metoclopramide.'

At that moment the patient's lips began to move, emitting little sprays of pinkish blood. He was trying to speak and Adele said, 'Hush now, don't try to talk, Mr Bryant. You'll be more comfortable soon.'

Karen was working on the chest but Ash noticed the lips forming words – 'Blind, blind . . . blind . . . blind . . .' – over and over, and looking down he noticed the eyes were closed and gummed around the lids. He pulled one of them back and observed the surface of the eye, red and sore, with no movement.

'Ash, metoclopramide and we'll put an analgesic line in.'

Later, after Mr Bryant had been x-rayed, Ash was able to take a few moments to find Josh. The paramedic was still a little sore over what he saw as Karen's continuing hostility, but he'd always got on well enough with Ash and was quite happy to go over the accident report once again.

'So he was hit by a carriage door as the train came into the station?'

'That's about the gist of it. We got there within twenty minutes. The BR boys had put him in the recovery position, which shows they must have learned something from all those first aid courses. There was considerable blood. I mean they'd had to close the platform. God, you should've seen the commuters. Already had one train cancelled this morning. They were screaming blue murder.'

'When you spoke to the staff there, was there anyone who'd seen it?'

'Yeah, this solicitor. He was a friend. He said he'd hang on and get in touch with the wife. He'd bring her in here.'

'She's here?' Ash hadn't known but then Adele would be handling that side of matters, speaking to the relatives, since she'd picked up the case first.

'As far as I know she's in the interview room. But this

other fellow who saw it, he said Mr Bryant seemed to have some kind of attack or something. He was flinging his arms around.' Josh checked the accident report, 'The platform was crowded, it was difficult to see anything.'

'But he was behaving oddly?'

' "Like he'd lost his balance or something", that's what the witness said.'

'OK, great, thanks, Josh, that's been a real help.'

'People should listen to us. We're not stupid.'

Ash clapped him on the shoulder and hurried back into the department. Dennis Ford, the clinical nurse specialist who had replaced Ken Hodges, was leading a young man with a massively bleeding hand through to the cubicles.

'Carpet layers,' he said, 'they shouldn't be let near Stanley knives.'

'Anyone in the interview room, d'you know, Dennis?'

'The wife of the pneumothorax, I think.'

'Great, thanks.' He carried on through, paused a moment in front of the interview room door, knocked gently and went in.

A woman in her late forties, smart but red-faced and puffy from weeping, looked up at him. A man, smart in a business suit, stood protectively beside her.

'Is there any . . .' she stuttered.

'Has anybody seen you yet?'

'Yes, the nurse. She said they're taking him to x-ray.'

'Then they'll be able to tell you more when he comes back.'

'Is he going to be all right?' she asked.

'I'm sorry, Mrs Bryant, I can't say yet. All I can tell you is that we will do everything possible for him.'

'Yes, of course, I understand.'

'But you can help us, Mrs Bryant, with some information.'

'Anything, anything at all.'

'The paramedics who brought him in said that just before the accident he'd been staggering.'

'Yes.' It was the well-dressed man. 'I told them that.'

'And you . . .?'

'I'm a friend of Ted and Brenda's. Same line of business. John Higgs. I said hello to Ted on the station this morning.' He turned away, evidently ashamed of the tear which had appeared at the corner of his eye, coughed and went on, 'He suddenly seemed to start staggering, waving his arms. I can't understand it.'

'Was he taking any medication?' Ash asked.

'Nothing,' Mrs Bryant said. 'Well, I mean except for his eye drops.'

'What were they?'

She shook her head. 'I can't remember. He had some trouble, soreness, I don't know, and went to the doctor and there was a prescription.'

'And he's been using the same prescription all the time?'

'The drops, yes. I got him some more only yesterday.'

'So this morning he used the new—'

'The new bottle. Yes. Is there something wrong?'

'No, no. I just wanted to check. Now, if you'll excuse me. Would you like them to send along some tea?'

Mike was strapping up a Colles fracture when Ash found him. The patient, a young workman, was enjoying himself in the department and looking forward to the time off he'd get with pay. He reckoned it was great, it'd give him a chance to enjoy the hot weather. As soon as he'd gone Ash told Mike what he'd found out about Mr Bryant's eyes.

'It isn't much, Mike, but with his behaviour on the platform and what he said about being blind, I reckon we should take a look.'

'You mean I should take a look?'

It was a tricky situation. Although the Casualty team

worked together and supported each other there were firm lines of responsibility and seniority. As the SHO, the junior doctor, Karen, was immeasurably junior to Mike, the consultant. At the same time, although Charlie or Duffy or even Ash might have more experience than she did, it would not do for them to direct her in any way. Mike, however, could take a look at any case and offer his advice, whether it was needed or not, and it would be a foolhardy SHO indeed who chose to ignore her consultant.

'If you could, Mike. I mean there's no other reason Mr Bryant should have started staggering like that.'

'I can think of half a dozen right off without even mentioning heart-attacks and strokes. But OK, it sounds like something may be up.'

'Great, thanks, Mike.'

'Don't thank me yet, this might blow up in your face.'

'Don't.'

'I think somebody wants you.'

Josette Lowell was waiting outside the Admin area. She gave him a half-wave, half-beckon.

'I should be so lucky!'

'Lucky, lucky.' Deevers hissed the words through his teeth as the window catch snapped open and the window itself slid up. A locking mechanism had been screwed into the sill but had not been set. Some people were mad, Deevers reckoned. They deserved everything they got. Not that he was a thief. He despised that kind of people. Weak, sneaking characters who never stood up to anyone. He didn't want anything that Martin Ashford had in this poky little flat. What he wanted were the things the guy had in his head: his peace of mind, the people he cared about and the hopes he had for the future.

He slipped off his shoes and left them on the sill. No

point in being obvious. He might leave a little present for Martin, something to cause him anxiety maybe, but nothing that would advertise the presence of the invisible man who was turning the pages of Martin's life.

He walked through into the kitchen, saw the two empty mugs, the bread still left out, the letters on the kitchen table. He read a couple and smiled at the one from the bank. He didn't have a mortgage himself but someone had once refused to pay up money they owed him. He'd told the guy he'd break his legs if he didn't come through. The guy didn't believe him. The guy was very, very wrong.

Back in the sitting-room he studied the photos on the mantelpiece. There was an old one of a couple, presumably Martin's mother and father; but the more recent ones just showed Martin with the woman and a younger girl who must've been his sister. Pretty. Had a sort of wild look to her. Perhaps she was a student or something. Maybe he should get in touch. It would be like that film, the one with De Niro, where he worms his way into the kid's confidence. Yeah, that would be good. Deevers sometimes thought of himself as being like De Niro. *Taxi Driver*, that was a great movie, he played it over at least once a month on the video. But maybe it would be difficult to find the girl.

The mother, she'd be easier to locate. Martin was the kind of guy who'd keep in touch with his mother. Probably gave her a call once a week, went up for a meal on Sundays. Would the number be in the phone book? How many Ashfords in the area?

He went out to the tiny hall where the phone stood next to a local directory. There was only one Mrs Ashford so that must be her. He noted down the address and number on the message pad by the phone and tore off the sheet. On the next sheet he drew an X, digging the pencil into the paper. That would start Martin worrying.

Where had it come from, had he done it himself? Maybe he'd think he was going crazy. Or maybe he'd reckon someone was going to X him out.

Deevers folded the paper with the address on it and slipped it into his shirt pocket.

The phone clicked and began to ring, shockingly loud in the silence. He breathed out slowly, his hand, held in front of his face, was steady, he hadn't even jumped at the shock. He was ice-cold. He reached out and lifted the receiver.

5

Balancing a tray on one hand while he paid, Ash looked round the crowded canteen for a free table. Josette was carrying a couple of coffees. She'd offered to pay for lunch; after all, she said, she was on expenses, but Ash had insisted. The food was OK here and it was certainly cheap enough for him to afford lunch for both of them.

'It's the old Adam,' Josette said, as they threaded their way across the crowded room. 'You can't stand letting a woman pay for a meal.'

'I'll make a deal with you,' he said. 'Come out with me after work and we'll go anywhere you like and I'll let you pay.'

'It's not that easy, Ash,' she laughed. 'Look, over by the window.' A couple of housemen were leaving their table and Ash and Josette made a dash for it, getting there just before a group of nurses.

'Sorry girls!'

'When are you going to transfer from A and E, Ash?' one of them, a pretty blonde, asked. 'We need someone like you in Orthopaedics.'

'Yeah, and I know what for, Sharon,' her friend laughed as the group drifted away to another table.

'I believe you're blushing,' Josette said.

'I'm impervious to embarrassment.'

'I'd noticed from the way you keep asking me out.'

'It's all these questions in your survey,' he said, trying to spear a radish which shot out from under his fork and landed on the floor. 'They're habit-forming. "Did the nurse introduce her or himself, did he tell you when you would be fed, where the toilet was, how long you'd have to wait?" We do these things all the time in A and E. I can't see why the hospital has to pay out money we really need for equipment on something like this.'

Josette handled her salad like an expert, managing to eat the lettuce leaves without smearing herself with dressing. It was a trick Ash had never quite mastered, and he was wondering if it would have been more sensible to have ordered a jacket potato with a filling.

'I just do my job, Ash. They pay me, I ask the questions. I provide them with conclusions. What they do with them is up to them.'

'They've asked us to make a two per cent cut across the board. And since we can't stop treating patients it means we're either cutting equipment levels or employing cheaper staff. And that means less experienced staff. And that means—'

'Don't lecture me.' There was a little inverted V of annoyance between her eyes. 'I know all the arguments. I also know that you'd try and cure everybody of everything if you could.'

'That's why we do the job.'

'But somebody has to pay, Ash.'

'Sure, the govern—'

'You and me. Through our tax. And the money doesn't go on for ever.'

'You don't have to tell me,' he smiled ruefully.

'I mean it,' she went on. 'We're all living longer and that means we're taking up more resources which have to be paid for by fewer taxpayers.'

'Oh great, so what do we do, find a clearing in the forest and leave the old people out there for a hungry lion?'

Her eyes flashed at him. 'That was offensive, Ash. I meet enough racism in this country. I didn't expect it from you.'

'Come on, Josette, that's rubbish and you know it.'

'I could say that in Africa families still count for something. That we don't shove our old people in homes, we actually listen to them and try to learn from them. Belief, religion, the invisible things still matter.'

'How did we get on to this subject?' he asked. 'Because I'm wondering if we could retrace our footsteps.'

'There you are, something does embarrass you. Religion.'

'I suppose so. I used to go to church with my mum. Even after I left home, but then, working here, seeing some of the things people do to each other, I suppose I lost my faith. Or at least I started putting my faith in things I knew could make a difference.'

'Like?'

'Like the treatment we give in A and E. If someone needs fluids, you put in a line and give them. If they're poisoned you do a wash through. If they're burned or crushed there are techniques that can lessen pain, improve breathing. These are real things, you can touch them. All the belief in the world can't suture a wound. I just want to do the best I can in each case.'

'That sounds like a good theory to me.'

'Yeah, but it does depend on . . .' He stopped as Mike Barratt arrived at the table with a tray.

'Mind if I join you? It's getting crowded in here today.'

'Not at all, Doctor,' Josette said. 'We were just talking about the department. Ash was telling me about the cuts you have to make.'

'Don't.' Mike shook his head and put on an expression of mock despair. Josette laughed. He went on,

'Sometimes I feel like locking the place up and going home. No, going on holiday for the rest of my life.'

'You'd get bored,' she said.

'Try me.' He took a mouthful of cheese roll and carried on speaking through it. 'Ash, the eye case. You were right.'

'What was it ?'

'The wrong prescription. When Mrs Bryant collected the follow-up drops they were something else entirely. If we – if you – hadn't spotted it, he'd be blind by now. Karen was devastated.'

'I can imagine she was. But then that's why we have a team, I suppose. Where was the prescription taken out?'

Mike paused, the roll between table and mouth. 'Do you have a reason for asking that?'

'Well, it wouldn't be the first misfilled prescription we've seen but I was wondering.'

'Taylor's in Lower End Road,' Mike said.

It was a sore point with A and E. This particular chemist, who by general agreement should have retired years before, had already been involved in a case of wrongful prescription. At that time, Julian had been the consultant and had pressed for a prosecution, even though the damage had been minor, but the professional body involved had exonerated the chemist and the matter had been dropped. Now things would be different.

'You're going to report it?'

'I suppose so. I haven't told Mrs Bryant yet.'

'How is he?'

'He'll pull through. Ruptured spleen, but he can live without that. He'll be off work for a few months but he's a tough chap.'

'Are you going to tell him?'

'I can hardly avoid it, can I? And since he's a solicitor I imagine he'll be pursuing old man Taylor for considerable damages.'

'And meanwhile he goes on prescribing.'

'I'll get in touch with the RCP this afternoon.'

'But they won't be able to stop him. You don't remember the last time. He's an arrogant man. He refused to accept any blame then and he'll be the same now.'

'There's still nothing I can do about it.' Mike opened his roll, looked in, wrinkled his nose and closed it again. 'You can't shut people down just like that. They've a right to a hearing. You should know that better than anyone.'

'Maybe someone should talk to him. Just ask him to stop prescribing for the time being.'

'What are you suggesting?' Mike asked. 'That I see him, or you do?'

'Someone should.'

'So you do get problems you can't solve with pieces of equipment,' Josette cut in.

Mike turned to her. 'Sorry?'

'We were talking, before you arrived, about belief.'

'Ah, the big one.'

'Are you all cynics in Casualty, Dr Barratt?'

'Please, it's Mike.'

Ash wasn't sure he liked the way Josette responded to the consultant. The two of them seemed pretty comfortable together. He was also annoyed by the way Mike had slipped out of answering his question about Taylor the chemist. He leaned forward to join in the conversation but as he did so his bleeper went off. All over the canteen hands went to pockets in instinctive response to the summons that usually meant some kind of emergency. Ash pushed his chair back. 'I'll see you later, Josette.'

She nodded, but before he'd left the room she was back in deep conversation with Mike.

He got to Admin in a couple of minutes. No one seemed unduly hurried and he looked around for some sign of a problem. Adele was examining an x-ray of a

47

green stick fracture and nodded towards the phone, which hung off the hook. 'Call for you.'

He felt a sudden swoop of nervousness. His mum? He must go and see her tonight and try to talk her round. He grabbed the phone. 'Yeah, hello?'

There was a pause, long and echoey, then a cough. 'Marty . . .'

'Benny?' It was his cousin all right, but what the hell was he doing ringing the hospital?

'Look, man, I need some help.'

'What d'you mean?' Benny never needed help. As far back as Ash could remember Benny had been the leader in their games, the one who got them into trouble and then out of it again with his outrageous stories.

'Marty, I've been hurt.'

'You've been in an accident of some kind? D'you need an ambulance?'

There was a pause, then a bitter laugh came down the line. 'I need a lot more than an ambulance, man. I reckon I need . . .' he stopped and for a few moments there was only heavy breathing.

'Are you OK, Benny?'

'It's all right, just wait a minute. OK, I'm fine now. Look, Marty, something's happened. I can't tell you right now but I sure do need you here.'

'It's the middle of the shift, I can't just walk out.'

'I know. That's fine. I called your place. Somebody picked the phone up but they didn't answer.'

'There's nobody there, you must've had a wrong number.'

'I dunno what I had.' There was another pause and this time it sounded as if Benny was talking to someone else. Then he came back on the line. 'Tonight. Come tonight.'

'Well, where are you?'

'Never mind. Can you get to the Golden Road estate?'

Golden Road was one of the most notorious estates in the town, a high-rise built in the early seventies which had been used as a dumping ground for problem families.

'What are you doing there? Where am I supposed to wait?'

'Someone'll find you. Right? Just be there by nine. Wait near the pub, you know it?'

'I've heard of it. The Horn of Plenty. It provides a high proportion of our clients on a Saturday night.'

'I bet it does. You'll be there?'

'Look, is this really important, Benny?'

'It's important. And bring . . .' Another pause. '. . . Bring some bandages, Marty. And something to help with pain. Something strong.'

A cold hand seemed to reach up his back and squeeze his neck. 'What've you done, Benny? What's happened? Look, if you're badly injured, you need proper help. A doctor.'

'Cut it, cousin. I need you, nobody else.'

'If I get mixed up in something illegal, it could finish me.'

'If you don't, then it sure as hell *will* finish me.' It was a flash of the old Benny coming through the pain-filled voice.

'I don't know. I have to think about it.'

'It's family. You have to be there. You owe me, Marty. You remember. Holding the rope. I held the rope for you. Now you gotta hold it for me, man.'

The connection was cut.

'You OK, Ash?' It was Sara Eeles, carrying an inflatable collar, looking a bit lost.

'Um, yeah, sure, I'm fine.'

'I wanted to ask you . . . ask you a couple of questions, if you've got a moment.'

Something had been upsetting her, that was for sure, but he didn't have time now. 'Can you see Charlie, or

Adele. I have to go. I need to . . . see someone.'

He hurried out and she stood looking after him, biting her lip.

Scrubbs had been scrubbed. Twice. He'd felt like nothing on earth and he still hadn't got hold of a drink. They'd given him lunch and then a cup of tea, which he'd managed to get down. After that he had had a nap and woken up feeling a bit better. A nurse had come along and told him they would take some samples later, though when that would be, she couldn't say. Not that time worried him much nowadays. Apart from opening time.

'Oh, that's a bit better, luv, isn't it now?' The white-haired head popped round the curtains. 'Mind if I come in, then?'

'Will it stop you if I do?' he grunted.

A wide grin split the face that hovered at the end of the bed. 'I can see you're a grumpy one. Still, you look a lot better now they've given you a shave and cut your hair. Mind if I sit down?' She didn't wait for an answer but plumped herself down in the chair beside the bed. 'What're you in for, then? Big feller like you, I should think you'd steer clear of a place like this.'

'Well I would, wouldn't I, but I didn't have no choice. Buggers just pulled me in. Still, orders is orders.'

'In the forces, were you?'

'I should think so. Sar'nt-major. Yes.'

'Sergeant-Major ? Where was that, then?'

'Korea. That's where I got my medal. Used to have it right here.' He tapped his chest and coughed. 'Haven't got a gasper about your person, have you, my dear?'

'They don't let you smoke in here, luv.'

'Oh, why's that?'

'It's bad for you, smoking.'

'So's this place.'

She giggled. 'Go on!'

'Never done me any harm, not the smoking.'

A silence fell. Beyond the curtains they could hear a radio playing the hospital request programme. After a while Scrubbs thought he ought to say something. He wasn't sure what, it had been a long time since he'd talked to anyone like this. In fact, come to think of it, it had been a long time since he'd done anything halfway normal – which included getting a drink.

'You – er – don't know anywhere a chap could get a small drink around here, do you, by any chance?'

'Go on with you!' she said again, thinking he was joking. 'Not a drinking man, are you? My Arthur was a man who liked a pint. Every night after work he'd stop in at the local. What's your local, maybe you saw him?'

Scrubbs searched his mind. Did he have a local? Was there anywhere that still let him in nowadays?

'The Horn of Plenty. Nice little hostelry.'

'No, Frank always went to the Jack of Both Sides. That's because it was at a crossroads, see, and it had two sides.'

What was she going on about ? He scratched his head. It still felt sensitive after the haircut but at least the stubble was decently military. 'I'm in for tests,' he said.

Barbara seemed to take the sudden change of direction in her stride. 'It's always the way. Tests and more tests. Can't leave you alone once they've got hold of you. I used to say as much to Arthur. When he was alive, of course. Now he's just an urn.'

'What, change his name, did he?'

Barbara shrieked with laughter. 'Ooh, what a one you are!'

Scrubbs gave her a puzzled look. Had he said something funny ?

'Fancy another cuppa? It's about that time of day.'

She was probably mad, he decided, but then he wasn't

noticeably twenty-twenty himself, not since the re-education programme out in Korea. Besides, he was enjoying himself, having a little chat. Clean feet, nice blankets, cup of tea when you wanted it. There definitely was something civilising about the ladies. Made him feel almost like he used to all those years ago, beyond the mist and the booze and the blackouts and the dreams. So why not?

'I don't mind if I do, thank you very much, Barbara.'

6

Ash sat on a bench that had been put up in memory of someone or other and looked out over the front of Holby General. His head was buzzing with the phone call. It was clear that Benny had got himself into some kind of serious trouble, something that put him on the wrong side of the law. The import-export business his cousin had always vaguely mentioned as the source of his money began to look increasingly dodgy.

All right, he didn't have any facts at all and it would be stupid to speculate, but if Benny wasn't in trouble with the law, then why had he refused an ambulance? And why had he called Ash? Because he needed him, that was why, and when Benny needed something he had no hesitation in going out and getting it. He'd always been the same, right from way back. Even on that day when he'd held the rope.

Ash had been eight and Benny a couple of years older. It was winter, the holidays after Christmas, and Benny had been staying over for a few days while his mum went into hospital to have a baby.

They'd been playing with their presents but both had reached that stage when they weren't really interested in the new toys any more and there wasn't anything on TV and Ash's mum had chased them out of the kitchen where she was cooking up swordfish stew. It was grey and cold outside, with flecks of snow beginning to drift slowly down out of a heavy sky.

'Let's go to the ghost house,' Benny had suddenly said, and Ash had felt exactly the same cold shiver of apprehension that he'd experienced during the phone call.

'We're not s'posed to, Benny, you know that.'

The house, a few streets away, was an old Victorian building which had been used until a few years before as a nursing home. Then it had fallen vacant and had been used by tramps and boozers. It was said, at least by most of the kids at the local schools, that one night this particular old drinker, an Irish woman called Maggie, had finished off a bottle of meths and, for no reason at all, started to burn like a fat candle. She'd run shrieking round the house in flames but by the time the fire brigade had arrived, all that was left were her two feet, from the ankles down, which were as white and untouched as a china doll's. Apart from that there was only a pile of ash and a great grease slick all the way down the stairs.

So the story went. And, the teller would go on, lowering his or her voice, if you went into the house now you could still see the greasy mark and sometimes, if you were unlucky, you'd hear the sound of steps and see Maggie's two white feet coming down the stairs, and if you were very unlucky indeed, you'd see the rest of Maggie as she burned.

'You scared then, Marty?'

'I'm not. Anyway, why d'you want to go there?'

'Bored. Nothing else to do. Anyway, they've got this thing there, the back of an old piano, with all the strings on it and it makes this great noise. Clark told me about it. He 'n' Pete went in there.'

'I dunno.' Actually he did. His mum had told him to stay away from the place, not because of the ghosts, though she believed in them, but because the house was falling apart and it was dangerous. And to tell the truth, he was pretty scared of meeting Maggie's feet, too. He'd imagined them often enough, long and white like two bony spiders.

'No, I don't think I fancy it.'

'You do what you want, I'm going. If you're not brave enough . . .'

He could hardly refuse that. Besides, Benny was a guest and Mum always said how important it was to do what the guest wanted.

By the time they reached the ghost house it was snowing heavily and the cold bit through the gloves and cagoules they were wearing. The front of the building was boarded up but Benny said there was a way in round the back, through a cellar window.

'We could still go home,' Ash had said, but Benny wasn't in the mood to stop now. He led them round the edge of the big old house to the back garden, which was piled high with dumped furniture and black rubbish bags and had a sour smell.

'There it is.' Benny pointed out a narrow black hole just visible through the ivy along the bottom of the wall. It looked like the kind of hole only a fool would climb through and Ash had the feeling that if he'd been watching a scene like this on TV, he'd be behind the sofa by now. Benny didn't seem to mind and within moments his feet were vanishing into the darkness. For a blissful moment Ash thought of turning and running off home. Then Benny's voice came out: 'Come on. It's OK. There's nothing to be scared of.'

Inside, the house wasn't too bad. It was dark and there were a lot of corners you couldn't see into and wallpaper hanging off the wall in tattered strips, but there were also signs of life: lots of bottles, piles of smelly old newspapers, swear words sprayed everywhere, which meant that ordinary people had been in here before and, presumably, had come out, too.

'It's up here.' Benny was halfway up the stairs.

'Wait for me,' he called. 'Don't leave me down here.' He scampered up, trying not to look at the dark mark down the wall which just might be grease. On the first landing there was still a tattered carpet which led up narrower stairs to the next floor. Benny went on and Ash followed.

Benny kicked open a door. There was a clatter, the sound of something falling. 'There it is.'

Peering past him Ash saw that the floorboards were missing. You could look straight down through the supporting beams into the room beneath. On the far side, half across the joists, lay the remains of a piano, most of which had fallen through and lay smashed fifteen feet below. The strings, however, hadn't fallen. Looking a bit like a square harp, they were caught halfway across the wooden supports, one end secured with a length of twine. Obviously Ash and Benny weren't the first up here by any means.

Benny picked up a length of wood and tossed it across. When it hit the metal strings there was a roar, a crash of sound which slowly died away. 'Great, isn't it. Really weird sound, that.' Benny was into weird sounds that year. 'We've got to get it and take it back.'

'How? We're never going to crawl over there.'

'Why not? It's safe enough.' Benny put a foot on to one of the beams and pressed. 'We can straddle them, get over there, tie on a piece of rope, get back then pull it across.

'What rope? We haven't got any rope.'

'Oh no ?' Behind them on the landing was a coil of sash-cord. As he picked it up, Benny's expression was triumphant and Ash had the feeling he'd set this up a long time ago.

'OK, Marty? We'll hold an end each. Just in case.' Taking one end of the cord, he straddled the joist in front of him and began to swing himself out. 'Mind the nails, there are still some left,' he said.

Ash looked down the narrow stairs and thought of Maggie's feet, the long toes scrabbling as they climbed blindly upwards towards the dark landing. He followed Benny out on to the beam. He had to use both hands to swing and pull himself along, so he wrapped the cord under his armpits, tying it over his chest. It was probably this that saved his life.

He heard a noise like a cough behind him and, thinking that someone, maybe a workman, had come in and heard them, he turned to look back at the door and saw Maggie standing there, her face swollen and slick and wreathed in flames like the Christmas pudding his mum had lit with brandy the week before. He shrieked and fell, arms flailing, until he felt an agonising pain round his chest and came to a stop, suspended on the end of the rope. Above him, Benny's face was grey with panic. In the doorway, as he turned, there was nothing.

'Bennnnyyyy!' he howled.

'Shut up.' Benny was gripping the cord, his knuckles white with effort. It began to slip and Ash screamed. Somehow Benny managed to jerk the rope and get enough slack to whip it round his hands. In moments it began to bite into the flesh.

'Don't let me go,' Ash pleaded.

Benny was leaning back with the strain. 'I won't let you go, Marty, I promise.' And Ash knew he meant it. He would hang on as long as he could and then he'd fall too. Because what he couldn't do was pull Ash up, he didn't have the strength; or lower him down, because the cord had bitten too deeply into his hands for him to release it. So they had stayed there, the two of them, shouting and, in the end, screaming for help while

Benny's hands grew numb and Ash thought his chest would be cut in half.

Eventually they were found. It can't have been more than a few minutes but for Ash it was forever, and Benny had held the rope all the time and saved his life. And now he was calling in the debt.

An ambulance came by, its siren splitting the silence. Ash looked up. The sun was beating down on to the dried grass and white paving, and he regretted more than ever putting on the heavy winter shirt this morning. He wouldn't be able to make the launderette tonight so he'd have to wash something in the sink and dry it overnight. He really needed to regain control of his own life, he thought as he got to his feet and headed back inside, where at least it was cool and the problems were comparatively straightforward.

'Muuuum, can I have the paddling pool. Please, Mum, can I, it's hot, can you do it for me, Muuuum?'

Janice Parker looked out the kitchen window into the back garden where seven-year-old Carly was playing. She knew she really should pull out the plastic pool from its cupboard, blow it up and fill it, but she just didn't have the energy. It was too hot to think. 'No, you can't. Go and play in the shade, under the trees.'

'Can I climb the trees, Mum?'

'If you're careful.'

Carly trotted off and Janice pulled open the fridge door, grateful for the cool air that blew over her legs. She remembered reading somewhere that in hot weather Marilyn Monroe used to keep her underwear in the fridge. If they didn't get some rain soon maybe she'd try the same thing. She wondered what Frank would think about that. It might put a bit of pep back into their relationship.

Not that there were any problems. Frank was a – well,

she was lucky to have him. Look round the large and immaculate kitchen with its ranks of equipment, look down the long garden with its striped lawn, look anywhere you like and you'd see how well he'd provided for her and Carly. Good holidays, too. They were off to Florida this winter, to see Disney World. Everything was perfect.

She pulled out a bottle of iced water, poured a glass and wondered about adding a touch of vodka, just to give it a little zing. But it was too early. She'd made it a rule never to drink before six in the evening. Not that she drank too much, neither of them did. Nice dry sherry, a decent bottle of wine with the pleasant dinner she'd cooked. She sighed. Sometimes she rather wished that Frank would drink a little bit too much; it might make him do something that wasn't perfectly respectable. That was one of his favourite sayings: 'Well, looks perfectly respectable to me.' He could say it about cars or plants, or almost anything.

Carly was pulling herself up on to the lowest branches and Janice called, 'Not too high.'

Carly waved. 'Look at me, Mum, I'm just like Tigger!'

Janice saw that she'd got one of her fluffy toys tucked into her belt. Carly was wild about the Pooh Bear stories and especially loved the one about Tigger getting stuck up the tree.

'Better make sure you can get down again,' she shouted. 'Remember what happened to Tigger. He had to let go and fall all the way down – bounce, bounce, bounce!'

Carly gurgled with delight and applied herself to her upward progress.

She was a real tomboy, always up to some mischief or other, falling over and bruising herself, getting scratches and stings; she was a regular customer at the surgery down the road and it was just as well that Dr Cowling had known her all her life, and knew Janice too, or she'd be on the at-risk register. As it was, anyone could see she was a well cared for child, loved and cherished but not spoiled.

Janice rubbed the cool glass against her forehead and cheeks. Maybe she should set up the pool after all, there was no way of telling how long this weather would last. Where had she put it away? Under the stairs in the big utility cupboard that Frank had built in for her? Or in the loft he'd converted so cleverly, creating an extra room which they used for storage – the house was quite big enough for the three of them – but which Carly could use as a sitting-room when she grew a little older? Oh yes, Frank was a great planner. He'd got it all worked out: career, promotion, the number of children they should have, the committees Janice should serve on, the good causes they should support. It really was a perfect life.

She opened the stair cupboard door and the light came on automatically. There were the piles of old newspapers, *Daily Mails*, ready for the fortnightly trip to the recycling point. The bottles for the bottle bank. The cans for the can bank. The wellingtons all lined up. The fuse wire ready just in case the fuse blew, the candles just in case it wasn't the fuse but a power cut, the gas burner stove so if it *was* a power cut they could still eat their dinner.

The pool was folded up on a shelf in a plastic bag with 'Paddling Pool' written on it. She pulled it out and took it back through into the kitchen. If she put it up just outside the back door, on the patio, she could keep an eye on Carly.

'Muuuum, look at me, I'm flying, I'm flying . . .' The words were Tigger's from the story but it was Carly who slipped and bumped the three or four feet to the ground.

Janice dropped the pool and ran down the garden. Carly lay spreadeagled on the grass. 'Owwwww,' she moaned.

'Carly, are you all right?'

'It's not me, it's Piglet.' She reached round and pulled the stuffed toy from the back of her waistband. 'I think I've squashed him.'

'What about you, Miss Tigger?'

'Oh I'm all right. Can I have the paddling pool out now?'

There was a bruise on her temple. Janice felt it. 'Does that hurt?'

'No. Ow!'

Had she been unconscious after she'd fallen, even for a moment? It wasn't far, but you could never be quite sure with children. Maybe she'd better take her down to the doctor, just to be safe. Just to be certain. She picked her up.

'Come on, Trouble. I think you'd better see your old friend Dr Cowling.'

'Can Piglet come too?'

'Of course. We can't leave Piglet on his own.'

She carried Carly back up to the house, thinking of the exasperated but understanding reception that Dr Cowling would give them. And there were one or two things she wanted to ask him about Carly's diet so it wasn't such a bad thing after all. Anyway, what else did she have to do today?

'Get that bloody woman out of here, Ash!'

Karen was trembling with fury. On the floor at her feet lay a slowly widening pool of blood and shards of broken glass. Josette Lowell stood by the door, her brows like a thunderstorm about to burst.

'I have a perfect right to be in this department, Doctor,' she hissed. 'I was told I would be given co-operation by the staff, not rudeness and arrogance.'

'If you reckon you can come in here and ask your bloody questions' – when she got angry Karen's accent reverted to south London – 'while I'm tryin' to treat a patient then you are about as wrong as you can be.'

Ash had heard the crash of the falling bottle and hurried through to Admin, where he found the two women bristling at each other.

'What happened?' he asked.

'Your colleague—'

'This woman—'

'Which woman? Dr Lowell?'

'Yeah, if that's what she calls herself. She comes in to my cubicle and starts askin' these stupid questions when I'm tryin' to deal with an RTA.'

'You were looking at the patient's foot. There was nothing else wrong with him. No reason at all why he couldn't talk to me.'

'Look, there was every bloody reason. He was my patient. I was treatin' him. You don't come bargin' in wivout a by-your-leave.'

'I don't recall that I did.' Josette's accent became even more precise and clipped. 'I seem to remember I said, "May I come in?" And I seem to remember that you said yes.'

'Well of course I said yeah, I thought you was a bloody relative, didn't I? I didn't think you'd haul out the *Encyclopaedia Britannica* and start reading it aloud and knock over two units of blood.'

Ash said: 'I'm sure Josette didn't intend to cause any offence.'

Karen looked at him open-mouthed. 'Josette, is it? Oh well, I didn't know I was trespassin' on delicate ground 'ere.'

'You're not,' Josette snapped. 'Mr Ashford was merely saying what was quite true. I didn't intend to cause any offence.' She paused and swallowed, mastering her anger. 'If I did, then I apologise.'

Without waiting for a response from Karen, she turned

on her heel and strode out. Karen bellowed: 'Porter! Is there a porter somewhere in this department?'

'Hold on, hold on, I'm here already before you asked.' Frankie appeared with a mop and bucket and began to clear up the blood.

'What happened?' Ash asked.

'Don't you want to go and comfort Josette ?' Karen gave the name a treacly sound.

'I'd just like to know what happened. She's doing her job. I don't see why you had to bite her head off.'

'Well you wouldn't, would you?'

'You're telling me it's none of my business?'

'That doesn't seem to be a problem with you, Ash.' She turned away and began to wipe a name, presumably the RTA, off the board on which all active patients, and their cubicle numbers, were noted down.

'I'm sorry, I don't understand.'

'Don't you? I would have thought it was pretty clear.' Her accent had settled back now but she was still angry. She went on: 'I would have thought anybody could see it, except me, of course.'

Behind her, Frankie pulled a long face but Ash didn't feel like grinning. 'You're talking about this morning.'

'You bet I'm talking about this morning. Mr Martin bloody perfect Ashford saves the patient's sight when the doctors don't even bloody notice.' She finished wiping with a savage swipe and flung the cloth on to the counter.

'I'm sorry, Karen. I couldn't be sure and anyway, you were busy. I had to check.'

'Without asking me.'

'Yes. What if I'd been wrong.'

'If you'd been wrong,' she snarled, 'it wouldn't have mattered a toss. I could've looked, checked it out, that would have been that. Instead you had to go and tell Mike.'

'Did he say something?'

She sighed in exasperation. 'He didn't need to. I might not be much of a doctor but I'm not quite stupid.'

'Nobody ever said you were, Karen. You're a good doctor. I've seen you enough to know that. It's just . . .' He shut his mouth. No point in making things worse.

'It's just what?'

'You're sometimes a bit too quick to make up your mind.'

'Are you saying I've got an attitude?'

'Can we finish this some other time? I'm supposed to be on duty.'

'We can finish it right now. I've made an official complaint to Charlie Fairhead about your behaviour this morning.'

He felt anger flare up. This was more than he needed. 'On what grounds?'

'On the grounds that you did not act in the best interests of the patient by withholding your suspicion that he was temporarily blinded.'

'You can't be serious,' he protested.

'Try me, Ash.' She nodded at Frankie, 'Thanks,' and hurried out.

'Blimey, mate.' Frankie squeezed his mop into the bucket. 'Looks like you got on her wrong side and no mistake.'

'If there was a mistake, it wasn't mine.' Was that true? Could he have approached the matter more delicately? There was no doubt that Karen was often prickly because of her background and maybe he had acted too independently, going off in his own direction. It wouldn't be the first time, and he knew that management regarded him as a bit of a firebrand. There had to be a chance that Mark Calder would regard this complaint, if it reached him, as just the bucket of water he needed to put out the flames.

The red alert sounded and without thinking he moved quickly towards Crash, pushing through the door just ahead of Sara and Adele.

The paramedics, a different crew from this morning, met them with the trolley bearing a woman twisting in agony, her hair wet with sweat, her belly swollen and spongy. An older woman, a nurse, pale and distraught but in control, followed. She was the one who snapped out a report:

'Petra Howarth, twenty-four, just given birth at home. She's passed a massive clot and still losing blood.'

'Get her on the table, fast, fast,' Karen was beside him. They both took hold and lifted together, moving the woman across. Adele was already removing the towel bunched between the legs.

'Get a line in now!' Karen said. 'Any other complications?'

'Good birth otherwise.'

'OK, fine. Now let's clear the bleeding.'

The drawsheet was already soaked and Adele slipped a pad in place while she swabbed. Karen moved into position. 'I don't think it's per vagina, probably a clot forming at the top of the vagina.'

Adele looked over her shoulder and asked: 'Is the uterus contracted?'

'Let's stop the bleeding first. Ash, is that line in?'

'It's in,' he said.

'Thanks,' she nodded, and bent back to her task. 'I can see clearer now. I think it's a cervical tear. We'll suture.'

She was working well and confidently and there was no animosity in her words to Ash. Outside was one thing but here, in Crash, there was no place for anything except total concentration. This was what it was all about in the end.

7

RSM Scrubbs first ventured beyond the perimeter of his defensive wall at 1400 hours. He established a bridgehead in a far forward position and there consolidated his advantage, doing considerable damage to the enemy before falling back on his original defensive position, where he discussed his strategic gains with his second-in-command, Mrs Barbara Harris. 'Thought I'd get lost out there. Place this size. Massive, my dear. Need a map.'

'Never could read a map, myself,' Barbara said. 'Preferred Anya Seton.'

'I'm not a reading man, not so as you could say. Never saw much point in it.' He was discovering things about himself he'd forgotten years ago. It was almost as if there was someone else inside him who was slowly beginning to emerge. Just now, on his way to the latrines, he'd passed someone carrying a lunch tray and caught the smell of baked jam rolypoly; it had sent his mind winging back to the army, to the very day he'd last eaten the dish, in the depot at Port Said, Egypt. A scorching day just like this one, but that never stopped the army serving a hot pudding and it didn't seem like it had stopped the hospital canteen, either. 'Baked puddings,' he mused.

'What's that, luv?' Barbara was knitting, quite happily sitting at the end of the bed. She seemed to have adopted him and had been providing bits and pieces, a biscuit here, a cup of tea there, all afternoon.

'I was just thinking, I haven't had a baked jam pud, not for years.'

'Arthur used to love them. Course, they don't believe in them any more.'

'Don't believe in 'em? I just saw one with my own eyes, right out there.'

'No, luv, not any more. Too much fat.'

'When I was a lad we used to eat our fat or get a clip round the ear.'

'Me too,' Barbara said, her needles flashing in and out of the tangle of wool, 'but not any more. Where've you been, anyway, Sar'nt-Major, if you didn't know that.'

'I've bin away. That's it. What're you making.'

A vague multi-coloured shape lay across her lap. 'Oh, I don't know,' she beamed. 'Something, I expect.'

The cervical tear had been sutured and sent to the ward, followed by the midwife, who was concerned about possible repercussions. Ash and Karen had parted without further words and the complaint was left in the air. Presumably Charlie would want to speak to him some time.

Of more immediate concern to Ash was the sight of Mike Barratt in conversation with Josette. They seemed to be getting on well. A little too well for Ash's liking. He'd tried to reestablish his role as guide and mentor in the department but Mike had smoothly but obviously deflected his attempts and Josette hadn't objected. Maybe they were going to dinner tonight? It left a bit of a sour taste in the mouth.

Mr Bryant, the pneumothorax, was being moved to the ward. His condition was more or less stable, although he was going to need a good deal of careful nursing before he could be discharged. Frankie and an agency nurse were pushing him through to the lift and Ash walked along for a while, asking how he felt now.

'Well, I won't say I'm chipper but I'm a good deal better than I was, thanks. I hear I have you people to thank for more than putting my carcass back together.'

'You mean your eye drops?'

'I do. Can't believe it: That young lass, the doctor, was telling me I'd been given the wrong bloody drops by that idiot Taylor.'

'That's what it seems like, Mr Bryant. It could easily be a genuine mistake. Misbottling by the manufacturer, something like that.'

Bryant could hardly move, his ribs and upper body were strapped firmly in place. His expression was impossible to read through the extensive bruising of his face but the tone of his voice, when he talked about the chemist, made his anger and contempt clear enough.

'I've known him for years, old Taylor. And I'll tell you one thing, young man, it doesn't surprise me a bit. There are things he's done for my Brenda that I've not trusted, though you'd never get him to admit it. Not in a month of Sundays. And I'll tell you another thing: this time he's gone too far. There's certain folk you should be wary of messing around and a solicitor is one of them. I told that lass, you keep your notes, love, because I'm going to sue the— Well, I'm going to sue him anyway. Soon as I get out of here.'

'And meanwhile,' Ash said, 'he'll still be filling out prescriptions.'

The lift came to a halt and the wide doors pulled back. 'Second floor,' Frankie chanted. 'We're getting off here.'

'Thanks for everything, anyway,' Mr Bryant said as they wheeled him away.

Ash waited until they were out of sight, then hurried through to the pharmacy, where he signed out various painkillers that were needed for the department and some that weren't. He felt as if eyes were boring into his back and when he slipped the unauthorised bottle into his pocket it was with the feeling that he had just stepped across a line which, whatever happened now, he would never be able to recross. Perhaps for that reason he kept his mind closed as much as he could, simply refusing to acknowledge to himself the fact of his theft of drugs from Holby General. It was surprising how simple it was. On the way up in the lift he'd been honest. Now, going down . . . he wasn't so different from Benny after all.

'Mr Ashford, you shouldn't be here.'

He spun round, shocked. Mark Calder was leaning at the back of the lift. He tapped his watch. 'Your shift finished ten minutes ago. Or are you staying round to help Dr Lowell?'

'I think she's doing well enough on her own.'

'Yes, she has quite a way about her, doesn't she? A high-flier, I'd say. Not for you and me, Martin. I remember when I was, well, working somewhere else, we used to say about certain secretaries, Managers Only, and about others, MDs Only. Well, I think Dr Lowell is Consultants Only. Hmm?'

One of the most unpleasant things about Mark Calder was the way he tricked you into admitting to yourself just how gross some of your own attitudes were. Ash had been thinking exactly that about Josette. 'I wouldn't know.'

'Wouldn't you, now.' The lift door opened. 'Excuse me. I still have a few hours to fill before I can get away.' He flashed a sneaky smile and hurried off. Ash collected his coat, calling in briefly at Charlie's office on the way.

'Charlie, did Karen have a word?'

'More than a word, I'm afraid. She was fuming.'

'I thought she might be.'

'Hurt pride mostly, I think.'

'Is there going to be a problem?'

'If she wants to pursue it, then yes, there might be.'

Charlie was concerned, he could see that much, and it worried him. The clinical nurse manager had been in the department longer than anyone, and he knew all there was to know about disciplinary procedures and had skated close to a few disasters himself in his time.

'It's one of those blurred areas,' Charlie said. 'Nothing you can look at and say this should have been done and that shouldn't.'

'I don't see what else I could have done, Charlie. If I'd just spoken out and said, "Why don't you check his eyes, Karen?" she'd've gone wild. You know how sensitive she is over her position.'

Charlie took hold of his shoulder and eased him into the office, shutting the door behind them. 'It's not really about that. I don't think it's even about you, Ash. Karen needs to impose her authority on the team. She knows she lacks experience, she's quite aware that most of us can handle patients as well as she can. How do you think she feels? How would you feel in that situation?'

'I don't know, Charlie.'

'Well you should think about it,' Charlie leaned across the desk to emphasise the point, 'because if you want to go for promotion you're going to find yourself leading a team one day. And when you walk in there, you're going to have to decide how to impose your authority, leadership, call it whatever you want, on a large group of people all of whom see themselves as every bit as good at their jobs as you are. In some cases better.' He held up a hand before Ash could speak. 'I'm not asking for an answer to that, I don't think there is one, but it might make sense for you to consider it.'

'And the complaint?'

'I'll talk to Mike, see if he can get through to her.'

'Maybe he's not the best choice, since I went to him in the first place.'

'Would you prefer Mark Calder?'

Ash mimed surrender. 'No thanks.'

'We'll sort it out somehow. You on for a lift tomorrow morning?'

'I'm beginning to feel guilty about this, Charlie.'

'No problem. I can't resist your coffee.'

'That'd be great then. I'll see you.'

On the bus Ash sat near the back to get what cool air there was and hoped his mum hadn't prepared anything elaborate for him. She usually liked to have something waiting when he arrived, a gumbo of some kind, or swordfish, which she went to great trouble to get for him, but today eating a mother's meal was out of the question.

The route from the bus stop to his mum's took him past the site of the ghost house. It had been knocked down and built over years ago, and now even the new community centre was beginning to look old. It must mean something, Ash mused. Probably that he was getting old himself.

He'd noticed recently that the stairs leading up to his mum's flat were getting dirtier; not just with rubbish bags being left out but with broken windows remaining unmended from one monthly visit to the next, paint peeling and empty cider bottles being left on the landings. Each time he feared what else might be left around to cause accidents and wondered how long Mum could continue living here in safety.

Her door was newly painted. Ash had done it for her, and the brass knocker and letter box, even the rim round the little spy-eye, had been polished to gleaming perfection. He pressed the bell and waited.

'Martin! It's too hot, you shouldn't have come out of your way.'

He gave her a hug and they went inside, where it was

pleasantly cool, with the curtains drawn across the opened windows to keep out the glare.

'Come on, Mum, you know it's no trouble.' It was always a good feeling coming back into his mum's flat. She'd moved here only ten years before so it wasn't exactly his childhood home, but all the ornaments, the furniture and the pictures were the same and the smell too, of furniture polish and clean washing. She'd always been a cyclone in the house, washing, polishing and cleaning after she got back from work. And cooking. The queen of the oven, he'd called her.

'Now, you just sit down, Martin. There's a nice salad for your tea waiting in the fridge. And a jug of that lemonade.'

'You shouldn't, Mum.'

'Why? What else have I got to do?'

'Well, at least let me fetch it through. No, sit down.' He almost held her in her chair and then went to the spotless kitchen. The salad was in the fridge as she'd said but there wasn't much else. He felt anxiety gnawing at him. She wasn't eating properly. He checked the cupboards. Semolina, lentils, beans of all sorts, but the packets hardly looked any emptier than last time he'd checked a month before.

He carried the salad and the jug of newly pressed lemon, with its ice cubes clinking, back into the sitting-room and sat down at the table. 'Could you open one of the curtains, Mum? Can't see a thing here,' he smiled.

'Ah, you people, always wanting the sun. You know, at home,' she still thought of the West Indies as 'home', 'when I grew up, folk didn't go in for all this sun-bathing. It's no good for you, all that sun. We knew it then and now they're discovering it all over again. You go to any hot country and you'll find they've got the sense to stay in the shade during the hot times.'

'I'm sure they have, Mum, but we have to enjoy it

while we can.' He jumped up and crossed to the window where he pulled the curtains back, flooding the room with light. His mum had an annoyed expression on her face, but not because of the light. It was obvious that she was thinner, more worn, her face tired and lined. 'You're still not going to the doctor?'

'He's no good, this local man. Hardly more than a boy himself.'

'Come on, Mum,' he sighed. 'It's me, Martin.'

'Eat your salad.'

It was his second salad today. He speared a radish on his fork. 'I'll eat my salad if you tell me how you're feeling.'

'I'm not a young girl any more. Feeling my age, that's all.'

'The stomach pains?'

'I wouldn't say they were pains.'

'Appetite?'

'I never was a big eater anyway.'

'Wind?'

'Martin, you mind your own business!'

'Don't you see, Mum, I want you to go to a doctor before you do become my business.'

Sighing, she turned away. 'I suppose if I have to . . .'

'You do, Mum. For me. I don't want to . . .' He faltered, unable to continue. His mother fixed him with her eye.

'You think it's serious, don't you, Martin?'

'I just think you should be safe, that's all.'

'You never could lie to me, boy.'

'This isn't about missing afternoon school or stealing an orange from the supermarket, Mum. It's your health and I want you to do something about it soon. Tomorrow.'

'Well, maybe I'll see this man.'

'Definitely you'll see him. Right?'

'Go on, drink your lemon.'

He did. It was as deliciously cool as ever he could remember. No one ever made it like his mum. Benny had said that. 'She should sell this stuff, your mum. She'd be rich.'

Benny.

'Do you ever hear from Benny, Mum?'

'That rude boy? Not a word. I've seen him around in that car of his, the big one he don't have no reason to drive. With those friends of his. You know, he bought me some flowers once, just last year. Arrived with this big bunch.'

'I didn't know that. You never told me.'

'That's 'cos I threw them straight out after he'd gone.'

'You never did.'

'I did my duty by Eugenia.' That was her sister. 'I looked after him while she had her babies. Hmm, couldn't stop having them, that girl. But that's all. I didn't want him round my house after that. But you don't need to ask about those times, do you?'

He didn't. It was in secondary school. A few years after the ghost house episode. Benny had been there too and they'd started to hang out with a few older kids, friends of Benny's. It hadn't seemed like they were doing much wrong to Ash. One of the guys had a car and they'd cruise around. Sometimes he and Benny would wait in the back while the others went off for a few minutes and then came back at a run, laughing like crazy. slapping hands and whooping as they skidded away from the kerb. There was dope passed around, though Ash didn't smoke and always declined the offer; there was Thunderbird fruit wine and music and a few girls who were the kind of girls he'd never have had the courage to talk to on his own.

And then, one night when he got back home sometime after twelve, there was his mother, waiting as he came through the door. He'd given her a cool grin which turned into a stupid smile. She marched over to him and slapped his face so hard his head literally rang. Then she slapped him again on the other cheek. He got angry. 'Don't you ever do that to me again,' he shouted, his eyes stinging with tears of shame..

She'd looked at him and said, very quietly, 'Your case is in your room, Martin. It's packed. You can take it now and go or you can unpack and stay. But if you stay, you work, you keep away from that trash you've been running with. Otherwise, you can leave right now. Before God, Martin, I don't want to lose you 'cos I love you more than I love anything, but I won't stand by and see you destroy your life like your cousin Benny.'

That's how it had been. He'd made his choice and stayed. He'd never regretted it.

'I was just wondering, that's all. If you'd heard anything about Benny.'

'If I did, then I wasn't listening,' she said in that maddening way she had when she wanted to close a subject. 'But never mind me, my time is all past time. What about you, Martin? You still don't bring a girl to see me since your Nikki went away.'

'She was never *my* Nikki, Mum.'

'You thought she might be. But there's no one, eh? Man like you, you should be thinking about settling down, having children while you're young enough to enjoy them. Your dad, now, dying like he did so early, that's what I regret for him, that he never had the pleasure of his children.'

'Oh come on, Mum,' he protested, 'it's hard enough managing on my own, if I had to support a family as well . . .'

She got up from the settee, holding her hand in the small of her back, and went across to the window where she pulled the curtains half closed. 'What if everybody thought like you? There would be no children at all. No,

75

you need someone to love and cherish, Martin. I know you, you're an affectionate boy, you need lots of loving, a good woman.'

'I've got a good mum. Who needs more?'

She smiled in pleasure at that. 'That's enough of your flattery. Now are you feeling strong? I've a few things I want from the shops so I thought you might walk down there with me.'

She was quite capable of carrying her own shopping, or at least had been before she'd got ill; her real reason was the enjoyment she got out of walking in the neighbourhood with her son. He knew she was proud of him. He wondered what she would feel if she knew he'd stolen drugs from the hospital. How proud would she be then?

Damn Benny, he said to himself. Damn him.

8

Janice Parker was pouring boiling water over the tomatoes ready to skin them for the salad when she heard
Frank turn into the drive. She didn't interrupt her work,
Frank hated mushy tomatoes in his salad. She poured
the boiling water out of the bowl, ran in the cold and
took a tomato out, cut the skin and began to peel it off.
She had finished all but one when Frank came through,
shrugging off his suit jacket.

'Don't throw the water away,' he cautioned as Janice
went to do just that, 'we can use it on the pots. They
must be dying in this weather. You did remember to
empty the teapot on the large one?'

'Hello, love. Good day?' she asked.

He took the bowl from her, slipped out through the
back door and emptied it into one of the many pots
which stood on the patio. Frank really loved his garden
and the effect the heat was having on it was like a personal attack. He stood for a while looking round,
studying the state of things. She saw his back tense and
when he returned to the kitchen his lips were pursed and
annoyed. 'Next door's cat has been in the flowerbed
again. I asked you to keep an eye on the wretched animal. I'll have to speak to them.'

'I'm sorry, love, I had to go out this afternoon. Carly
had a little . . .'

He'd gone back out, vanishing in the garden shed before reappearing with a shovel which he held in front of him like a weapon. He advanced upon the flowerbed at the end of the garden and used the spade to remove whatever sin next door's cat had left there. He carried it, at arm's length, to the compost heap and flipped it in.

'Sorry, Jan, what was it you said, Carly was what?'

'Oh, she just had a little tumble, off the tree.'

'She wasn't climbing the thing again, was she?' He went off and a moment later she heard him calling up to their daughter, pretending to be a big furry bear who was going to come growling up the stairs to eat her all up. Janice could remember a time when it had been her own delighted laughter that had sounded as Frank came lumbering up to the bedroom, but not any longer.

'Here she is, here's yummy supper,' growled Frank, carrying a squealing Carly through and sitting down with her at the kitchen table while she told him everything she'd done during the day.

Janice made a couple of gin and tonics for them, slipping a good deal more gin into hers than Frank's.

'Can I have one?' Carly asked.

'Not for you,' Frank laughed. 'Just me and Mummy because we work so hard. Cheers, love.' He took a sip – always a sip, never a slug – and set his glass carefully down. 'I said I'd give James a hand with his mower engine after supper.' James was their other neighbour, who didn't have a cat. 'Doesn't seem to be running smoothly. Moira said why don't you come over too and watch some TV with her.'

Janice nearly shouted Whoopee! But she didn't. She never shouted. Frank didn't like it. 'I don't know, love. It's a bit late for Carly and I don't want to leave her alone in the house.'

Frank nodded in agreement with her good sense. 'You've got a point. I'll apologise to Moira. Anyway, they're coming over for drinks at the weekend.'

'Yes, perhaps Moira and I could watch TV then.' She took a drink. 'Besides, I want to get on with Carly's dress.'

'How's it coming?'

'Fine, It's no problem really.' They could easy afford all the dresses they wanted for Carly but Janice liked to make them and Frank thought it was a good hobby for her. She'd once suggested making a suit for him but he hadn't really felt that this would be right; not that he could give any reason and the patterns she'd showed him had been every bit as sober as those he habitually wore, it was just that having your wife make your suits wasn't quite right. Not in the upper reaches of the insurance business, anyway.

'What's for supper?' he asked, looking at the bits and pieces that would go together to make a salad niçoise.

'Salad niçoise,' she said. 'And poached pears.' He liked his puddings, did Frank.

'Splendid. Perhaps a half-bottle of something sparkling. The Vouvray, do you think?'

'Whatever *you* think,' she said. Carly was drawing on the kitchen table with a crayon, a big waxy circle with waves across it. 'It's the moon,' she said, 'and this is the sea.'

'There isn't any water on the moon,' Frank said.

Janice took another drink. It was amazing how much better the world began to seem after a gin and tonic. 'Then why do they have all those seas? The Sea of Tranquillity. The Sea of Fertility?'

'They're just names,' Frank said. 'That's all.' He put Carly down, got a damp cloth and wiped the crayon off the shiny white surface. 'There's no water at all. Silly mummy, eh?' he said to Carly.

'Silly mummy,' she said.

*

It was after seven when Ash left his mother. She had finally promised she'd go to the doctor within the next couple of days. He wasn't sure how much the promise was worth but it was something.

The evening was, if anything, hotter than the afternoon, as if the heat had gathered and consolidated itself over the city. Everywhere people were moving on to the street. They stood in crowds outside city-centre pubs, they congregated on front steps or just hung around, too hot to do anything much.

Ash had to change buses near the town centre and walking through to pick up his local bus he found himself passing Taylor's chemist's shop. It was open late dispensing prescriptions, though there were few people waiting. It was no different from half a dozen shops like it in the town, the windows displaying soaps and make-up and a rack of fluffy slippers visible inside.

Ash stopped by the door. There was a scent of perfume coming out. After a moment's indecision, he went in. A girl stood behind a small make-up counter. There were racks of health foods and herbal teas, everything you'd expect except a sign saying: 'Beware, this prescription may injure your health.'

The pharmacy was at the far end of the shop and he could see the light catching a bald head back there, beyond the security window. He went to the counter and an elderly man, the owner of the bald head, with a round face and little half-moon spectacles in gold frames, beamed out at him.

'Yes, Sir. You have a prescription?'

'Er, no I don't. I wanted to have a word with you, Mr Taylor. If I could.'

'The smile became a little less sure? 'I'm sorry, I don't think we've met?'

'No. We haven't. My name is Martin Ashford. I'm at Holby General. In Casualty.'

'Yes?' He picked up a prescription sheet. 'You don't mind if I work while you talk. I am rather busy.'

'Not at all, please.'

Taylor peered at the sheet, blinked a couple of times and began to sort through various packets and bottles.

'We had a patient in today. A Mr Bryant. Edward Bryant.'

Taylor didn't react.

'There was an accident at the station. Serious injuries.'

'Go on, young man.' Taylor didn't look up from his close examination of labels.

'The thing is, he was injured because he couldn't see. He was taking eye drops prescribed by you. He'd got the wrong prescription.'

Taylor looked up sharply. 'Nobody has said anything to me.'

'They will,' Ash said. 'There will have to be an enquiry. Mr Bryant will ensure that if nothing else. He's a solicitor.'

A frown crossed the old man's round smooth face. 'Bryant, did you say?'

'Yes. Eye drops. He was given them by mistake.'

'Are you sure of this?' The voice was sharper and the smile had vanished from the face. 'Because you can't come in here accusing people of things without getting your facts right. What evidence is there of any malpractice?'

Ash tried to speak calmly. 'I'm not accusing you of anything, Mr Taylor. I want to help.'

'That's why you come in here with these stories? Well, I have no time for this kind of bullying behaviour. Please be good enough to leave at once!'

'But don't you see—'

'I see you want to make trouble.'

'There is trouble already.' The girl at the make-up counter was looking anxiously down the shop, her attention drawn by Taylor's angry tone.

'You're accusing me of being incompetent.'

'I just thought you should know what happened, that's all. And I hoped . . .'

'What ?'

'That maybe you would stop issuing prescriptions today. Now. So that there aren't any more mistakes. I mean, if there is an enquiry, it would look better if you'd stopped as soon as you knew something had gone wrong.'

'Nothing has gone wrong. This is all hearsay. You can't prove a thing.'

'A man nearly went blind today. He suffered serious injuries. I'm not placing blame. I just don't want it to happen again.'

Red now, and furious, Taylor came out from the security hatch. 'It's because of last time, isn't it. You tried to do this before. Put me out of business with your enquiries. Well, it didn't work then and it won't work now.' He began to push at Ash, shoving him back through the shop.

'Mr Taylor, are you all right?' the girl asked.

'Yes, thank you, Penny. This gentleman is leaving and if you ever see him in this shop again, please call me.'

'You're betraying your trust,' Ash said.

'Get out! Get out!'

A moment later he was back on the pavement, a passing couple giving him a curious look as Taylor slammed his door and glared out.

'Bloody fool, what did I think I was doing?' he said to himself, shoving his hands deep into his trouser pockets, where he felt the bottle of stolen pills turn like a snake under his palm. Poking his nose in, acting before thinking, too ready to get involved in other people's problems. They were familiar words which had appeared on all too many of his personnel reports. They'd write it on his grave one day: he leaped before he looked once too often.

The thought made him grin. Then he saw his bus and ran for it, jumping on to the platform as it pulled away from the stop. He had been trying to help, hadn't he? Just like he'd been trying to help earlier today. And look where that had landed him: with a possible disciplinary hearing that would really screw up his promotion chances.

The car was hot. He was almost melting, but he didn't get out; he sat looking up through the shaded top of the windscreen at the flats and the windows where, one by one, the lights were beginning to come on.

People were coming home from work, sitting down to their suppers, and a night in front of the TV with their wives. Except he had no wife to go home to. Sherry was gone forever, he'd never see her face again, never feel her tremble under his touch, they'd never share a drink or a meal or a laugh. Not that there had been many of those near the end when she'd been getting out of hand more and more.

He felt his head tighten as if someone was turning a screw on a hose clip. He slammed his fist into the steering wheel, barking the knuckles. The pain felt good, almost as good as when he smashed his fist into someone's face and saw the bruises form and the blood, bright and red, start to flow. There was an exhilaration when you were fighting. Nothing else mattered in the world except you and the other guy and knowing what you were going to do to him.

A curtain moved and a window was closed up on the fourth floor. He caught the flash of sun on turning glass and then saw the old woman pause, looking out over the city. Maybe Mrs Ashford liked looking at the lights too. He wondered if he should go and see her now. Knock at her door, introduce himself as an old friend of Martin's and slip inside.

No, it was too soon; it would be too easy for someone to see and remember him. Because people noticed, there was something about the way he was: if he went into a bar, drinkers turned round, gave him room, didn't mix it. Respect, that's what it was. Even if they didn't know his reputation, they could feel the danger, the way he might explode at any moment.

A black kid was passing, walking with that rolling ain't-I-wonderful gait they had, running his hand along the cars parked at the kerb. When he reached Deevers' car he lifted his hand and walked round. They respected him, even when they didn't know him, and soon Martin would respect him too.

He flipped the ignition and peeled away from the kerb, making a U-turn and heading back into town.

As soon as he'd let himself in Ash peeled off his shirt and went through to the bedroom to grab something cooler. He took a couple of dirty shirts from the laundry basket, filled the basin, added some powder and shoved them in to soak. Then he put on the kettle for a coffee. He'd have a shower before going out to see Benny but first he wanted to grab a few minutes' sleep.

He had a feeling he was going to be late tonight and Charlie would be knocking at his door tomorrow at a quarter to seven. Late nights didn't make for good decisions and good decisions could save lives.

'Pompous idiot,' he laughed at himself, going through and falling back on to the bed. He closed his eyes, thinking, I'll never sleep, and slept at once.

He woke to the sound of the doorbell and thought, bloody hell, I've slept right through. A look at his clock reassured him. It was twenty past eight, he had time in hand. The bell rang again and he went though to the hall.

'I'm sorry.' It was Sara Eeles, the Project 2000 nurse.

What on earth did she want?

'Come in,' he said, standing aside.

She walked past him. She was out of uniform, wearing loose fit blue jeans and a white body. Her hair was untied too, and fell, deep chestnut, around her shoulders. She was, he realised, an attractive girl.

'I er, was asleep. Busy day. Umm . . . look, can I get you a coffee?'

She nodded. 'Thanks. I really am sorry about disturbing you at home.'

He ushered her through into the kitchen. 'No, that's OK. Really. I needed to wake up. I have to go out.'

She blushed. 'Oh, I'm sorry, I'll go.'

'No, no.' He felt like a brute. 'I didn't mean now. Later, that's all. I've got a while. How do you like your coffee?'

'White with no sugar.'

'Not slimming?' he said, looking at her waist, then looking away, embarrassed. She had a very good figure. A little like Nikki's.

'I just don't like it,' she said. 'Anyway, working in Casualty, I should think I could eat double what I do and still burn up calories.'

'It does get pretty hectic at times.' The kettle was still warm and didn't take long to boil. He spooned coffee into clean mugs. 'You know,' he said, 'this morning when I was making coffee I was wondering why glamorous women never called on me. I figured I was using the wrong brand – but here you are.'

She blushed again and smiled and her face came alive. He couldn't resist smiling back. He felt easy with her, relaxed. It was a totally different feeling to the one he experienced with Josette Lowell. There he felt on trial the whole time; here he felt no kind of threat at all.

'So, Sara, what can I do for you?'

'I wanted to speak to you at work but . . .'

'Yeah, I'm sorry, I was umm . . .'

'No, I quite understand. I mean I should have realised.'

'Hold it, Sara,' he said. 'I think we both have to stop apologising to each other or we'll never get anywhere.'

'Oh yeah, I'm sorry.' She burst out laughing. Then her face settled and she took a deep breath. 'I'm really worried about my position in A and E. I can't seem to get on the way I should. I keep rubbing people up the wrong way.'

'How do you mean?'

She cradled her mug in both hands and blew the steam off the top. 'People resent me. Some of the nurses, anyway. As if I'm pushing in where I'm not wanted. It's like they think I'm acting superior because I'm a Project 2000, but at the same time they accuse me of not knowing anything.'

'That's hardly your fault,' Ash said. 'The whole idea of Project 2000 is to build up on theory before coming into the department.'

'Is that how it was when you started?'

'Hey, no, I studied under Florence Nightingale. No, we tended to have more of a balance between work on the wards and theory, which is fine in its own way but it does sometimes mean that you lose out on the scientific aspects of nursing, and nowadays they're more and more important.'

She was taking in his words with all her attention. He thought that she really was remarkably good-looking. Not beautiful like Josette, but someone you'd like to take to a pizza bar. He almost asked her there and then but remembered where he had to go later tonight.

'I want to be a good nurse more than anything.'

'We all do,' he said.

'So why do people get annoyed when I ask questions? How can I learn anything if I don't?'

'Of course, you've got to ask, yeah. But what you

should try and understand is that sometimes people are busy. They're concentrating on a patient and it's not a good time to start asking what the correct practice might be.' He saw her flinch and went on hastily, 'It's not your fault. You have to try and understand that situations are different. Sometimes it's fine to talk in front of a patient, others it's the worse thing you can do. Most people want to help. Don't you have a monitor yet?'

'No, what is it?'

'Someone you work alongside. Helen Chatsworth, the last Project 2000, worked with Adele. She drove her crazy but she ended up knowing a lot more than when she started. Charlie should've set something up.'

'Well, I've only been in the department a few days. Maybe he hasn't had time.'

'Talking of which,' he indicated the clock, 'I have to be going.'

She was disappointed. 'I wondered if perhaps, I mean I live quite near here. I've got a room in this house I share. If you wanted to drop in and have a coffee any time.'

'Yeah, that'd be nice. Thanks, Sara. And look, maybe I could speak to Charlie Fairhead and get him to set up a monitor for you.' He sensed he was doing it all wrong. That she was hurt and expected something else from him. 'I know you'll find it difficult, unlike anything you've been taught but please, stick with us and you'll find it begins to fall into place.' Maybe she expected him to become her monitor? He went to the door and held it as she left.

'Thanks, anyway.' She went and as he stood there watching her go down the stairs he realised how much he'd have liked her to stay. But how could he have told her that at the same time as he was obviously throwing her out?

'Sara!'

She stopped and looked back at him.

'It'll be fine. You'll see.'

He couldn't read a thing from her expression, not a single thing. He shrugged and went back inside to shower and change. It wasn't going to be the night out he'd expected when he'd asked Josette to come for a meal but he had an uncomfortable feeling that it was going to be a memorable one all the same.

9

'They brought this fellow in, he's really bad, they said. He ought to be somewhere else, they said, but they haven't got any room so they've put him in here.'

Barbara was excited. Scrubbs supposed a new arrival was something that broke the monotony. He pulled his dressing-gown round him and fumbled up the belt. 'Brought who in?'

'This fellow, I told you, Sar'nt-Major. He walked into a train.'

'He what?'

'He said so. Frankie the porter said so. Nice lad. Said he walked into a train. That's what he said.'

'Blimey.'

'He's a big fellow, though.'

'Uh,' Scrubbs grunted, 'he'd need to be. Train all right, is it?'

'You can see him if you want,' Barbara confided. 'He's got all these tubes going in, and things, sort of technical things.'

'Ah well he would, having walked into a train. You'd need technical things for that.'

'Do you want to take a peek, then?'

He wasn't quite sure how his legs would stand up to a walk down the ward. His thirst was beginning to get pretty bad, tea didn't help and the withdrawal symptoms seemed to have settled, for some reason, in his legs, making them buzz and feel like bendy old rhubarb stalks. He knew nothing would help except a drink and yet he'd begun to suspect that maybe, with a bit of luck and a lot of hard work, just maybe he might be able to get through the night without one.

'All right, c'mon then, let's have a look at him.' He stood up unsteadily, arms out for balance. Barbara took hold of one hand.

'There you go, Sar'nt Major. That better?'

'Thank you, Barbara, I reckon it is.'

What a shock, to be holding a clean hand after all this time, a woman's hand with (he sneaked a look) nicely cut nails.

'Are you all right, Sar'nt-Major?'

He turned away and answered gruffly. 'Course I am. Are we going or not?'

They set off down the ward. The lights had been lowered and many of the patients were asleep or dozing. At the far end, near the nurse station and the little cubicle loo, they found Ted Bryant festooned with lines and monitors. He was breathing calmly and seemed asleep, though when Scrubbs took hold of the bed end with a free hand, his eyes opened.

'Hello,' he mumbled. 'What's up then?'

'Looks like you are, mate,' Scrubbs answered. 'They said you walked into a train.'

A fleeting grin appeared on Ted's face. 'Well I'm still here, and I'm not planning on going anywhere. Where's Brenda, is she here? Must be breakfast time. Can't be late.'

He drifted off. Barbara said: 'Drugs. Look.' She pointed to a line passing through a tiny box which clicked like an old-fashioned watch, and then into Ted's inner elbow. 'They can keep you asleep for weeks in this place. You could spend your whole life dreaming.'

'Wouldn't fancy that,' Scrubbs muttered, 'not with some of the dreams I have.'

He started back towards his bed, suddenly feeling very tired. How long was he going to be in here and what about these tests they were supposed to do? What exactly were they about? After seeing Ted Bryant he began to feel more than a bit nervous. Once they got you into these places, they didn't have to let you go. It would be like it was back in Korea, when the communists captured him. My God, he couldn't go through that again.

'You all right, Sar'nt-Major?'

'Er, yes, nothing wrong, what could be wrong?'

'I don't know, but you're pulling me along like you was our Nigel.'

'Who?'

'You know, that Nigel Mansell. Drives racing cars. He was world champion.'

Sweat rose up suddenly all over his back, as he remembered Korea and the prison camp. The noise, day after day; worse, night after night. And the footsteps outside the hut, passing or stopping. Life or death for some poor sod. He shook his head. God, he knew why he needed a drink now. To blot out the memory of those days.

Someone opened a window and the breeze turned the sweat to ice. He started to shiver.

'Are you sure you're all right, luv? You don't look so good to me. Maybe I should call a nurse.'

'No, just leave me alone, will you? Leave me alone.' Letting go of her hand he blundered into his curtained-off cubicle and fell on the bed, his whole body shaking.

Golden Road estate had been built in the early seventies by a council which thought that at last it could deliver the best in housing to ordinary men and women. Using the latest techniques, the builders had put up the blocks in double-quick time, fulfilling an election promise of speedy results. Soon families were beginning to move in and the estate was featured on Television's *Tomorrow's World*. Its walkways were praised for giving easy access to the purpose-built shopping precinct with its neat row of greengrocer, butcher, minimarket, baker, betting shop, chemist; everything, in fact, that the newcomers could want. In the basement of each block there was a washing room, there were crêches, community flats, a local bobby and a local pub, the Horn of Plenty.

Twenty years later the precinct was a row of black holes with only a minimarket, behind steel shutters, and a betting shop remaining. The walkways were escape routes for gangs of kids, the basements were open toilets, the community flats housed squatters; only the pub seemed to go from strength to strength.

Tonight it was pumping out music so loud that Ash could feel the thud of base notes pulsing like hammer blows through the hot damp air. Drinkers were gathered around the open door, pints in hands, faces running with sweat, skin looking diseased under the glare of sodium streetlamps.

Ash's T-shirt was wet already. He wiped his face and remembered his dream, of being alone in an operating theatre, sweating, not knowing what to do. He needed a cool drink but didn't want to go into the Horn in case he missed his contact.

A gang of kids lounged by. The leader, maybe sixteen or seventeen, was pale, looking like a zombie under the lights, his head shaved back to the skull, a white T-shirt plastered to his chest like a second skin, emphasising the muscles. His eyes swam back and forth, lazily waiting to make contact with someone. Ash looked away, the kid and his mates were out for trouble and he didn't intend to provide it.

'You be Benny's mate, then?' A touch on his shoulder

and he was looking at a slim black kid with big glasses which reflected the neon sign outside the pub.

'I could be.'

The kid grinned. 'You be Marty Ashford?'

'I be stupid to come down here,' Ash said, 'but, yeah, you got your man, Sheriff.'

'He said you were OK.'

'Benny?'

'That's what he said. I dunno, maybe he's wrong.'

'I'm here.'

The kid stuck his hand out. After a few moments Ash decided he was supposed to shake it. 'Hi.'

'Hi. I'm Vernon.'

'Nice to meet you, Vernon.'

'Come on. ' The kid nodded and started across the street towards the nearest of the tower blocks. The zombie and his mates had stopped a few paces down the road while the kid had been talking. Now they began to drift back, six of them, spread out across the blistered tarmac. The kid didn't seem fazed; he strolled up to the zombie and said something, as if he knew the guy, indicating Ash with a jerk of the thumb. The zombie had to bend low to catch the kid's words, and when he stood up he grunted to his mates and they slid away into the darkness.

'What was that all about?' Ash asked.

'It was about saving your ass from Iceman there.'

'You did that? How come he listened.'

The kid grinned, his teeth as bright as a knife blade. 'You don't be asking that kind of question. You just come along with me.'

Leaving the precinct, for all its shabbiness, meant leaving the lights behind. Once there had been lighting throughout the estate, bulkhead lamps illuminating every dark corner. Now there were just dark corners which the kid navigated like he'd lived here all his life.

Which he probably had, Ash reflected with a shudder. Sometimes, through the hot darkness, he saw the glitter of eyes, the sudden glow of a cigarette, and heard the sounds of people doing things to each other which couldn't be done in the light of day.

The kid didn't hang around; twisting through alleys, up and down walkways, he hurried on until Ash had no idea where he was. At last, they went inside, pushing through swing doors in which the glass had been replaced with wood, which had in turn been splintered and broken and patched with dull, unpainted sheets of metal.

'Come on, come on.' Vernon started up stairs, vanishing for a moment as he turned a corner. Ash hurried after the flash of his trainers.

'Wait a minute.' He didn't want to be left alone here. God knew who or what might come out of some of the flat doors, which gaped open on to lives that were unimaginable to him.

'We here now.' The kid knocked a couple of times. 'Susie, it's me.'

'You got him?' a girl's voice answered.

'Course I got him. You think I'm stupid? Open the door.'

After a few moments, during which keys turned and bolts were pulled, the door opened.

'OK, move it, mister.' The kid pushed him through into the narrow hallway.

A low growl that made his guts turn watery came from a pit bull. It was straining at the steel links of its leash and Ash noticed that some of them had been marked by teeth. About two feet high and four broad, it looked like you could have hammered iron spikes into rock with its head and it wouldn't have noticed.

'You don't be scared of Steel,' Vernon said, lightly steering him past. 'When he wants you, he'll be coming to get you.'

94

The kid went through into a kitchen. The girl, who was in her twenties and might have been pretty if she wasn't so drawn and tired, said: 'He's in the bedroom.'

Ash followed her down a dark passage. In a room off it he heard a baby crying. At the end the door was half open and light spilled out.

'Go on,' the girl said.

He pushed the door open.

'Heeey, Marty, I knew you'd come. I knew I could count on you.'

Benny was half lying on an unmade bed. He wore trousers and shoes but no shirt. A towel was draped across his shoulders and he used it to wipe his face. His left side, nearest the bed, seemed to be in shadow but as Ash advanced into the room he caught the smell of disinfectant and saw the torn flesh at the base of Benny's rib cage. It was like an eruption, dried blood crusting in peaks. Empty pill decks were scattered round the bed and a bottle of bourbon, almost empty, stood on the floor within reach of Benny's hand.

'What happened?' Ash knelt by the bed, training taking over as he eased Benny towards him so he could get a better look at the wound.

'I had some trouble. These people, they didn't like what I sold 'em. They got real mad, Marty. It was like *Nightmare on Elm Street* in there for a while.'

'This is a gun-shot wound, for God's sake.'

Benny cried out in pain as Ash's finger probed the extent of the damage. 'Of course it is. What d'you think these people do, flick towels at each other?'

'This is serious.'

Benny shut his eyes. 'I know it is, man. I think the bullet is still in there. I think I can feel it.'

'I'll check for an exit wound.' He reached carefully round. The flesh was smooth and unbroken. 'I think it has to be.'

95

'How bad is it, Marty?'

'Let me look, give me some time here. I need more light.'

'Susie, get some more light.'

Ash couldn't see if the girl was watching but in a few moments she appeared with another lamp, which she plugged in and placed on the bedside table. In its light he was able to get a better view of the wound.

'Well?'

'Well, you're not bleeding any more, that's something.'

'Bled like a pig to start with. Towels soaking in the bath through there.'

Ash palpated the back. Benny winced.

'Any sharp pain?'

'Just a sort of ache then there's this.' He writhed away from the probing hand. 'That's it. A real sharp pain.'

'It's probably a nerve. I need to see if any structures have been damaged. Bones or organs. There shouldn't be anything here but you can never tell. Have you eaten anything, drunk anything?'

'You seen the whiskey. Susie made some soup.'

'You were able to eat it?'

'A little.'

'No blood coming up ? No coughing?'

'No.'

'You been to the toilet?'

'Yeah.'

'Any blood there?'

'Hey, why'd I be looking at that?'

'You looked.'

'Yeah. There was some kinda pink stuff in the bowl after, you know.'

'Probably the stomach. I need to get you into hospital.'

Benny grabbed his arm. There was surprising strength in the grip. 'No, man. I could get myself into hospital. I have to stay here.'

'You can't, Benny.'

'Don't tell me, Marty. I can't leave here. I go out and I'm dead.'

'I need some clean dressings. Have you got anything?' He was talking to the girl.

'Everything is messed up.'

'What about the baby. Are there nappies?'

'Yeah. Disposable.'

'Get them. And I need to wash my hands.'

She showed him the bathroom. There were clothes, hers and the baby's, hanging over the bath. In it were the towels, soaking out blood. He filled the basin with water as hot as he could bear and washed his hands. He should've brought some gloves, but how could he have known.

Back in the bedroom Benny had eased himself down on the bed so he was lying flat. When Ash looked at him, he winked. 'It's OK, Marty, you don't have to worry about no Aids or nothing. I'm clean.'

'I just have to worry about losing my job, right?'

'Come on, nobody is ever gonna know. Dig it out and sew me up and that's it, I'm out of your life.'

Susie came back with the nappies. He improvised a dressing out of one. 'You don't seem to understand, Benny. I think the stomach or maybe the bowel is torn.'

Briefly fear flared in Benny's eyes. 'What're you saying, Marty?'

'This is more than I can handle. There might be internal injuries. Have you any idea how much force there is behind a bullet? How far away was the person who did this?'

'We were in this place. A club. I guess he was—' Benny's face was grey and he stopped to catch his breath.

'The pain is bad isn't it?'

'It's bad, Marty. I didn't want you to think I couldn't take it.' He smiled wanly. 'Can you give me something?

I gotta have—' He began to suck in air and let it out in a moaning sigh. 'Jesuuuus, it hurts, it hurts.'

The girl Susie had him by the arm. 'You've got to help him. Give him something.' She was getting frantic.

'Get me some water, quick.' She did so and Ash took out the pills he'd stolen and gave Benny some nubane.

'That'll take a while to work,' he said. 'I think I need something to drink.'

'You come through,' she said, and he followed her into the kitchen where Vernon was sitting at the table with a Tab, the baby on his knee.

The fridge was well stocked and Susie asked, 'Beer or what?'

'Water'll do.' It was cold, blissfully cold, and he tipped it back in a couple of swallows.

'You be hot, man,' Vernon said. 'You want more?'

Ash said he did. He sat down at the table, across from the kid. The kitchen was neat, like the rest of the flat, and had microwave, freezer, everything you might need. The furniture was modern, it couldn't have been more than a few months old. These people were living too well for Golden Road estate.

He took a drink. 'You want to tell me what's happening here?'

The kid shrugged. 'You be better off you don't be askin'.'

'That man through there is very ill. If I'm going to help him I need to know a few things.'

'You are going to help him?' Susie said.

'If he lets me. Can we start by finding out who you are?'

'I'm Benny's woman,' she said proudly. 'This is his little girl.' She took the baby from the kid's lap.

'I didn't know he was married.'

'I didn't say we was married. Don't you listen? And this is my little brother.'

'You don't have to tell him anything, sis,' the kid scowled.

'You stupid? Course we have to tell him.' She turned to Ash. 'Benny was working this deal with some guys. They were importing the stuff, he was cutting it and selling it on.'

'Stuff?'

'You know. Blow.'

'Cocaine? That's what you're talking about.'

'That's about it,' she said. 'Benny, he's got a reputation as a man you can trust so he does the business round here. Only what he had to sell this time, someone cut it with the wrong stuff.'

'It happens,' Vernon said. 'There's a long way to come, they send it through Nigeria. There are a lot of folk who might get sticky fingers.'

'You mean Benny sold somebody some bad cocaine.'

'You could say.' The kid was all professional but he didn't look a day over fourteen.

Susie went on: 'There was trouble. They was threatening Benny, which is no good. A man has to stand by his reputation so he takes out his cutlass—'

'Stop. I don't want to hear. This is getting insane.'

'Benny didn't have no guns, he don't hold with guns. But these guys, they were carrying and they shot my Benny.' She began to cry, big tears which dropped on to the baby's sleeping face. 'And I don't want him to die.'

'Then you'd better make him understand he's got to go to hospital.'

'He said you're his friend, from way back.'

'I knew him when we were kids, yeah. But that doesn't mean I can make him better just like that. He needs a laparotomy . . . I mean, we have to explore the stomach and the bowel to make sure there isn't serious damage. You can't just cut into someone—'

The door crashed open and Benny came through, one

hand holding the dressing over the wound. He staggered to the table and slumped down, grinning at them. 'You'd be surprised, Marty, what you can do if you have to.'

'I know what I can do and know what I can't do and taking a bullet out of you without sterile conditions, without a proper doctor, without any back-up at all, is what I can't do.'

'Can't do or won't do?'

'I don't have the skill to operate.'

'You've seen it done?'

'Of course I have.'

'Then you can do it. I know you ain't stupid, Marty.'

He held his head in his hands. 'Can't you see, Benny? If I do this and you die then I'm finished. They'll put me in prison and throw away the key.'

'You're s'posed to help people, aren't you?' Susie said.

Benny said: 'You don't do this and I'm finished. These people are still looking for me.'

'What d'you mean? I thought they shot you, Benny. What else do they want?' A terrible suspicion began to steal over him. 'Benny, what did you do to them with your . . .' He couldn't say the word cutlass, it made it all sound like Captain Hook and Peter Pan and it wasn't. 'Did you hurt somebody?'

'Marty, I cut his arm off. So you could say I hurt him.'

'Do the police know?'

'These people don't use the police. They have their own police. I have to go away for a while, that's all. Things'll cool down. Just patch me up enough so I can run, Marty. That's all I ask.'

'You don't understand—'

'If you don't, they're gonna keep looking and sooner or later they'll find me. Here. With Susie and the baby. And when they come, I'll fight.'

'Me too,' the kid said.

100

' 'Cos they won't have no reason not to ice us all. Every one of us. Susie and the baby too. So you better think about that, Marty. Just like you're thinking about me holding that rope for you all those years ago.'

'If you do get away, will Susie and the child be all right?'

'Yeah. It's me they want. The others are bonus. If I'm not here—'

'Then give yourself up now. I can call an ambulance, get you into Casualty tonight. We can arrange police protection.'

'Not in prison, you can't. I'm asking you, Marty. You going to hold the rope for me?'

'I don't know. I . . . have to think.'

'You do that. Come back tomorrow night. The kid will meet you same place, same time. And leave that stuff, that painkiller. I'm gonna need it.'

Ash emptied the pills out of the bottle and gave directions for the dose. Benny caught his eye. 'I said you weren't stupid. You ain't even leaving the bottles around, just in case. Well, that's the kind of smarts I need.'

Ash felt like taking a pill himself, his head was so tight and full of pain.

At the door, while the kid waited to guide him back to the real world, Susie took his hand.

'Save my man for me, Marty. Save my little girl!'

10

Iceman leaned out over the edge of the walkway, look-ing down at Vernon and the big black guy as they slipped in and out of the shadows, heading back to the pub. He'd thought of taking them earlier but the kid had slipped him some stuff and besides, this guy Benny who looked after the kid's big sister could be trouble. Except nobody had seen him around for the past few days and he wasn't normally the kind of dude to play quiet and low. He tapped his teeth with his thumbnail the way he always did when he was thinking. Was there something to be made out of this situation? Money, a score or just trouble? Iceman liked trouble. It passed the time and kept the guys in line.

The rest of them were hanging around along the walk-way with a couple of girls. That was all the thinking they did, about who they could get off with and how far they could go. Depressing really. They'd never get out of this place. But Iceman was different. He had it inside him to be big in this town. Maybe even in London. He just needed the first score.

He was seventeen and hadn't been at school for a cou-ple of years. They hadn't been able to teach him anything anyway. What was he supposed to do, make boxes in Woodwork and find a career doing that for the rest of his life? Big joke. They didn't have careers on the Golden Road estate, they didn't have anything. Most of his time he spent at the local gym, where he did a bit of humping and sweeping for the chance to work out on the equipment after they closed. He'd thought of physical culture. He had the body for it but not the patience. Besides, how many ever made it right through to the top? That's what he wanted to be: top of the world!

'Hey, Iceman, what're you thinking about?' Petey was slow. He'd always been that way, the kid who got pushed around because he was there to be pushed around. There was some kind of problem inside his head and he went crazy at times. Mostly though he was just slow.

'Money, Petey. I'm thinking about money.'

A couple of the others drifted along. Tony, who was Indian but was called Tony anyway, and Gary Speke, who was always pushing to be the leader. He draped his long arms round Petey's shoulders.

'Hi, Gary,' Petey said, not so sure about this move, if it was friendly or not.

'We need to raise some capital,' Iceman said.

Gary snorted and tightened his arm round Petey's neck. 'Why don't we sell Petey to a hospital for spare-part surgery?'

'Because,' Tony said, 'we wouldn't get much for him.'

'In that case,' Gary shoved Petey against the edge of the walkway and grinned right into his face, 'why don't we just junk him right now?'

Iceman exploded. One moment Gary had his elbow hooked round Petey's throat, the next he was hanging by his feet, the concrete path twenty feet directly below his head.

'Lemmego!' he howled, looking up at Iceman's face. He felt the grip on his ankles loosen and howled again: 'Don't lemmego! Please, for God's sake!'

The rest of the group came rushing up, drawn by Gary's shrieks. Iceman held him, straight armed, the muscles swelling with the effort. 'Maybe we should junk *you*,' he hissed, and jerked Gary up and down so that everything fell out of his pockets and rained down on to the path.

'Come on, lemmeup, man. I didn't mean nothin', lemmeup, Ice. I didn't mean nothin' at all.'

With a weigh-lifter's jerk, Iceman pulled him up in one movement and set him back on his feet. 'Yeah, that's your problem, Gary. You don't mean nothing. You better go and pick your stuff up.'

'Sure. Hang around, I'll be back.'

'Hasta la vista, baby,' Petey snickered. Gary didn't look at him.

Ice said: 'One day he'll really do you, Petey, and if I ain't around, you'll be dead.' Petey went white.

'I'll stay out of his way.'

'You do that. Meantime you do something for me.'

'Sure, Ice, I'll do anything for you.'

'Hang around Susie's kid brother. See if you can find out what happening over at their place.'

'You think there's . . .'

'I dunno. I think maybe we should try and find out, that's all. Meantime I think I feel like a kebab. Let's go see Zorba the Greek.'

There was general laughter at this. The old kebab van run by 'Zorba', who was Turkish rather than Greek, but who cared about that, was a constant target of the gang. They ate there two or three times a week and rarely paid. The estate was their territory and they regarded the kebabs they took as tribute. Besides, if Zorba didn't come through, they'd trash his van.

By the time Ash got back it was after midnight and he was wrecked. He put the kettle on and sat staring blankly at the kitchen wall. He had a nasty taste in his mouth from the kebab he'd bought on the way out of the estate. The van had been the dirtiest he'd ever seen and the meat fatty and indigestible. He'd thrown most of the thing away and wondered about the kind of people who had to live on food like that. What did it do to your body?

The water was boiling and he made his coffee extra strong. While it cooled he went through to the bathroom, rinsed and squeezed out his shirts and hung them in front of the sitting-room windows. He left the curtains open; the room faced east and the sun should dry the thin material before he got up.

Back in the bathroom he took his medication. One of his greatest fears was forgetting and not noticing as he slipped into ketosis. Diabetes was something you learned to live with; it had given his life a pattern ever since he could remember and, in a strange way, he was almost grateful to the disease for teaching him a discipline he might not otherwise have had.

As he sipped his coffee he began to go over the evening's events in his mind. There was no doubt that he did owe something at least to Benny, but at the same time he knew very well that even back in the ghost house Benny had used him, virtually tricked him into going along. And after the accident, as he had been hanging there on the rope, Benny must have realised that his only chance of getting out of it without serious trouble lay in saving Ash and emerging as a hero.

He looked in the fridge and checked there was still milk left in the carton, then poured some bran flakes into a bowl and added sugar and milk. He carried the bowl and his coffee through to the bedroom and sat on the bed, still trying to work out some kind of answer. He couldn't go to the police and hand his cousin over. He couldn't refuse treatment but neither could he help someone who had almost certainly committed a serious crime. Never mind the drugs – and Ash had seen enough of the misery they had caused in Holby to mind them a great deal. There was worse: the injury. What had Benny done, what did you have to do to make someone want to kill you?

He lay back and groaned aloud: 'I'm out of my depth. I just don't know what the hell I'm supposed to do.'

He shut his eyes and, for the second time that day, he was asleep, the bran flakes untouched and the coffee unfinished on the bedside table.

While Ash slept others lay awake in their various beds around the city.

Janice Parker watched the reflected headlights from a passing car slide slowly across the bedroom ceiling. Frank lay sleeping beside her, his breathing hovering on the edge of a snore. He'd gone next door and helped mend the mower, coming back with oily hands and a satisfied expression. They'd watched a little TV, had a cup of tea and two biscuits each – Janice had bought some custard creams, which were Frank's favourite – and then Frank had yawned and said he was tired and they'd gone to bed.

After a while she knew she wasn't going to sleep. Carefully, so she didn't wake her husband, she slipped from under the sheet, pulled on her dressing-gown and went out on to the landing. It was a cloudless night. The moon was almost full and dark moon shadows lay across the landing carpet. There was a gurgle from Carly's room and she went in. As always the smell of her sleeping child summoned up all her protective, loving feelings and she knelt by the head of the bed and listened to Carly breathing in and out, just as she had in the first days after her birth.

Carly's hair was damp with sweat and she'd pushed the duvet back. Janice didn't pull it up – it was a hot night and she was surprised anyone was sleeping. She knew she wouldn't be able to rest now for a couple of hours. She went downstairs to the kitchen and made herself a cup of tea. Sitting at the table there she wondered what she could do to fill in the time tomrrow.

Mike Barratt lay cradling his wife Frances in his arms. They had made love and now she was sleeping, relaxed, a slight smile on her lips. He could hear the sound of a radio, some pop station, not loud but annoying all the same. It was one of the boys. Frances's children from a previous marriage, not his. He wondered if he ought to go and ask for the sound to be turned down. But what the hell, it wasn't that loud and it wasn't that late and the kids were on school holiday.

He changed his position slightly, moving his arm out from under Frances. She murmured but didn't wake. He shut his eyes and immediately saw Josette Lowell as she had been when she'd left his office earlier.

She'd stopped a moment by the door, turning back to say what time she'd arrive in the morning. A simple enough movement but seeing her there he'd experienced a moment of pure desire. She was beautiful, yes, but it was more than that; she had the kind of presence and self-awareness that movie stars must have. And he'd known that if he asked her out for dinner, she'd accept. And he'd also known that Frances was going to be away tomorrow at an antiques fair in Lincolnshire.

'I'll see you then, Mike.'

'Hold on a second, Josette.' He'd got up from his desk.' I just wondered if you might be free tomorrow night.'

'As a matter of fact, Mike, I am. Yes.' When he hadn't said anything she'd continued, 'Did you have something in mind? A late question-and-answer session?' The smile had been knowing.

'Dinner, that's all. If you're staying in a hotel it must get boring.'

'Only ignorant people let themselves get bored, Mike. But yes, I'd love to have dinner. Anywhere special in mind?'

'I'll sort something out.'

'Great. I look forward to it.'

And now he was faced with – what? It was hardly the great wife betrayal. He was only having a meal with a professional colleague. They'd probably discuss staffing levels and the patient response to the monitor exercise.

He sighed and said to himself: even you aren't simple enough to believe that one, Mike Barratt!

Sergeant-Major Scrubbs lay rigidly to attention in his bed, his eyes wide, seeing a different time and place, seeing Yongan prison camp in North Korea, where he'd been sent after they captured him.

First there had been the long march when three hundred prisoners of war, fighting under the United Nations banner against communist North Korea, had been force-marched hundreds of miles across inhospitable country. It had been winter and the cold was worse than anything he'd ever known. A constant pain in feet and hands that never left you, day and night, and that you never wanted to leave you because once it did, and your limbs became numb, you knew you'd got frostbite. And that meant amputation, which in these primitive conditions meant gangrene and death. Of the three hundred who set off, seventy-three arrived at the camp.

That was the easy part.

The communists didn't want military victory alone,

they wanted to convince their enemies that they were right and to do this they had invented a system which would soon become notorious throughout the world. They called it re-education; the world called it brain-washing.

For weeks on end he was kept in a brightly lit cell without sleep; then they allowed him rest, five minutes after which they woke him, told him he'd been sleeping for twenty hours and gave him breakfast, then another ten minutes and another breakfast until his mind was totally adrift and he didn't know where or even who he was.

After that they started the re-education. Twenty hours a day sitting facing relays of teachers who screamed the sins of the West into his face. And after a while he discovered something strange. He didn't hate these men in their tightly buttoned dun brown uniforms; on the contrary, he wanted to please them, he wanted to listen and learn everything they had to teach. That's when the kindness began and he became a comrade and they told him he would be filmed so he could condemn the atrocities committed by the United Nations troops against the freedom-loving peoples of Korea.

He never got to make his statement. A settlement was worked out and the armies went home and the prisoners were released. They gave Sergeant-Major Scrubbs what they called a reorientation course. It lasted two weeks. They gave him his back pay and two months' leave. He wasn't married, except to the army, so he had nowhere much to go.

He booked into a cheap room in Blackpool, took the pictures off the walls, removed all the furniture except the iron bedstead and one chair. He repainted the room white and sat on his chair with his back to the window. It was the only way he could find any peace inside his head.

After that he'd returned to duty and the dreams had started. He'd seen the medical officer, who told him to get a grip on himself. When he started having the dreams while he was awake, he knew he had to do something.

The only thing that seemed to help was drink. The sergeants' mess sold it cheaply. There was nothing else to spend his salary on and it got him through the days and nights until his time was up and he went back to civvy street. Then it was just the drink and there was only one way: down into forgetfulness.

And now he was climbing out of it and the nightmares were still there, they hadn't gone away at all, they were waiting and they had all the time in the world.

The curtain at the end of his bed was pulled back. Probably the night nurse checking on him, he thought, but it wasn't. Mumbling under her breath, Barbara came in, her hair down, clutching her dressing-gown. She headed for the chair beside the bed, pulled up her nightie and sat down.

Horrified, Scrubbs realised she'd made a mistake. She thought she was in the toilet cubicle at the other end of the ward. 'Barbara!' he hissed.

She didn't respond. Half asleep, confused, she wasn't aware of him. He grabbed the emergency button and pressed it frantically.

Footsteps sounded and a nurse appeared. 'What is it?

At that moment it became all too clear what it was. 'Oh dear, love,' the nurse said. 'Little mistake, eh? Never mind, we'll soon have you comfortable.' She took Barbara's arm and gently led her out. 'Someone will be along, Mr Scrubbs, in just a moment, don't you worry. Come along now, dear.'

As they went through the curtains Barbara seemed to come fully awake. She looked at the chair, at Scrubbs and uttered a cry of shame and horror. The nurse comforted her and led her away but Scrubbs had seen the look and knew how she must be feeling. Whatever the nurse said, Barbara would never be able to face him again. It wouldn't have mattered if it had been another bloke. You could laugh that off. But not between a man and a woman.

After they'd cleaned up and left him alone he lay there thinking. He knew he couldn't stand this any more. Barbara's shame, his dreams. He knew what would put them right. A drink would solve everything and he had a good idea where he'd left a stash of cider bottles.

Pushing back the sheets he slipped his feet out of bed and on to the floor. The lino was cool, about the only thing that was. He didn't know where his clothes were but he knew he'd be able to pick something up and he didn't need much, just enough to allow him to slip out unnoticed.

He stood up and quietly left the ward.

Dr Karen Goodliffe let the smoke drift lazily between her lips and spiral up to join the hazy blue layer that hung like a web just below the ceiling. Beside her, Andy slept. She took another drag and wondered how long he'd stay around. He was an OK guy; they got on, enjoyed the same films, read the same books and were both members of the local Labour party. And he had a great body, the kind of slim, wiry shape she liked. There wasn't anything deeper but that was enough for now.

It wasn't Andy who was on her mind as she lay there, the joint slowly burning down to her fingers. It was Ash and the bloody stupid trick he'd pulled that morning. It made her look a fool and that, more than anything else, made her furious. She thought of Droopy the cartoon dog, who used to say: 'You know what, that makes me maaaad,' in his slow old voice. She began to smile, despite her annoyance, then giggle.

Andy snorted and woke up, squinting at her through the smoke. 'What?'

'I was just thinking.'

'Thinking? At this time of night? What about?'

'Droopy.'

He turned and looked at her curled naked across the bed.

'Hey, who's droopy?'

Ray Deevers ran the video back to the place where De Niro walks up to the pimp and shoots him in the guts and then goes inside to rescue the girl. It was a great sequence. He played it over and over, even though Sherry hated it. She didn't understand. Well, she wasn't understanding anything now. She was smoke, halfway to the ozone layer.

He popped another can and drank. It was so damn hot you couldn't sleep, you could hardly think. He wondered about giving Martin a call, waking him up, letting the silence really get to him or maybe even asking if he'd noticed the X on his phone pad. He almost did it, too, but he was too damn tired and anyway, he'd got a better idea. Something that would hurt a lot more than missed sleep.

He finished the beer, and ran the video back again.

Everywhere people were trying to sleep in spite of the heat and some of them were succeeding. Ted Bryant was dreaming of batting against Fred Trueman, dispatching balls to the boundary. His wife Brenda was in a deep, dreamless trough conjured by the pills her doctor had given her. Benny was asleep too, watched over by Susie. Iceman lay awake, though, in his mum's flat, wondering if Benny still had a crew or if he was on his own and what could be made out of the situation. And in a sterile room in Holby General a young girl was awake in a world of dragons and adventures, her eyes glittering in the moonlight.

11

'What is this? It looks like a brick.' Charlie hefted the loaf in his hand.

'It's healthy.' Ash was ironing his uniform shirt badly.

'Not if you drop it on your foot. It's heavy, Ash. Where did it come from?'

'The health food shop just down from the hospital. You know the place.'

Charlie began to hack a slice from the loaf. 'Oh, right. I treated someone from there last week.'

'Yeah?'

'Heavy bread syndrome. You don't have a power saw around the place?'

'Look, Charlie, leave my bread alone. It's roughage.'

'So's a pair of corduroy trousers.'

'I happen to like the taste. Wholemeal. Really, it's good for you. I know you have this terrible hidden vice of eating fried breakfasts.'

'Can't be hidden if you know about it.' Charlie popped a couple of slices in the toaster and pressed it down. 'Is that from Duffy?'

A postcard showing a beach in Portugal lay on the work top.

'Yeah.' Ash pulled on the shirt. Charlie flipped the card over and read the back.

'I miss her, you know,' he said. 'You work with someone for so long, it's like they become part of you.'

'Maybe you two should have got together. In a more permanent way.'

'C'mon.' Charlie flipped the card back and looked at the beach. 'She's happy with Andrew. It's better for the children that way. And, anyway, our relationship was work, it was professional and sometimes I think that's the deepest kind of friendship you can have with someone. Not that there weren't times . . .' He sighed and looked at the picture on the postcard as if he might have been on that beach with Duffy.

The toaster popped. Ash caught the slices and howled as they burnt his hand. 'Keeps the heat, proper bread. Pass the spread.'

Charlie looked at it. 'Sunflower *Even Lower* Fat Spread?'

'I told you, you have to stay healthy in this game.'

'I'd rather eat those trousers. You ready?'

'Five minutes.'

He'd slept well, with no dreams that he remembered, waking at a quarter past six feeling refreshed. Sometimes the world was topsy-turvy. Go to bed with nothing much on your mind and you had nightmares, crash out after an evening spent with a gangster who wanted you to take a bullet out of his side and you slept like a baby. 'Let's go, Charlie. C'mon, no time to waste.' He pulled on his jacket and, the second slice of toast still in his hand, hurried into the hall, where he stopped in his tracks and picked up the phone pad.

'Charlie, did you draw this?' He held up the cross. The thick pencil lines had been driven deep, almost ripping the paper.

'Nope.'

'Well someone did.'

Charlie took the pad from him and put it back beside

the phone. 'It must've been you. Who else has been here?'

Ash didn't answer but while they drove to the hospital he went over it in his head. It hadn't been him, unless he was going crazy, and he wasn't – if you were, you wouldn't think about it. Or something like that. And the only other person who'd been in the flat, apart from Charlie, was Sara Eeles. Had he upset her that much? Anyway, why an X? He'd have to ask.

Charlie managed to get his positioning right and slid his card through the meter without difficulty. There was a space in the shade, which made a difference. The day was as hot as yesterday and the weather forecast promised even higher temperatures by the afternoon.

'Much more of this and we'll start sticking to the tarmac,' Charlie said as they walked towards the department.

'I wish it would break, that's all,' Ash was already feeling sticky. 'It's building up to a thunderstorm. Art Hunter in Gynae was telling me that their air conditioning went out twice last week.'

'The fabric is falling apart.' Charlie indicated the looming bulk of Holby General. 'It looks OK from the outside but you start peeking under the surface and you'll find it's all wearing out. Wiring, ducting, insulation, circulating pumps – it doesn't last forever.'

'Not like you and me, right?' Ash grinned and held the door open. Charlie hobbled through, staggering up to the desk where Mie was taking over from the night receptionist.

Ash still missed Norma. She'd been a fixture of the place, like a squeaky door that was annoying but when it wasn't there any more, you felt the lack. He wished he could have done more for her.

Mie settled behind the counter. She gave Charlie a puzzled glance. 'Mr Fairhead, are you all right?'

'It's his fabric,' Ash said. 'Looks fine on the surface but underneath – aaarrrgh!'

'Are you sick?' Mie didn't always quite see Ash's jokes. 'Shall I call someone?'

'I don't think so,' Charlie said. 'I'll try to make it through the day.'

'You'd be fine if you ate decent bread.'

'Thank you, Mr Ashford, for your dietary tips. Now, if you'll excuse me, I have a department to run.' He slapped Ash on the shoulder and headed off through the swing doors.

'He really is OK?'

'Sure, Mie, he's fine. Just a little joke.'

'Oh. Jokes are very difficult, they don't translate so well.'

Behind them the entrance doors banged and a young woman came hurrying in with a baby in her arms. She rushed across to Mie. 'Please, help me, she's not breathing.' She was near hysterics but holding herself under rigid control in a manner that told Ash this probably wasn't the first time. He took the child from her and noticed the veins visible under the skin.

'Asthma?' he asked.

The woman nodded. Ash didn't waste time. He hurried through to the department, knowing Mie would take care of the mother. Another day in A and E was beginning and he hadn't even had time to take his coat off yet.

For Mehmet Ali the prospect of another day was enough to bring the sour taste of fear into his throat.

He sliced down through the cabbage, halving and then quartering it, before chopping it up into quarter-inch strips, which he tipped into a plastic bag and put in the fridge. The area where he worked was filthy. He tried to keep it clean, his wife Ayse spent hours with scrubbing brush and cloth, but the building was so old that dirt seemed to bleed out of it. He just prayed that no one from the council would ever come and check.

When he'd gone for his food trading licence he'd borrowed his cousin's truck and said he was preparing the food at his cousin's address, which had passed inspection before. It had been a lie. In fact he had hired a lock-up garage for his truck and had put in a fridge and some worktops. The rent was low – it would be, the row in which the garage stood was a back lane running behind food shops and a couple of restaurants and was used for rubbish collection. And as Mehmet knew all too well, rubbish means rats.

The garage was hot and stuffy and he was tired. He'd stayed open until two o'clock and hadn't got to bed until three. On the Golden Road estate he often did his best business in the hours after the pub closed, when customers weren't bothered about the look of his van but just wanted something to soak up the drink. As a good Muslim, Mehmet didn't drink and couldn't understand why anyone would want to get drunk night after night. Granted, life on the estate was hard. Most of them didn't work and had little chance of improving themselves. But then most of them didn't try.

Mehmet himself had no qualifications to speak of but that hadn't stopped him from struggling to get on. He'd worked all the hours he could to save enough money to buy the kebab van and hire the garage so he was his own master. Now it was up to him. If he worked, he'd get on. Except that it was never that easy.

The van he'd bought was old and clapped out. Every morning it was touch and go whether it would start or not. Then there was the cost of the meat, the vegetables and pitta bread, and the soft drinks, crisps and sweets he'd added to his lines. There was the petrol, the gas cylinder to heat the portable grill on which the meat turned. All of these were draining his savings but they were nothing compared to the kids on the estate who seemed to regard Mehmet as their natural prey.

Some of them would throw stones or shout insults at him as he tried to sell. Others were worse. Especially the one they called Iceman. He and his gang stole from Mehmet. They taunted him with names, calling him Zorba or Peeps, and demanded kebabs and cans of Coke and never paid. They were driving him out of business.

He thought of his wife Ayse and their little boy, Hayri. They depended on Mehmet, without him they would be lost. His grip tightened on the handle of his chopping knife. It was eight or nine inches long, a thin wedge of shiny steel tapering towards a wicked point. It could whip through cabbages and cucumbers, it could slice meat like butter. He kept it very sharp.

A large fly buzzed past his face and settled on the worktop. He smashed it flat with the palm of his hand and wiped it off against his apron. Time was passing, he should be on the move. After loading the veg and meat aboard the van he opened the garage door, climbed into the cab, muttered a quick prayer and pressed the starter. Nothing happened.

'What are you do to me?' he demanded. The van stayed silent. 'Please, work for me. Do not let my wife and child go hungry today. Do not shame me!'

Mehmet was inclined to be excitable. He'd been in trouble once or twice before, losing his temper when people annoyed him or, worse, striking out at inanimate objects like the television or cupboard doors when they didn't function properly. Sometimes he had the feeling that no matter how hard he tried, the world was against him. 'Work, you stupid van! What do I buy you for if you do not work!'

He tried again and this time the van must have got the message because the engine shuddered into life. He backed out into the blinding sunlight, jumped from the cab and shut the garage door without noticing the pool of petrol which lay on the concrete. He got back in the cab and drove off towards the estate.

'Hydrocortisone and then a corticosteroid by mouth,' Mike Barratt said. 'But she'd better see her GP.'

Adele nodded. 'I'll tell the mother. And the child can be released now?'

'Certainly. Relief is virtually instantaneous.' The asthmatic child was breathing easily and Adele was just off to fetch the mother. Mike folded another page on his clipboard and scribbled a signature. He looked rough, like he'd had a long night.

'You get called out or something?' Ash asked as they walked back to Admin.

'No, couldn't sleep, that's all. The heat.'

'Yeah, it's a pain.' He rubbed the child's name off the board. So far they weren't that crowded. The seven to three shift was generally the lightest, unless there was a big accident out on the motorway; somehow casualties seemed to occur more frequently in the afternoon and evening.

'Oh, by the way,' Mike went on, 'your man Scrubbs.'

'What about him. In for tests, wasn't he?'

'The Ward Sister called down. Apparently he left.'

'Discharged himself?'

'Walked out. Some time during the night. There was some kind of problem, a mix-up; someone thought his cubicle was the loo and when they went to give him his tea in the morning, zilch.'

'Well, they're always howling for beds up there anyway. They should worry.'

'Could you just have a word with the sister? It's Mary Wilcox. You know Scrubbs quite well, don't you?'

'We have met before.'

'Just to reassure her, that's all. Oh, hi, Josette. You're early today.' Mike beamed.

'Couldn't keep away, Mike. I've come to love the old place. Morning, Ash.'

'Hi,' he said. She looked as fresh and beautiful as ever. Mike obviously agreed from the smile on his face. Ash thought about Mark Calder lounging in the lift and saying, Consultants Only. 'How's it going?' he asked.

Josette had a pile of forms. 'There's been the odd hiccup but it's going fine. Mike's been a great help.'

'I'm sure he has,' Ash said drily.

'If you could nip up and see Sister Wilcox?' Mike prompted.

'Well, I'll leave you two together.' He backed away and went through to Reception to catch the lift.

Frankie was chatting to Mie, showing off the medical knowledge he'd picked up since beginning to work in A and E.

'Becotide rotocaps, the one hundreds,' he was saying. 'That's the asthma treatment you'll find most doctors opting for nowadays. Only for the little kids, well, you'd be looking for something a good deal less— Er, hello, Ash. How's it going, old mate?'

'Fine, Frankie. Mike Barratt did ask if you could pop through. He's got a tricky myasthenia gravis he'd like your opinion on. You know, should he go for neostigmine or prydostigmine?'

'Passing the time of day, that's all,' Frankie protested. 'No need to get shirty.'

'You could always get another few boxes of fanfold for Admin. I think we're getting low.'

The lift arrived and he stepped into it before Frankie could reply.

'Wait!' Sara came hurrying through Reception pushing an elderly lady in a wheelchair. Ash held the door back as she manoeuvred the chair in.

'Thanks. We're just going up to Cardiology. Mrs Marnham is going to see the specialist.'

'So you're feeling a bit better about things today?'

'You know how it can get sometimes. Everything overwhelms you, it all seems too much. I'm sorry I wasted your time.'

'You didn't, Sara,' he said. 'I really mean that. If you have any problems then . . . Oh, by the way . . .'

'Yes?' She looked at him eagerly.

'Did you draw something on my phone pad?'

Her face clouded over with disappointment. She was not the kind of person who could hide her emotions, everything was reflected in her expression. 'Draw something. What?'

'A cross. An X.'

'Like Malcolm X, you mean?'

'No, just an X.'

'Why would I do that?'

'I didn't say you would, I only wondered if you had. For some reason.' It sounded pretty lame to him now.

'Of course not. I don't go—'

He had no choice but to blunder on.

'If you were disappointed that you couldn't stay.'

'You arrogant sod.' Tight-lipped and white she turned away from him. 'You think you're so wonderful that I'm plotting revenge because you didn't ask me to stay for a nightcap? Or did you have something else in mind?'

She was furious.

'No, I . . . It was . . . I didn't . . .'

The lift juddered to a halt. Sara snapped, 'No, obviously you didn't.'

She swept out with her patient, who said, 'That's right, my dear, you tell him. These men think they can have anything they want. Well it's time . . .' The querulous old voice faded away down the corridor.

'Hmm, well handled, Martin,' he murmured to himself as he walked along to the ward. However, that did leave him facing the obvious question: who the hell *had* drawn the X on the pad? Could it have been some friend of Benny's to tell him not to back out of his promise to return to the housing estate? Or an enemy of Benny's? Maybe he'd done it himself after all. Crazy, it was crazy.

Sister Wilcox was a cheerful Scot in her fifties. She offered him a cup of tea which he accepted and then he went along with her to the office.

'Mr Scrubbs was admitted for tests yesterday by Dr Goodliffe. Yes?' said Sister Wilcox.

'She was worried about the state of his—'

'Everything, I should think,' she cut in. 'He was not what you would call a fit man.'

'He's quite well known around Holby,' Ash said, taking a biscuit from the tin she offered him. 'I think he was in the army a few years ago. I remember seeing him around when I was a kid.'

'A drinker. One of life's victims I would say.' Her expression was concerned. 'There was something about him. Not such a bad sort, once we'd got him cleaned up a wee bit. He was pretty whiffy when he came in.'

'You don't get a lot of chance to stay clean when you're living rough. There isn't really any point.'

'Well, here are the papers.' She handed them across. 'No reason for us having them now.'

Ash took them. 'Thank you anyway. If I see him around I'll ask him to come back but I can't see that he will. To be honest, there was never any point in admitting him in the first place.'

'Thank you, Ash, for your vote of confidence.' Karen was standing in the doorway. Angrily she snatched the papers from his grasp. 'Sister Wilcox, isn't it usual to speak to the doctor responsible in these cases?'

The sister was embarrassed but you didn't get to her

position by being flustered easily. 'Of course, Doctor,' she answered frostily. 'I quite understand how you feel. I apologise.' Her smile was about as apologetic as the pit bull at Benny's.

Karen nodded and backed out. 'I'll see you later, if I may, Mr Ashford.'

After a pause Sister Wilcox said, 'What a remarkably angry young lady. Your SHO, I presume?'

'Yes, and I'm afraid I don't seem to be able to put a foot right with her nowadays.'

'Well, far be it from me to criticise a doctor, but when I started out, an SHO would generally have the sense to listen to his or her nursing staff. However, things are different now, I've no doubt, though, being told off by someone young enough to be my daughter is not . . .' She stopped before saying anything indiscreet. 'Will you have another cup of tea before you go, Mr Ashford?'

'No thanks, Sister. I'd better be on my way. Thanks for you help.'

'It's nothing.' She walked through the ward with him and pointed out an old lady knitting. 'That's Barbara, she was quite a friend to your Mr Scrubbs. She was the one who had the accident last night, though she's forgotten all about it now. But she is asking about Mr Scrubbs. She calls him the Sergeant-Major. If you do see him perhaps you could mention that someone here misses him.'

The problem was finding the bloody things. Scrubbs knew that in a sober moment he had stashed at least a couple of bottles of the strong cider for which Holby was famous in a hiding place along the canal. That had been in the winter. Now it was summer and everything was different, the canal banks overgrown with brambles and reeds.

Perhaps he'd imagined it, but he was sure he could

remember finding the wallet that someone had dropped near the bridge with the two ten-pound notes still in it. Most of the money had been used straight away at the off sales part of the Horn of Plenty, where they'd filled up jug after glorious jug with draught cider rough enough to strip paint. But some spark of prudence had counselled him: put something aside for a rainy day, Scrubbsy. You never know when you might need it. Well he needed it now.

Getting out of the hospital had been a doddle. He'd found his way to some kind of store room where there were piles of overalls, rain jackets and overboots. God knew what they were for. It didn't matter, anyway, what counted was that he was able to find stuff that fitted him – no easy matter when you were six foot four – and within a few minutes a figure in orange overalls and a fluorescent yellow jacket was on its way across the car park and down to the canal.

Where he'd been searching for the cider ever since, his thirst getting greater as the sun came up and his need for forgetfulness growing as more memories from the camp began to crowd around him. For a start, there was his old mucker, Sam Smith. Sergeant Sam Smith, he was sure that was the name. Otherwise, what was it doing floating around in his head? He and Sam had been captured and done the long walk together and he was certain that Sam had died outside Da-Lo on the mountain road, exhausted, unable to go on. The guards had gathered round him and the last thing Scrubbs had seen was their rifle butts rising and falling and the sound of blows and cries that got weaker and finally vanished altogether.

And now here he was, looking just like he used to with that cheeky grin, sitting on the riverbank soaking his aching feet in the water, his tattered army boots beside him on the path.

'Eh up, Scrubbsy. Took you a while to get here.'

'Wha—? I, uh, didn't expect to see you, Sam. Not sort of down here.'

Sam lifted a foot. The sole was black and bruised, the skin torn. 'Nah, great little billet you got. Nice bit o' fishin', no officers to bother you. I'd say we got it made, me old mucker. On the mike, that's you and me.'

Scrubbs wondered if he was seeing things, but he'd bumped into enough oddities over the past twenty years not to be thrown by one more. 'I dunno about you, Sam,' he said, 'but I could murder a drink.'

'You and me both. Hey, there were a few times on the road to Da-Lo when we could've fancied a couple of pints.'

'Well, I've a bottle of cider or two, if only I could remember where I put the buggers.'

Sam stretched and lay back, his arms folded behind his head. 'Ah, never could remember anything, Scrubbsy. Forget your trousers if someone didn't hand 'em to you. You stuck 'em up under the culvert, where it comes out of the water works.'

For a brief moment Scrubbs felt the touch of fear. How could Sam have known that, because he was right, Scrubbs remembered it now. He'd forgotten but Sam had known, so . . .

'That's right, Scrubbsy. Of course I'm real.' He clapped his hands. 'I don't sound like no ghost you ever saw, do I?'

Pulling out a tin of Old Holborn he began to roll up while Scrubbs hurried off to the culvert, where he found the two bottles stuck into the mud and leaf-mould. He washed them off and hurried back. 'You were dead right, mate.'

Sam lit up and the rich fruity smell of rolling tobacco filled Scrubbs' nostrils. He took a deep breath, unscrewed the first bottle, licked his lips and drank, shutting his eyes as the cider filled every inch of his body with pure joy.

'Ahhh, that was good.' He handed the bottle across to Sam, who took a drink.

'It is an' all, mate. Sets you up, right?' There was a glint in Sam Smith's eye.

'Sets you up, mate?'

'That's right.' He began to put his boots on, easing his bruised feet carefully into the cracked and dry leather. 'Looks like they've recalled you to the flag, mucker. Them communists ain't finished yet. Not by a long chalk. I reckon we owes 'em something, you an' me, Scrubbsy. I reckon we ain't gonna give 'em the satisfaction of killin' us off before we finish this march. We'll make it, you and me, right to the bloody bitter end.'

Scrubbs tipped the bottle, squinting past it at the sun. 'Never surrender, right, Sam?'

'Right, Sergeant-Major.'

Scrubbs lurched to his feet holding a bottle in either hand. The dayglo jacket billowed around him as he began to trudge forward, step after step, day after day on the long march that had never really ended. Every so often he paused as if to wait for someone or turned and talked at the empty path, holding the bottle out.

12

Sara had the blood pressure cuff over the girl's sweater when Ash looked into cubicle four. He slipped in and rearranged the sleeve so the cuff was on the flesh. Sara nodded but didn't say a word. She was obviously still angry with him. The famed Ash charm was clearly operating at less than par today.

There was a commotion coming from Reception and he hurried through. A couple of workmen were leaning over Mie's desk shouting at her while their mate, white-faced, was slumped on a chair.

'What's the problem, Mie?'

'Here, you a doctor?' One of the workmen grabbed his shoulder.

'Will you let go, please.'

The young man did so but went on shouting. 'I asked you a question. Are you a doctor, 'cos my mate over there is bleeding to death and this stupid woman won't do anything to help.'

'If you'll just wait a minute.' He turned back to Mie. 'Have they registered?'

'Yes,' she said, a tremble in her voice. She didn't yet have the experience to deal with aggressive patients or their friends. Norma would have shut this lot up in seconds flat. 'He's bleeding from the mouth, they said.'

At this moment the injured workman vomited blood all over the floor.

'Told you so, didn't I?' the young workman crowed.

'Shut up and tell me what happened.' Ash was already beside the injured man as he spoke, helping him to his feet. Adele had appeared and, taking in the situation, she said: 'Cubicle two.'

'Got belted in the guts with a roof beam we was lifting,' the young workman shouted after him. 'If he cops it it'll be your bloody fault.'

Ash thought they were probably nervous about their working practices and the insurance cover. An awful lot of building work in the city was carried out on the black economy with no proper protection.

'OK, we're going to lie you down and see what the problem is. Can you breathe all right?'

'Yeah, I reckon.' The voice was weak.

'All right, don't talk. I want you to lie on your side to make sure the passages stay open.'

Karen slipped in beside him. Another of his fan club. She began to work, cleaning out the mouth with suction, asking what had happened. When Adele and one of the agency nurses arrived she said, 'I'll want x-ray, blood tests and cross-matching. I think we should ask the surgical reg to have a look at him.' Then she snapped at Ash: 'Can you see if there is family to be called?'

It was a dismissal pure and simple. He'd started with the case, he should have stayed on it. Adele gave him a sympathetic glance as he went. There was no point in pushing the matter, Karen clearly wasn't in the mood to listen to him now.

Frankie had cleaned up the blood in Reception and the place stank of disinfectant. The workman's mates were sitting talking quietly and looked up when he came through.

After chatting to them, and confirming that they'd

been working without a proper contract, he got Mie to call the patient's wife and asked her to let him know when she arrived.

Josette was waiting in Admin. After he'd written up the workman on the board, she said, 'You were pretty sharp out there just now.'

'Me?'

'To those two young men. Is that generally the way you speak to patients when they're worried and anxious?'

'It depends on the patient and the circumstances,' he said. 'I mean circumstances change, don't they, from day to day.'

She shuffled her papers. 'I'm not sure I understand.'

'Oh come on, Josette. I thought we were getting on well yesterday. And this morning . . .'

'We're still getting on well. I was just asking you a question, that's all. No need to be defensive, Ash.'

'I don't mean that,' he said. 'I thought, yesterday, that we might get to know each other a bit better.'

'Did you now?' Her laugh was deep and sexy. It sent a shiver right through him. 'We'll have to see about that, won't we? After all, I do have my job to do. If I can deliver, then I'll have time to think about off-duty activities. Hmm?'

'Deliver what?'

She waved the papers. 'My conclusions. What else? The Hospital Trust consider this monitor exercise of the highest important.'

'Well I'm glad we're so valuable down here in A and E.'

'Oh you are. You could say they regard you as a benchmark for the whole Trust. Look,' she flipped open a page of computer print-out. 'It's possible to link the overall spending of all hospital departments to each other. Now if we can take one as an example and, say, lower its budget a percentage point without altering its effectiveness, then we should, in theory be able to apply the same cuts' – she corrected herself – 'the same savings across the whole hospital.'

'Do you mean that the Trust know what results they want before you do the tests and it's your job to arrive at the figures they expect?'

'Ash, you have a suspicious mind.'

'We've already had to lose two per cent. We can't cut any further. Anyway, I thought this was all about patient response. Asking them how they feel they've been treated.'

'Of course. That's what everything is about nowadays. The point of delivery. Do the public feel that they are getting a good return for their money. Education, health, the railways. It's the same thing.'

He took hold of her hand, agitated. 'No it's not, Josette. The general public, as you call them, simply don't understand enough about medicine to know what kind of deal they're getting.'

Gently she laid her hand over his. 'Ash, this is very important to my company, and it's important to me, too. I don't want anyone to lie, I just want to do my job, that's all. And I need your help, and the help of everyone in Casualty, so that we can all make the system work better.'

He pulled his hand from under hers. 'You should think of going into politics, Josette. You're good, you're very good. Let's all make the service better by cutting the budget even further. It doesn't matter how bad it is as long as people believe it's getting better. Anyway, they can always go private.'

'I think you've got the wrong end of the stick about this, Ash.'

'I'm not stupid,' he said. 'I can see what's in front of my eyes.'

131

'Are you sure there's not a little jealousy here?'

Before he could answer, Mike Barratt came through with an x-ray plate which he shoved on to the view screen.

'You two getting on all right?' he asked as he considered the shadow on the unknown lungs in front of him. 'No problems, Josette? Everyone being helpful?'

'It's going fine, Mike. And I'm looking forward to our dinner tonight, too. I'll be ready for a little time out.' She smiled at Ash and left.

Mike blushed. 'Impressive young woman. I thought, er, since she's stuck at an hotel . . . which must be boring.'

'That you'd invite her back for dinner with your wife and family. That's very thoughtful, Mike. I'm sure she really will appreciate a little home cooking. She looks like a home-loving sort of girl to me.'

Mike cleared his throat. 'Hmm, quite.' He looked miserable, caught out. Then he brightened slightly. 'What do you reckon?' He tapped the shadow on the x-ray with the tip of his pen.

'Is it a tumour?' Ash looked more closely. 'I haven't seen anything quite like that before.'

'No, you wouldn't have done. It's TB.'

'What? There isn't . . . we don't have it any more. It's beaten in this country. A thing of the past.'

'Nevertheless, that's what I think it is.'

'My God, we are slipping back, aren't we. Josette should really appreciate that.'

Mike pulled the sheet clear of the clips. 'What?'

'Nothing, nothing at all, Mike. Just . . . Just nothing.'

The morning stretched in front of Janice like a desert. It was that hot and that empty. She'd given Frank his breakfast. The same thing every morning: cornflakes and two slices of toast, a cup of coffee – but only after she'd taken him his first cup in bed. Then he'd check through his briefcase to make sure there were no papers that had gone missing overnight. And how she hated that little check. Where could they go, who on earth would ever want to steal Frank's papers? After that he'd put on his shoes – it was slippers in the house – give her a kiss and go round to the garage.

When he'd gone the house was silent until she woke Carly, who got up a bit later in the holidays, and gave her breakfast. Today, her daughter had scalded herself slightly on the kettle. Nothing serious, no need to bother the doctor unless it got worse.

Carly seemed quite happy playing in the garden so Janice decided she really would get the paddling pool out this afternoon. As long as she was careful, of course. Carly had pale skin and needed a good barrier cream if she was going out in the sun. Janice shook her head and let the thought fly away.

Shopping. That's what they could do this morning. She didn't need a lot. The whole family drove out to the Megamarket on Friday evenings to stock up for the week, but there were always a few things she overlooked. Perhaps she could call in at the library, too, and see if anything new had come in.

She was a fan of medical romances and often read four or five a week. They were generally pretty silly if you thought about the plots. That's what Frank said, though he read only non-fiction, but what the hell, she liked them, so why shouldn't she read them? There was little enough else in her life.

'Carly,' she called, 'what are you doing?' The child was sitting very still in the middle of the garden, one hand on her hip, the other out like an Egyptian dancer.

'I'm a teapot, Mummy.'

'Oh, you are.' She went out. It was hot, very hot, already, and Carly's shoulders were red and peeling. 'Will you pour me a cup of tea?'

'Of course,' Carly leaned over, making glugging noises with her lips. 'Oh dear,' she said.

'What is it?'

'I didn't use a strainer, Mummy.'

'That's all right, I don't mind a few tea leaves.'

She took her invisible cup back inside and mimed drinking it. She wished she had Carly's ability to create her own endlessly interesting world around her. As it was – and she looked at the sterile kitchen – her world was slowly killing her with boredom. And yet what could she do? She'd made her bed, now she must lie on it.

She wondered briefly about Carly's scald. Maybe they should call in at the doctor's to check. Only they couldn't go again, not really. But if it was something more serious . . .

'To the traditional classes of wound: abrasion, contusion, laceration and incision, we should perhaps add the class of puncture. This would be described as a penetrating wound which enters a body cavity and damages structures within that cavity, that is nerves or vital organs. Though we must also take into account the effects of shock upon the injured organs.'

Ash shut the book. There was no way he could operate on Benny to remove the bullet inside him. He didn't even know how to read the map, never mind use the compass and actually find his way through the inner organs of his cousin without doing some terminal damage. It was his nightmare made real. Because he couldn't walk away from it. Just like the rope that had been wrapped around Benny's hands too tight to remove, so the ties of family and obligation were too tight for Ash to shake off. He had to find an answer, even if it was the wrong one. He had to *do* something.

There was no one he could talk to about it, either. He

could hardly go to Charlie and say, hey, my cousin got shot in a drug deal and I owe him a lot so what do I do? He could imagine Charlie's face. Mike? He'd say call in the police. Of course he'd say that. What else could he say? Adele, any of them, they'd say the same thing: don't get mixed up in this.

It was coming up to eleven, he was due a break. He'd hoped to see if Josette was going across to the canteen and have coffee with her, but that wasn't on any more. Then he thought that there was one person he could talk to, someone who'd give him straight answers to his questions.

He thumbed the button. Lisa was dozing in her sealed chamber, surrounded as always by the net of lines. A fluffy toy lay on the pillow next to her bald head. She looked so vulnerable and young that he wanted to find someone, anyone, and demand to know why this was happening, who was responsible. Her eyes opened. 'Hey, what's up, Doc?'

'Hunting wabbits,' he said.

'You got any yet?'

'They're just too clever for me.'

'That's rabbits for you. Hey, what's the difference between cabbages and bogeys?'

He thought about it. 'I don't know, Lisa. Why don't you tell me?'

'You can't get kids to eat cabbages.' She laughed, her smile huge across her emaciated face. 'Pretty good, huh?'

'I always ate my cabbage when I was a kid.'

She focused on him through the glass. 'Yeah, I bet you did, too. Thanks for the book, by the way, it's good. You ever read any of her stuff?'

'No.'

'You should try, you'd like it. She writes well about

135

women. There aren't many people writing SF who can do that.'

Sometimes he had to remind himself that this was a thirteen-year-old girl he was talking to. She seemed so mature.

'I have a problem, Lisa.'

'Good. Normally I'm the problem around here. People come in and you should see the way they look at me. They see this sick girl and they don't see *me* at all. What is it, Doc? Girlfriend trouble?'

'I should be so lucky. At the moment I only have to talk to a girl and I put my foot in my mouth.'

'You can talk to me, Doc, though I don't s'pose I look much like a girl any more.'

'That's not true,' he said, 'you look fine.'

'I saw a mirror the other day. I look like one of those aliens out of *Close Encounters*.' Her voice changed suddenly and became full of hope and yearning: 'Wouldn't it be great if that mother ship came down one night over Holby, right over this hospital, and we could go away in it and see . . . everything. The spiral nebula in Andromeda. Orion. Jupiter and beyond!'

'I expect they'd try and arrest the driver.'

She laughed. 'I bet they would, too. So what's up, Doc?'

'There's this bloke. I know him from when we were kids and I owe him one. I mean he saved my life. It was his fault in the first place but all the same.'

'Go on, I like this story,' she said.

'Well, I didn't see him for years. We went in different directions.'

'Right,' she said. 'You were the good boy he was the bad.'

'I think you've been reading my script, Lisa.'

'It's all I have to do except be sick and feel terrible. I think I'll end up reading everything in the world.'

'Anyway, Benny, this guy, he's in trouble and he wants me to help him. But I can't.'

'You mean you don't want to, Doc?'

'I can't. I don't have the skill to do what he wants.'

'Uhh-oh, he's badly hurt?'

'He is. He needs a proper doctor but if I get him one, then he's going to be in a different kind of trouble. Police trouble. And it's not just him. There's a girl and a baby too.'

'This is complicated, isn't it?'

'It is. Whatever I do someone is going to get hurt.'

'Let me think about it for five minutes.' She thumbed off the intercom and lay back. He could see her eyelids, without eyelashes, close slowly over her huge eyes. She was right, she did look like an alien. Maybe one night she really would wake up and see a light outside the window and it would be the mother ship coming to take her home. And maybe not. He pressed his forehead against the glass. It was slick.

'OK, I've been thinking, Doc.'

'Right. And?'

'Daffy Duck.'

'Lisa, what're you talking about?'

'What's Daffy Duck like? I mean would you say he was trustworthy?'

'Nope. He's actually pretty . . . despicable. When you come down to it.'

'Right. So that's your problem, Doc. You're too nice. You need to be despicable. Stop being so sweet, think about yourself for once. Be selfish. Turn him in.'

'I can't do that, Lisa.'

'Why?'

'I'd feel like . . .'

'What's your problem? You think you're better than the rest of us? You never do anything bad? You've been a good boy all your life. You know, Doc, sometimes I

137

look at you out there and I really hate you. I hate you for being so nice when I'm so messed up. Now go away. I'm tired, I want to read my book, I want to go away on a flying saucer. Go away, I don't want your problems.'

She thumbed off and wouldn't answer any more. Even when he banged on the glass, she didn't look at him.

13

People just didn't understand the way Brian felt about Isabella. She was, quite simply, the most beautiful creature he'd ever seen. He carried a photo in his wallet and sometimes, if he was in a pub having a few drinks, he'd get it out and show people, hoping that, for once, someone might understand.

They never did, of course.

It was blind prejudice, he decided; you couldn't expect them to rise above their nature, and in time he'd stopped talking about her and kept the photos to himself, though he had on one occasion sent some transparencies of her to a magazine which printed readers' pictures. There had been quite a response to that. Even a couple of offers, and although he hadn't considered them, there had been hopes that Isabella might be pregnant and, in that case, he had written back, the zoo would be quite happy to think again.

Isabella was a star, there was no doubt about it. She had her fans who came once a month at least to admire her and when a school party visited, her sheer size and beauty was sure to quieten even the rowdies. There was, Brian used to say, something about an Amazonian bird-eating spider as big as a dinner plate, as big as a big dinner plate, that inspired respect.

People said: 'Ooh, it's a tarantula,' but they were wrong. The tarantula was just one, fairly small species among many. Brian reckoned that there were still quite a few new arachnids waiting to be discovered out in Amazonas.

He had found Isabella himself on one of his collecting expeditions for the Holby Zoological Society. He'd been in the forest, walking through the cathedral-like spaces under the thick leaf canopy after a heavy storm. Huge trunks arched upwards through the gloom like pillars – you saw little sun in the forest – creepers and air roots hung down and drips and sometimes small waterfalls fell from the leaves and branches which formed a layer strong enough to walk on more than thirty feet above the ground.

Occasionally there were holes torn in the canopy, where old trees had fallen under the weight of water and new ones had not yet raced to take their place. It was under one of these that his eye caught a flash of light, like diamonds, and he saw her on a log, her back jewelled with raindrops. She was not a web-spinner, she was a hunter, and she reared up, her front legs waving, her eyes gleaming like cold stars, and he was lost. It was love at first sight.

'Has anyone seen my mug?' he asked, rubbing his glasses as if that might enable him to find the lost article. He was a tall man, stooped, thin, dried out, you could almost say, by the tropical sun under which he had spent so much of his life. He had moved to Holby to take over the new arachnid house, built by a grant from a multi-national and linked to the chair in Biology he held at the university. His teaching load was light and he spent as much time as he could at the zoo, among the objects of his affection, for Isabella was only the greatest of many passions. There was a Jamaican Goliath spider, rumoured to have been the species which inspired the touchy heroes, as Brian saw them, of the film *Arachnaphobia*; and a funnelweb from New South Wales, only an inch and a half long but probably the most deadly spider in the world (though it did not belong to the genus Latrodectus, which included most of the poisonous biters like the redback, black widow and the Russian karakut, all of which were represented).

His colleagues thought him a rather odd chap, but then he was a brilliant scientist and nobody was paying him for his relaxed social manner. Still, he did like to have his own mug and could get quite annoyed if it wasn't in its place.

'Here it is, Dr Rommleson.' Andrea, the group secretary, who generally got lumbered with the coffee-making, produced the missing mug and filled it with coffee.

'Getting a little warm, Andrea. Quite tropical, in fact,' Brian said as he accepted his drink. 'We'll have to monitor our heating very carefully. We don't want our friends getting too hot. Never know what it might do to them. They don't like it when their routine gets upset.'

'I'm sure they don't,' Andrea said.

She didn't like them, either, and her one consolation for working here was that at least the English weather was so dull and cold that the tropical species would die in minutes if they ever got out of their special environment. Only now, with this heatwave going on day after day, she was beginning to wonder.

Brian finished his roll, brushed the crumbs off the magazine he was reading, and said, 'Better get back to it, I suppose. Isabella is in a frisky mood today. Won't show herself, keeps hiding in the foliage. I told her she was a naughty girl but she just won't come out.'

His colleagues smiled weakly at the familiar joke. Ever since the installation of the new arachnid house, which had been built to resemble a rainforest environment with creepers and tropical plants, visitors had been having trouble actually locating the inhabitants. After all, as Brian never tired of pointing out, a million years of evolution had gone into making them hard to spot.

He shook his head over the idiocy of the general public as he slipped his coat off and let himself into the moist, warm environment. The smells of the rainforest, sour and overripe like old earth, assailed his nostrils and he breathed in with pleasure.

'Where are you hiding, Izzy?' he crooned, peering here and there through the fronds. Half a dozen smaller species were visible but not Isabella. Perhaps she was about to give birth. He knew that she would be extra touchy at that time. Maybe she'd hidden herself away to surprise him later.

Water dripped in front of him from the point of a fleshy yellow leaf. He looked up. Was there movement?

'Izzy?' he whispered, craning round to see over the leaf. There was a movement there, definitely. He stepped back, catching the trunk of the plant, sending a shudder up its whole length. Legs flailed and scrabbled at shiny leaf surfaces. Brian flung up a hand but it was too late. Something struck his face and everything went black. Pain began to dig cruel fingers into his flesh, and agony exploded in a thousand different places as if he was on fire.

When Dr Rommleson didn't appear for lunch – it was pepper soup, one of his favourites – Andrea was dispatched to summon him. Gingerly she tapped on the glass of the arachnid house, hoping to attract his attention. She wasn't going in to fetch him, no chance. He'd have to miss his lunch if he didn't notice her. She tapped again and called out 'Dr Rommleson,' though there was faint chance he'd hear her behind the thick glass.

Then she saw his leg, lying there on the ground. At

142

first she thought he was working on something, then she wondered, pointlessly, if he'd fallen asleep; finally she asked herself why there was a massive gloved hand gripping his face. A hand with no arm, a hand with eight fingers. After that she lost her lunch and staggered to the nearest phone.

Brenda Bryant sat holding Ted's hand as she passed on the best wishes of neighbours, friends and even the gold-fish. He smiled at that because he'd never liked them.

'You're a lucky man, Ted,' she said.

'If I'm lucky,' Ted could move his arm now and indicated the paraphernalia of lines and wires that hung all around him, as well as the strapping and binding and the cannula in his chest, draining off the fluid from his lung, 'then I'd hate to be unlucky.'

He wheezed and laughed and shut his eyes. 'I'll tell you one thing, love, they're right when they say it only hurts when you laugh.'

Brenda unpacked some grapes. 'I thought you might like something fresh.'

'Oh, I've the nurses for that,' he chuckled.

'I can see you're getting better. I expect they'll be glad to see the back of you, Ted.'

'No, they've been very good. It's bloody hard work in here.'

'Don't swear, love.'

'Well it is, and I'll say it any time you like: nurses deserve twice what they get. You never know till you need 'em, and then you'd pay them anything on God's earth to see you right.'

Brenda had never seen her husband like this before. The accident had made a difference. 'Are you going soft on me, Ted?'

'Never, lass. Not on your nelly. And not on that infernal bugger Taylor. My God, when I get back to work I'll take him to the cleaners like he's never been taken in his life.'

'Don't get over-excited, love. Have a grape.'

'People like that are dangerous. I could've . . . well, never mind me, how many other folk have come unstuck because he's too old or too careless to do his job properly? As soon as I'm back in that office . . .'

'It may be some time,' Brenda said. 'You're going to need a good long rest before you can be up and about again.'

Ted frowned. 'I was never one for resting, you know that, Brenda, love. And while that man Taylor's still giving out the wrong stuff . . .' He paused.

'Yes, love?' Brenda leaned forward as he pulled her hand towards him. 'Easy, love, you're hurting me.' She tried to free herself but the pressure increased. A rictus passed over Ted's face and his body twisted in pain. He tried to speak but couldn't get the words out.

Still with her hand trapped in his fierce grip, Brenda cried out, 'Help, somebody help my husband!'

Doors crashed open. In no time nurses seemed to be all around, Sister Wilcox prominent as she leaned briefly over Ted and snapped out: 'Cardiac arrest. Get him to Crash.'

Normally an arrest would have been dealt with on the ward, with doctors summoned by their emergency bleepers, but in Ted's case, with his serious chest injuries, external massage was not going to be possible. The team in Crash would be prepared for the alternative techniques that would be needed.

They were waiting as Ted was wheeled through the door and moved into action immediately. It was something they'd done a thousand times in their careers: Ash, Mike Barratt, Adele, working smoothly together with speed but no hurry. For Sara Eeles, assisting the resuscitation team, it was an object lesson in all the techniques she'd had explained to her in lectures and seen in training films.

What she hadn't had explained, and what she wasn't ready for, was failure. The team tried everything: injections of atropine and adrenaline, external massage, even the defib paddles, sending shocks of 300 joules through the body, despite the risk of further internal damage from the movement of broken bones. And in the end Mike stepped back and shook his head. Sara could see him going through a mental list, his lips moving slightly, before he looked around at the others. 'We're not getting anywhere. I think we should stop. Is everybody OK with that?'

The team nodded and stepped away.

Looking at the bulk of Ted Bryant's body, so large and somehow insulted now that life had deserted it, Sara wanted to shout: you can't stop. Please, please, we're supposed to make him better, not walk away.

Adele nodded. 'We've done our best. I agree with Mike, we can't do any more for him.'

Mike said: 'Resusc abandoned at' – he flicked a glance at his watch – 'twelve twenty-two. Adele, will you speak to Mrs Bryant?'

'OK, Mike. Sara, would you like to come with me?'

She wanted to say no, not me. It's too much, I can't cope with this. Then she felt a slight pressure on her shoulder. Ash had his hand there giving a reassuring squeeze. He nodded, as if to say it's going to be tough but you can do it. She didn't feel any more confident but there was something about his face, about the way he smiled, that gave her the courage she needed to get through the ordeal.

Because an ordeal was exactly what it was.

Telling Mrs Bryant that her husband had died, after all he'd been through over the past forty-eight hours, was the worst thing Sara had ever done. Afterwards she felt as if she'd committed a crime. Adele told her she'd handled it all right, but she knew that she'd done nothing, just stood there like a post and watched an elderly woman's world slowly fall apart.

Adele had taken Mrs Bryant to see her husband's body. Sara didn't have to go through that, she rushed upstairs to the rest-room and started making herself a cup of tea.

Ash found her there ten minutes later, standing frozen at the sink, the half-filled kettle in her hands.

'Sara,' he opened her grip and finished refilling the kettle. 'What is it?'

'It wasn't all right,' she said angrily, her voice choked with tears. 'It was the most bloody awful thing I ever had to do.'

'You'd never seen an arrest before?' Ash asked.

She shook her head.

'I'm sorry, somebody should've thought. It's . . . it's pretty awful, isn't it. Seeing someone die like that.'

'They talk about it, we had lectures,' she said, 'but it doesn't mean anything. It's people, that was a man with a wife and – I don't know, a car, a cat, a budgie.' Her voice was getting louder, approaching the edge of hysteria. 'He had a whole life and it just stopped. Bang. That's it. Finished. No more chances. I talked to him yesterday. He couldn't say a lot but he was so grateful for what we'd done. It made me feel really proud to be a nurse. To be training. And it's all for nothing.'

'Not for nothing, Sara.' The kettle was boiling. Ash made her coffee sweet.

'I don't take sugar,' she said as she saw him spooning it in.

'Drink it anyway. It'll help.'

'I don't need help,' she snapped. 'I need . . . I don't know what I need.' No longer able to contain her feelings, she burst into tears.

Gently, Ash took her into his arms. 'It's OK, Sara. It's OK.'

'I . . . I don't think I'll ever be able to get used to it,' she sobbed. 'I just haven't got what it takes to be a nurse.'

Ash took his arms from around her and gripped her shoulders, looking straight into her face. 'If you ever do get used to it, Sara, that's when you don't have what it takes any more. All of us feel like you. How do you think we keep going, keep caring? Because it hurts every time we fail.'

'You feel like that too?'

'Every bloody time.' He loosened his grip and let her slide forward against him again. Her hair smelled fresh, slightly of lemon. When she looked up at him, her face wet with tears, so vulnerable in her pain, he felt an immense need to protect her, though he knew he couldn't because they all had to come to their own terms with the nature of the job. 'I wish there was something I could tell you that would make it easier,' he said, 'but there isn't. It's what we live with. The only thing I can say is that the good things, when you see someone you've really helped walk out of here, then that makes up for everything.'

She sniffed and smiled through the tears. 'You promise?'

'I know, and that's even better. You'll see.' He brushed a strand of her hair back from her face.

'God, I must look a mess,' she said.

'No, you look . . . ' What was he going to say? That she looked beautiful? Because she did. 'You look great.'

'Thank you.' She leaned forward and kissed him briefly on the cheek. Then she froze, they both froze. The contact of lip and face had awakened something in them and after a long moment they kissed.

'Very touching. I must say.'

Ash pulled back. Josette Lowell stood in the open rest-room doorway, a smile just touching the corners of her mouth. Sara moved away, wiping her eyes. 'Excuse me.'

She rushed past Josette and a moment later there was the sound of the wash-room door opening and closing.

'A bit young and tender for you, Ash? I thought you preferred the more sophisticated woman.'

'She was upset. She's just seen somebody die.'

'Isn't that a fairly common experience in a hospital?'

He emptied and washed out Sara's coffee cup while answering. 'It doesn't make it any easier to cope with; especially not the first time.'

'But then if you have a shoulder to cry on, that makes all the difference in the world.'

'I'm not quite sure what you're saying, Josette.'

'Oh, I'm sure you are.'

'Do you mean I was acting unprofessionally?'

'I think kissing pretty little nurses on duty might be seen in that light.'

He felt anger gust through him. 'She was upset. She needed—'

'Guidance, comfort. Maybe. I don't think she needed a clinch with Martin Ashford, heart-throb of A and E.'

'That's rather offensive, Josette. You're saying I would take advantage of her confusion.'

'You were ready to take me out to dinner yesterday. Are you taking . . . what's her name?'

'Sara Eeles. She's a Project 2000.'

'Is that your score, Ash?'

'You made it clear enough that you weren't interested, Josette.'

'I thought I made it clear that I didn't want to mix business and pleasure.'

'Tell that to Mike Barratt.'

The grin became a broad smile. 'Ooooh, the old green-eyed monster. Is that what it all comes down to? You men are so predictable.'

'That's nothing to do with it.' He had the uncomfortable feeling that she was tying him in knots. Where, he wondered, was it leading? 'If you don't have anything else to say, Josette, I am busy.'

'I don't have anything at all to say, Ash. How could I have? I don't run this department, all I have to do is carry out my survey, make my report on how efficient or otherwise the staff are, on how well they are serving the public. I know you don't agree with that approach but you, of course, have your own unique approach to staff relations, don't you. Now, I too have work to do. Excuse me.'

For a moment he felt like throwing the mug in his hand at the closing door. If this kind of thing was what management was all about then he didn't want anything to do with it. She was virtually blackmailing him, threatening to disclose the fact that he'd been seen kissing a nurse on duty, abusing his position in the department. And why? Presumably just in case he took it into his head to publicly register his opposition to the monitor survey. Not that he had any intention of doing so – she was just covering herself. She really was a politician, they could use someone like her in the union.

Still, kissing Sara was a stupid thing to have done but he couldn't have said it was going to happen a second before it did. Surely Sara hadn't known either. And what about Sara. Was she all right? And how *did* he feel about her?

Problems. Too many problems. He put the mug away and left the rest-room.

14

Mrs Ashford looked at the sandwich she'd just made for herself and shook her head. She didn't feel like eating. Martin was right about that, as he generally was where her health was concerned. It had been quite a while since she'd enjoyed a meal and she was a woman who'd always loved cooking, and eating too, as her size testified. But not any more.

However much she tried to hide it from her son, she was very worried indeed about her state of health. And yet she couldn't bring herself to go to the doctor. It was true what she'd told him. He was too young to remember his daddy going into hospital, saying, 'I'll only be a week or two, darling.' And he hadn't even felt bad. It was just the doctor telling him to have a check-up.

Outside it was as hot as ever, the sun beating back from the concrete paths of the estate. It was the kind of weather Mrs Ashford loved, to tell the truth. Most years it took the aches right out of her bones but this year the worry had come to replace it. Still, while we live in this Vale of Tears, she reflected, we have no right to escape from our burden of woes. And there was much to be thankful for; her children for a start. And this flat of hers where she could gather all her memories.

She put the sandwich back in the fridge. Things would

sort themselves out in time, one way or the other. Let the Lord decide, she thought. Then she saw she was out of milk and decided she'd better go down to the shop straight away. There were a few other things she needed too: cleaning materials, some paper towels for the kitchen. There was always something.

She put on her hat and a light jacket and gathered up a couple of string bags. They were so much better than all those plastic ones that you used and threw away. In her childhood they had never thrown away a single thing – everything had a use and a reuse.

The stairwell was cool, and for once no one was hanging round there, not that her estate was as bad as many. The landings had been cleared of rubbish as well, which was a real improvement.

'Good afternoon, Mrs Ashford. How are you today?' Mr Kent was a widower who, like her husband, had worked for British Rail, retiring as chief signalman. He always used to say they should get together, her and him, because Ashford, Kent was a well-known railway station and would be even more so when the Channel tunnel started rolling. He lifted his panama hat in greeting. He was a real gentleman, a Barbadian who had the kind of good manners the English no longer even recognised.

'Good morning, Mr Kent. I'm going on all right. I suppose. And how are you?'

'So so, my dear lady. I see you are going shopping. I too am about to patronise the local supermarket. Perhaps I might accompany you?'

'It'll be a pleasure. A job shared is a job halved.'

'Very true, dear lady.' He held the door for her and they stepped out into the glaring heat.

Mr Kent offered his arm, though truth to tell Mrs Ashford was a good deal fitter than he was; but she took it anyway since today she really didn't mind a little support. 'I remember wet summers, Mr Kent. With the children stuck at home because of the rain. I just don't know what's happening nowadays.'

'Well, they do say it's the ozone layer or the rainforests or maybe its the government. I've given up trying to understand this world.'

They walked along to the road, following the estate paths rather than cutting across the withered grass, since they both came from a generation who tended to do what public notices requested rather than ignore them. For a moment they paused by the bus stop and the man at the wheel of the dusty Vauxhall tapped his fingers on the dashboard in annoyance. Then they passed by, walking slowly down the hot pavements, heading towards the pelican crossing that would take them over to the precinct.

The driver eased off the handbrake and pulled slowly away from the kerb. The dice swung in the back window. He picked up sunglasses from the sun-hot seat beside him and slipped them on.

The old couple were almost at the crossing now, looking left and right before stepping off the pavement. The driver began to whistle tunelessly through his teeth as he increased the pressure on the accelerator.

'We have a little problem.'

Ash had never seen the paramedics so numbed. They had experienced just about everything A and E had to offer, from the worst domestic call to a full-scale air crash, but Josh was white, his eyes wide, his whole body bowed away from the stretcher. Mickey Parsons, his temporary partner, was every bit as nervous, his face green as if he were about to vomit any moment.

'The patient . . .' he mumbled. 'Er, it's . . . Oh, God, it's gross.'

Karen came hurrying through and caught the last words. She was not pleased: her relationship with the paramedics had never been good but this was the last straw. 'What kind of report is that, Mr Parsons? Am I supposed to be able to gather the patient's state of injury, his name and any other relevant information from "Ugh, it's gross"? Let me take a look. Jeeeeesus!' She sprang back, her face white. 'It is gross! I can't touch that. I hate spiders.'

The paramedics gently lowered the stretcher on to the crash bed.

'Aren't we going to move him off?' Ash asked.

'You move him, mate, I'm not,' Mickey retorted. 'I run a mile when I see the little buggers trapped in the bath.' He held his hand to his mouth and backed out. Josh followed, waving the patient notes, which Ash took. He handed them to Karen. 'OK, Doctor, it's all yours.'

'No way, I can't.' She was, he saw, terrified. It wasn't a question of dislike or pulling herself together – this was something altogether deeper. She backed away towards the door. Mike came through and she said, 'How d'you feel about spiders, Mike?'

Ash was bending over the patient so Mike was unable to make the connection. 'I don't have any problems,' he laughed, 'just as long as they're smaller than me.'

'I think this one probably is,' Ash mumbled, 'but not by much.' He shifted to one side and Mike came closer.

'Holy God, what is that?'

Karen had shoved the patient notes into his hand on her way out. He scanned them rapidly. Behind him the door to Crash eased open and half a dozen heads peered round.

'If you've nothing better to do,' he snapped. The heads disappeared. Dennis Ford, the new CNS, came through. He squatted beside Mike and Ash. The spider regarded them, its legs spread across the patient's face, the body obscuring the features.

'Oh my God,' Dennis breathed. 'It's like *Alien*.' All three men shuddered then Mike jumped like a scalded cat as something touched his neck.

Adele looked down. 'It's a spider. That's all.'

'Come on, it's eating his face,' Dennis said.

'I don't think so,' Mike said. 'The notes state that this is Dr Brian Rommleson, a biologist. He was found with the spider on his face, it had presumably fallen there. He was unconscious. Pulse is slow. Ash, will you do BP, please. Dennis, on your way out will you call the tropical medicine people. Mie will have the number. And Immunology, please. Get the reg down here fast. And can you find me an expert on this creature? We need to know if it's poisonous.'

'Oh sure, and who's going to get close enough to find out?'

The patient moved, a shudder passing up his body. Instantly the spider tensed, its feet digging into the flesh slightly to keep its position.

'It's probably scared,' Adele said.

'Well I think first we need to get it off his face.' Mike extended a pencil towards it. The two front legs left the face and the whole body tipped back.

'Careful!' Ash shouted, 'those things can jump!'

Mike backed away fast. The spider resumed its old position.

'BP erratic. Pulse thready. I don't like it.' Ash said.

'I don't either, but what the hell can I do here? We have to get this damn thing off his face but if it's biting him and it's venomous, and we touch it, then it's going to pump even more into him. It could finish him off. I don't know a lot but I do know that spiders are among the most poisonous creatures on this planet.'

The door crashed open. Dennis leaned in. 'You'll love this. Our expert. They advise us to get in touch with Dr Brian Rommleson, right here in Holby.'

'Brilliant. Did they have any advice?'

'They said it's the heat that is keeping it active. Normally if it got out of the cage, it'd go to sleep.'

'Ah, hush-a-bye baby,' Adele said.

'They say that it probably isn't venomous, not being that size . . .'

'Great.'

'. . . But they can't be sure without seeing it. They're sending someone.'

'Scientists,' Mike growled, 'don't you love 'em? OK, anything else?'

'Immunology is on his way down.'

'So what the hell do we do now? Wait? Put his head in a fridge?'

Something had been tickling in the back of Ash's mind and, on Mike's words, it sprang into the light of day.

'Hair dryer.'

'Would you like to explain?'

'We get a hair dryer, turn the heat off and blow cool air over it. It'll go to sleep and we'll be able to slip it into a box. There's a dryer in the rest-room, I noticed it earlier.'

'OK, let's do it.'

Ash was through the door in seconds. The dryer was where he'd seen it before, and it was working. On the way back down he passed Sara. She wanted to talk but he didn't have time to stop. 'It's OK, everything is fine,' he flung back as he vanished round a corner.

Back in Crash the situation was the same, except that Mike now held a stainless steel sterilising tray in one hand, the lid in the other like a shield. He positioned them just in front of the spider, so that if it ran or jumped forward it would end up trapped.

'You sure that steel's strong enough?' Adele asked. Mike was about to give a serious answer when he realised she was joking.

'I think you're enjoying this, Adele.'

She didn't say anything but her shoulders shook with mirth.

'Turning on,' Ash said. He checked the air coming out the nozzle. It was cool, not cold, but it should lower the

155

creature's temperature. From a couple of metres he directed the jet, bringing the dryer gradually closer. The spider began to tremble.

'Hold it.'

Ash backed off a couple of inches.

'All right.'

He began to advance again. This time there was no obvious effect. Inch by inch he brought the nozzle in towards the massive body.

'Gently, gently . . .'

The spider moved like lightning. One moment it was on the face, the next it was scrabbling in the shiny container and Mike, white-faced, was jamming the top on. He put the tray behind him on the floor and turned immediately back to the patient. They could see now that his face was covered with spine-like hairs from the spider's body and that round each puncture the flesh was swollen and red.

'Tweezers! Let's get this stuff out!' Mike shouted.

All three leaned over the patient's face and began removing the spines, dropping them carefully into a dish. The flesh was mottled and pitted but the swellings seemed to subside a bit as they worked.

'There's no sweating or trembling,' Mike noted, 'though the lack of consciousness means we can't check for stomach cramps. I think it's unlikely he's been poisoned. I would've thought shock from the pain of the spines, which I imagine are at the very least irritant—'

'Ah, very interesting.'

'Jim.'

The immunologist had appeared without any of them noticing, so intent were they on the patient.

'Your CNS filled me in. It's fascinating, I haven't seen one of these before. We had a scorpion last year.'

'Oh, that's nothing, Jim. We've got Arnold Schwarzenegger Spider.'

'If it's a bird-eater—'

'Hey,' Ash said, 'it's a man-eater.'

'Well then, it's probably not poisonous. They have a nasty bite, though. Big jaws and they do tend to carry a few tropical nasties around in the germ line, so I think we should get our man here into isolation for a while. We could shoot him up to Trop in an ambulance if you've one spare.'

'Ha bloody ha.' Mike snarled. 'What about these spines? How bad are they?'

'Well, it's likely to be a protein of some nature so we can neutralise with antibodies. An antivenin. But if possible, no tranquillisers or painkillers injected – generally they don't help. An Epsom salt wash will probably be as effective as anything.'

The spines were all out by now and Adele prepared a salt solution which they swabbed on. The patient's breathing and pulse began to settle back to normal.

The immunologist pulled back the eyelids. 'Got an ophthalmoscope handy, Mike?'

'In Admin. What're you thinking – that the eyes might have been affected?'

'I think they're probably all right. Best to check. I reckon we'll walk the rest. But let's have a look at this monster, anyway.'

'Sure. All yours. It's in the steel tray.'

There was a moment of silence as they realised, at the same buttock-creeping moment, that the tray was on its side and empty.

Town had been hot and crowded and by the time Janice and Carly got back home they were both ready for a long, cool drink.

Carly had an orange juice and so did Janice, though she slipped just a sniff of vodka into hers. It had been a busy old morning, what with rushing into the library and then off to the department store, where they had got some socks for Daddy and looked at furnishing fabrics, though they weren't thinking of changing the furniture. Still, they'd got a lovely new quilt cover for Carly's room and some bits and pieces for the kitchen.

Janice opened the kitchen door and let the little breeze from the back garden blow through. 'It's even hotter than yesterday, I think.'

'I think so too. Can I have some ice-cream?'

'We haven't got any, and besides, you've had lunch in town.'

'We have,' Carly said. 'We've got a box of Neapolitan in the freezer and two Mars ice-creams.'

'They'll be frozen solid,' Janice said. 'You'll break your teeth.'

Carly displayed her mouth with its spaces. 'They're all coming out anyway. Daddy says I'm running the tooth fairy off her feet.'

'Lucky tooth fairy,' Janice said, and tipped just a teeny bit more vodka into the orange. 'And if you do eat all the ice-cream you'll get fatter and fatter and fatter until . . .'

'I burst!' Carly shouted. 'That would be really messy, wouldn't it? I bet Mrs Prince wouldn't clean that up.' Mrs Prince, who cleaned three times a week, was not one of Carly's favourite people. She had a terrible habit of sweeping all Carly's farm animals, which she arranged with great care across her floor, into their box whenever they were left out. 'Yeah,' Carly considered the thought, 'I think I will burst. It would serve her right. Gooey me all over the house.'

Janice, who felt pretty much the same as Carly did about Mrs Prince, laughed. 'But I'd miss you. Who would I talk to? Who'd be my friend?'

'I s'pose. All right. If I can't have the ice-cream, can I have the paddling pool out? Please? Please, Mum?'

Kids, they always had a bargain to offer – and they

always had something they wanted to do so urgently it just couldn't wait. 'All right. But you'll have to help me blow it up.'

It was a long job. They'd got a pump somewhere but Janice had lost it, or that's what Frank said, implying that he couldn't possibly have misplaced it so it had to be Janice and they certainly weren't buying a new one when the old was still somewhere, etc., etc., blah, blah.

Together they pulled the plastic bundle out on to the lawn and shook it open. Then they sat down together and started blowing. And blowing and blowing, until Janice was seeing stars and Carly had run right out of puff. At last, though, the sides began to rear up and sausages of air ran round, driving out the wrinkles until the red and yellow pool was erected.

'I'll work the hose, I'll do the hose.'

Carly loved to squirt everyone and everything within range but today Janice said, 'I'm sorry, love, there's a shortage of water and that means we can't use the hose on the garden. I can fill your pool up but mustn't water the plants.'

'Poor plants. I bet they're thirsty.' The child's concern was immediate and all-consuming.

'I'll tell you what, then. When you've finished in the pool you can use your bucket to put the water on the flowers instead of letting it run down the drain.'

Carly's face cleared immediately. 'Come on then. Fill it up.'

She unwound the hose from the shed and fixed it to the garden tap. She knew Frank wouldn't approve but he wasn't here, so who cared. She even laughed a little as she directed the hose into the pool. It filled quickly enough and within moments Carly was happily at play, splashing and filling and emptying toys with total attention.

Janice went back inside and poured more orange juice

and another touch of vodka. She wondered if perhaps it would have been better to put the pool at least partly in the shade but that would have meant siting it down at the end of the garden under the trees, where she wouldn't be able to keep an eye on Carly. Besides, it was too hot to play outside for long and Carly had been liberally coated with sun-cream.

She went through to the sitting-room and sat down in front of the TV. There must be something to watch, to help pass the endless time. Maybe Oprah Winfrey would be on. Or a quiz show. Or *The Young Doctors*. Anything, really.

15

Ted Bryant's case notes detailed the wrongfully dispensed drops, though they didn't actually name the chemist Taylor. Ash was concerned that in the aftermath of the man's death, the whole thing would be forgotten or dropped. He could understand that Mrs Bryant might not feel able to pursue the matter but he wanted to be sure that someone, even if it had to be himself, would keep on Taylor's track. 'The man is a public menace,' he said.

Mark Calder didn't respond. They were in Mark's office, Ash, Charlie, Mike and the clinical director, Hilary Kingston. A woman in her fifties, she was Mark's immediate boss and every bit as shrewd and sharp as he was himself. There had, it was rumoured, already been a number of occasions when she had hauled Mark over the coals for lack of efficiency. Ash would have loved to have seen it.

The meeting was the monthly liaison with the Trust board, in which opinion was supposed to rise up and down the ladder of command. Usually it ended in mutual recriminations and measures forced through by one or other side. Or so Charlie said. Ash wasn't of sufficient seniority to attend but had been called in today on the matter of Taylor and to underline Mike's concern about the eight-legged visitor who was, even as they talked, somewhere in the bowels of the hospital, perhaps waiting to jump out on unknowing patients or staff.

Mike was speaking, backing up Ash's statement. 'We simply cannot allow this kind of sloppy dispensing of prescriptions.'

'But is it really within our remit?' Mark asked. 'I don't know how you feel, Hilary, but I can't help thinking that the Authority ought to handle this. The Royal College, the Society of Pharmacists, whoever.'

'Anybody,' Ash cut in, 'except us?'

Hilary Kingston looked at him sharply, as if imprinting his face on her memory for future reference. 'Mr Ashford, am I to take it that you have already visited Mr Taylor's business premises and, how shall I put it . . .?'

'You can put it any way you like,' Ash shot back. 'I went to plead with him to stop issuing prescriptions, for everyone's sake.'

'I have to say,' Mrs Kingston went on as if he hadn't interrupted, 'that this could be seen as an unwise move. A very unwise move. You know that Mr Taylor has complained to the Hospital Trust about this harassment?'

'Someone had to try and talk to him. A man has died.'

'Of a heart-attack,' Mark said. 'There is no proof of any connection between the eye drops and Mr Bryant's seizure on the station. Granted, the wrong drops *were* issued but we can say no more.'

'You just want to avoid any trouble, don't you?' Ash answered. Mike leaned forward and laid a restraining hand on his arm but he shook it off. 'It's all part of the same thing: your attitude, this monitor exercise, the budget reductions. Never mind what actually needs doing, as long as everything looks all right and the customer, the almighty customer, thinks they're getting value for money. For less money.'

Mark smiled like a tiger. 'I think you've gone a little too far there, Martin.'

Mark using his Christian name in that patronising way made Ash feel about four years old.

Mark went on: 'I think you should apologise to Mrs Kingston.'

For the first time Charlie spoke. 'I think Mr Ashford was expressing a very real concern that all of us in the department feel. If Mrs Bryant should get in touch with the press, or if there is another case like this one, and the papers find out, we are going to look pretty silly if we haven't even passed on a warning.'

Ash gave Charlie a grateful glance but the clinical manager ignored him. Charlie was an expert at these confrontations and knew that the only way to get through them was to use your brains not your lungs.

Mrs Kingston made a note on her pad. 'Point taken, Mr Fairhead. I will attend to it. The last thing we want is Holby General appearing uncaring in the community. Right,' she looked at her watch, 'meetings should never take longer than an hour and this one is already ten minutes old. We have a lot of business to get through. Need we keep Mr Ashford?'

'There is the question of our visitor,' Mike said.

A sour look passed across the normally rather superior features of Mrs Kingston.

Mark craned forward across his desk. 'Ah, yes, the giant killer spider from Planet X. Right?'

'It's not a killer,' Mike said, 'but it can give a nasty bite and its fur is liable to produce an allergic reaction if it touches flesh.'

Mrs Kingston peered around her. She was not, obviously, a spider fan. Mark took note of her reaction. 'What do you think, Hilary? Reckon you might find it hiding in your handbag?' He guffawed. Mrs Kingston began to display the symptoms with which Ash had become all too familiar over the afternoon. A sort of green tinge to the face and an all-over shrinking movement as if the skin were literally crawling.

'Surely,' she said, 'it's not such a great problem. Don't these things die in this country?'

'They do,' Charlie said, 'because of the cold. Hospitals, as you have said many times when complaining about fuel costs, are never cold.'

'We managed to speak to Dr Rommleson after he came round,' Mike said. 'He's a charming man, very upset about all the trouble he and Isabella, that's the spider, caused us. A bit odd, of course. Wouldn't hear a word against Izzy. He said she was quite right to act as she did. Even went so far as to say that when he died he hoped to be taken to South America where he could be eaten by spiders.'

A hand over her mouth, Mrs Kingston rose to her feet and headed for the door. Even Mark was beginning to enjoy this one. 'Shall we hold the meeting until you get back, Hilary?'

She drew a breath and returned to her seat. 'If we can just get through it, please. We have one admittedly quite large spider loose in the building. Surely it is not beyond the skill of the local council vermin control officer to find and destroy it?'

'She's actually rather valuable,' Mike said.

A warning frown crossed Mrs Kingston's face, it said: so far and no further. She snapped out: 'Mark, you will call the council as soon as the meeting is over. Right. Is that settled? Can we leave this spider alone now?'

'Not exactly,' Ash said. 'There is a problem.'

'Go on.'

'When we talked to Dr Rommleson he was explaining Isabella's odd behaviour.'

'And?'

'It seems she's pregnant. About to give birth.'

164

'To little spiders?'

'That is the general idea,' Mark said. 'How many?'

'Two or three – hundred.'

A wheeze rather like a balloon going down terribly slowly came from Mrs Kingston. 'You mean we have two or three *hundred* bird-eating spiders on the loose in this hospital?'

Mike said: 'It's highly unlikely that most of them will survive. And there aren't exactly a lot of birds to eat in Holby General.'

'What about mice, cockroaches, I don't know, voles? And some of our older patients aren't exactly quick on their feet. I think I'd better inform the Trust management board about this as soon as possible. Does this doctor of yours have a date for the blessed event. Events?'

'Could be a day, he says, could be a week.'

'Let's hope it's a week and let's hope we find it or . . .' She paused.

'Or what?' Mark Calder asked.

'Or somebody is just going to have to go down the ducts after them, Mark. Mr Ashford, I don't think we need detain you any longer.'

When he got to Admin there was a call waiting. He picked up the phone with a sinking feeling, and as soon as he heard Benny's voice he was back in that over-heated flat with the anxiety and the animal stink of the pit bull as it strained at the leash.

'Hello, Benny.'

'Marty, how you doing?'

'Oh, you know, so so.'

'Ain't you gonna ask me how I'm doing, Marty?'

'Benny, how're you doing?'

'I'm in pain, man. It hurts pretty bad. Even those pills don't seem to do the business any more. I need your

165

help and I need it soon. You gotta come to me tonight, Marty, and you gotta clean me up so I can get out of here.'

'Benny, you have to understand.' He looked around to check no one was near enough to overhear. Karen was talking to an agency nurse, Adele and Dennis were helping a patient with a head wound through to the cubicles. 'I can't operate on you. If I do, you'll probably die, and you'll certainly be in worse shape than you are now.'

'Are you backing out?' The voice was heavy with menace. It made Ash realise that his cousin had another life, a life in which he threatened people, where arms were cut off and guns were fired. 'I told you, Marty, I need you. You have to help me, there's no choice. OK, you can't take the bullet out but you can sure as hell make it so I can travel. I need stuff to keep me going. You get it for me.'

Anger began to stir inside him. Not the indignation he felt over Taylor the chemist, or the fury he sometimes experienced over injustice at work, but something deeper, which reached right back to his childhood and those hours he'd spent with Benny, not only in the ghost house but later, when they were getting drunk and running wild. He didn't let it surface. He hardly knew it was there yet, but it lent him enough steel to snap down the line: 'Don't threaten me, Benny. Don't ever do that again.'

There was a pause and Benny's voice, when it returned, was calmer, almost caressing. 'Hey, I didn't mean to hurt you, Marty. You and me, we go way back together. Right? We were always the ones, Benny and Marty. That's all I want now. Some of the old magic. Just a little of your time, Marty.'

After a long wait he answered: 'I'll do what I can, you know that.'

'I know it, man. I'll see you tonight.'

'I don't know when I'll be there, Benny.'

'It's OK, the kid'll wait for you. He'll be there when you need him. You can trust him. I'll see you.'

The line went dead. He looked at the receiver in his hand and felt like he wanted to smash it against the wall. He didn't. He went through into Reception to see who was waiting and found his mother.

The after-lunch crowd was good. Mehmet Ali found himself working flat out for an hour or so and when things began to slow down at last he looked in the cash drawer and saw a whole drift of pound coins and even a few fivers.

The percentage of unemployment on the Golden Road estate was about as high as it could go, but there was always enough for a few drinks. After all, as Mehmet said to himself, when you've got no job and not much hope of ever getting one, you need something to cheer you up. And there was also the fact that quite a few of the men had work on the side, a few hours a week they did for cash in hand. It was inevitable. If they declared it they immediately lost part of their unemployment benefit. Mehmet thought that governments were stupid. They didn't have even as much sense as a small shopkeeper like him.

'Gissa doner, mate.'

He took a few wafer-thin slices off the meat turning in front of its gas grill. The temperature was almost unbearable inside the van and he was dripping with sweat.

'Salad?' he asked.

The customer nodded and belched. Filthy manners some of them had. 'Dressing?'

The guy looked down at his flies and nodded. He was well away, the stink of beer rising off him as he swayed and fumbled in his pockets for some change.

One day, Mehmet thought, he would get away from

here and buy a brand-new van with beautiful lettering on the side and he would park at the corner of clean wide roads where people were polite. He handed over the kebab. The customer slapped down a couple of pounds and breathed alcohol fumes into the back of the van. Mehmet gave him his change and he wandered away.

So far Mehmet hadn't been bothered by Iceman's gang but that didn't mean a lot since they weren't likely to get up much before midday. Even so, he emptied the cash drawer of most of the money and stashed it in a coin bag under the counter. He'd never yet been robbed, generally it was a matter of free food and drink and a five quid 'parking fee', but he'd made up his mind, he was finished with running away from these people. He had to fight back or he'd never get out of this place.

'Attention! Aaaaat – wait for it – Eaaaaase!'

'Mr Sergeant-Major?' Mehmet had known the old drunk for more than two years, ever since he'd been selling on the estate. Though some drinkers were a nuisance, Scrubbs was generally quiet enough, though sometimes he could go wild. Mehmet remembered one occasion when the old man had lifted the back wheels of some kid's car right off the ground. Luckily it didn't happen often or somebody could have been seriously injured. Scrubbs was a figure of fun to the locals. Today he was dressed in the most amazing bright orange boiler suit and a glaring yellow jacket.

'What are you wearing, Sergeant-Major, my friend? You look like traffic lights.'

Scrubbs looked to one side and mumbled something, then seemed to be listening. Finally he nodded and stepped forward, leaning on the little counter so that the whole van tipped towards him.

'Never reckoned to find a NAAFI van out here, old son. Still, good to see you anyhow. Me'n my mucker'll have a wad and a cup of char, I reckon. Done over twenty kilometres today. And you ain't got no snout, have you?' He mimed smoking, which gave Mehmet the clue. He offered a fag. Scrubbs looked at it. 'Got spats on.' He broke off the tip and accepted a light. Mehmet had never seen him smoke before and from the way he coughed and hacked, he certainly wasn't used to it.

'I didn't know you smoked, Mr Sergeant-Major.'

'Rations, ain't it. Sergeant's mess. Get 'em quarter the price. Ah, that's good.'

He blew smoke out and offered the cigarette to the air behind him. For a moment he froze then nodded. 'Yeah, ta,' to no one and came to life again.

Mehmet poured tea into a styrofoam cup. 'Here you are, Mr Sergeant-Major. I didn't see you yesterday. I heard there was some bother?'

'Guards. Bloody communists. Good fighters, mind. I'll say nothing bad about 'em as fighters. Better than the bloody Yanks, I'll tell you. Better than us, I reckon, else how come we're the prisoners and not them?'

'Um, well, I don't know.'

Scrubbs winked. 'That's 'cos you're not a military man, mate. Me'n Sam here, we know because we've faced 'em on Hill Twenty-seven. My God, that was as tough as I've ever known it. You know what?'

'No, Mr Sergeant-Major, I don't.' The old man was often a bit strange but Mehmet had never known him like this before. He was far more coherent than usual but seemed to be living in a totally different world.

'They used to play loudspeakers at night. When we was in our trenches waiting for the assault, they'd play this bloody woman: "Soldiers, think of your wives and children. Why don't you go home to your little babies and your wives. They are lonely. Maybe they find another husband if you not there." On and on they went all bloody night. Used to get to some of the lads. Them

169

that was just married, like, and worried about the kids, the wife.'

He crushed the cup, and the undrunk tea ran over his hand. His eyes were far away, seeing other sights, his ears hearing other sounds. 'That's it then, lads,' he bellowed, attracting a few curious stares. 'Time for the off. Don't let 'em see you giving up. Let's show the little yellow bastards how the British soldier marches. Hup, hup, hup!'

He lurched away into the afternoon shadows of the tower blocks, which were stretching out across the tired grass and baked mud. Mehmet wondered if he should tell someone about Sergeant-Major's condition. There didn't seem much point, really. Whenever they took him away, to a home or a hospital, he just turned up again after a few days.

'Got a Coke there?'

He reached down to the cool-box and took one out. Sergeant-Major would look after himself. There was no point in worrying about the whole world. He had his own interests to look out for and that was hard enough.

16

'Mum, what are you doing here?'

She looked terrible, her eyes red with weeping, a hankie screwed up in her hands. He knelt beside her. 'Mum, what is it?'

'Oh, Martin . . .' She could say no more before the tears came and she hugged him.

'What is it?' he insisted, his fear ballooning inside him. Had her stomach got worse?

She sniffed and wiped her face with the already sodden handkerchief. He pulled out his own and gave it to her. 'Thank you, Martin. Oh, that poor man. That poor, poor man!'

'Who, Mum?'

'Mr Kent. Such a gentleman and look what happens. I'll never forgive myself, never.'

'Please, Mum, stop a moment.' He took her hand in his. 'Just tell me what happened. Do you want a cup of tea?'

'I don't think I should leave here, not while Mr Kent is . . .' Tears sprang to her eyes again.

'We'll use the interview room, there's no one there at the moment.' Over his shoulder he called to Mie: 'Do you think you could get a cup of tea for my mum? We'll be in the interview room.'

'Of course, Ash. You should have said, I didn't know. I would have called for you at once.'

'It's OK. Come on, Mum.' He took her through.

'I was going shopping,' she began, once she'd settled and had drunk some of the tea Mie had brought. 'And who should I see but Mr Kent. Well, we're old friends as you know, Martin.' He did. He liked the ex-railwayman immensely and had sometimes wondered if Mr Kent and his mum might not get together one day. 'He was going to the shops too so we decided to go together. We thought maybe we would stop off after and have a cup of tea at that new place . . .'

'Mum, get on with it.' She'd always been a great teller of tales and still found it difficult to give a straight list of events.

'Well, here we are walking out, the two of us, and we get to the crossing. You know the one, just at the corner of Bread Street near the playground. There's nothing on the road and we start to cross and – oh,' her hands went up defensively at the memory. 'Suddenly Mr Kent, he grabs hold of me and pulls me back. And he's shouting out, "Be careful, Mrs Ashford!" and then he's lying there on the road with his shopping bag beside him and his glasses all smashed up. I don't know where it came from.'

'A car hit him?'

'That's what I'm trying to tell you, boy. He grabbed me, stopped me and goes and gets hit himself, poor man.'

'Did you see the car?'

'I didn't see nothing, except Mr Kent lying there like he was struck down stone dead.'

He felt almost sick with relief. 'You wait here, Mum. I'll go and see if there's any news about Mr Kent.'

'That's all right, I'm not going anywhere.'

He hurried through to the department and checked the board. Mr Kent was marked as RTA in cubicle five.

He found Karen and an agency nurse working on the patient. Karen gave him a far from friendly look as he came through the curtains. 'Yes, do you have a problem, Ash?'

'Mr Kent, here. He's a friend of my mother's. I just wanted to see how he is.'

'He'll be a great deal better if you let me get on with my job.'

The agency nurse raised her eyebrows as if to say: Wow, what a tiger.

'Is he in any danger?' Ash could see a couple of lines in already and gelofisin going through. The breathing was regular and there was no intubation so that seemed a good sign.

Karen sighed. 'He's in shock, there's a broken pelvis which is going to take some time to mend. No damage to any organs as far as I can see. You can tell your mother to get ready to spend a while helping her friend learn to manage his crutches.'

'He's coming round,' the agency nurse said. 'Hello, Mr Kent. How are you feeling?'

Ash leaned past her. 'Mr Kent, it's Martin.'

The eyes focused, blinked a couple of times. 'Can't see properly without my glasses, Martin. What happened?'

'You had an accident. You were with Mum. There was a car.'

'Hmmm, bloody fool. Came straight at us. Must've been drunk or blind. How is your mother?'

'She's fine. A bit shaken up, that's all. She's waiting outside. They'll let her in to see you in a while. I – er – Doctor Goodliffe will let you know when she can come through.'

Karen snapped: 'You're sure I can handle that, Ash? You wouldn't want a second opinion?'

'You should tell her to go home, Martin. I'll be fine for now. No point in her waiting around.'

'I think she wants to, Mr Kent. And you know what she's like when she's made up her mind.'

'There's no moving her.' He smiled and closed his eyes again.

Karen said: 'Ash, do you mind?'

'OK, I'm sorry, I didn't mean to get in your way.'

She turned her back on him and resumed work without answering.

Mike was coming out of Charlie's office with a folder full of papers. He grinned at Ash. 'What d'you reckon to Mark being sent down the tubes to get our visitor?'

'It's *Alien*, for sure,' he said, then went on, 'Mike, could you do me a favour?'

'Yeah.'

'My mum is in reception. An old friend got knocked down by a car. Karen's treating him now. But I'm a bit worried about her, er, general health. You know, the shock of something like this. I wonder if you could, if you have a moment, perhaps just give her a quick check-out?'

'Doesn't she have a GP, Ash? He should do that.'

'I know, but since she's here, she does really come under us, doesn't she?'

'Is this the same senior staff nurse who was complaining only the other day that a good quarter of our patients should be seeing their GPs and not taking up our time?'

'Just to be safe, Mike?'

'I don't know why I do these things. I'm too good-natured.'

'You're a saint. You know, every morning when I wake up, I thank God that I'm privileged to work with such a fine, noble—'

'Stow it!' Mike swatted him with the folder.

'Ouch, that hurt. Shall I get her?'

'Go on. Maybe I should do this privately. Seventy-five quid OK by you?'

174

'Don't. The bank bounced my mortgage yesterday. I need to borrow money, not spend it.'

'Cubicle one, then, but make it fast.'

He couldn't believe it. How had the crumbly moved so fast? They were supposed to be *old* – which meant slow and feeble, half deaf, half blind, rocky on their pins. Only this old sod had spun around like a ballet dancer, grabbed Martin's mum and swung her out of the way seconds before he would have nudged her into her own son's Casualty department.

Oh, it would have been such a sweet scheme. Imagine Martin's face when he saw her. And it would have hurt like hell. No doubt about it, Martin was the kind of bloke who really loved his mother.

Deevers spun the wheel and joined the traffic heading west round the inner distribution road. He reckoned he should probably get off the streets. When he'd looked back, after clipping the old guy, he was sure he'd seen someone else at the crossing taking his number. Maybe he was wrong, of course, and anyway the back of the car was pretty filthy, it would be hard to read the plate accurately. But best not to take chances. He had too much business to get through before . . .

He pulled out of the traffic and took a left, heading into the maze of small streets that made up the western suburbs of Holby. His house was a house like any other, an end-of-terrace with a small garden out the back. There had been a garden in front but he'd concreted it over so he could park off the road. His neighbours had complained.

Once.

After that they'd had the sense to keep their mouths shut and their noses out of his business. He drove straight on to the forecourt and squealed to a halt. Next door a curtain twitched. Sod 'em, he thought, getting out and slamming the door as loud as he could. After this afternoon's cock-up he'd welcome a snide remark. But none came and he let himself into the house.

He had to admit, it was getting pretty bad. It hadn't been cleaned since Sherry had died. And he'd give her that, for all her faults, she kept the place spotless. Now it was beginning to stink in the heat. The sink was full of unwashed dishes and cups. There was a plastic rubbish sack spilling across the floor. Crushed beer cans and fast food containers littered the sitting-room. He had to get a grip on things, stop them sliding the way they had been since Sherry had been taken from him.

He went through to the sitting-room and pulled open the curtains. The place was such a tip that he closed them again, but not before the sun had fallen on the photo of Sherry and him on their wedding day. He picked it up and looked at her. So beautiful, so innocent, and now she was gone, because of those bastards at the hospital. 'I swear to you, Sherry my love, I swear he'll pay. Oh yes, he will. I'll make him crawl and beg your forgiveness, Sherry. And then . . .'

As always, he had to stop at that point. What was he going to do afterwards? He didn't know. Maybe things would become clear when he'd finished with Martin. Yes, that was it, his head would clear and he'd be able to see where to go, what to do next. Perhaps he should sell the house. It was too big for him now. Or maybe he should find another woman. Yes, that sounded like good sense. A man needed a woman, needed her love and support, needed her obedience.

In that case he'd better clear up. You couldn't invite a woman into a place like this. Maybe Martin had a girl? Somebody who would need a little comfort after Martin's accident? Well, it would have to be Martin, now. His old woman wasn't going to walk under a car twice.

He went through to the kitchen, got out another black sack and emptied the dirty crockery into it. The noise of breaking was sharp, like his brain was being cut with little razors. He picked up the beer cans and food containers and shoved them in too, then tied up the neck and put both sacks out into the back garden. Action, that was what he needed. He was getting soft. They'd given him time off at work and he'd added a couple of weeks' holiday owing to him, so he'd been missing out on the company gym.

He worked for a private security firm, they'd taken him on when he'd come out of the army after realising he wasn't going to get promotion. That had been a bastard all right. 'Bad attitude,' they'd said. 'Not fit to accept responsibility for leadership.' Well, he'd proved them wrong, hadn't he; he was climbing up the company ladder pretty damn fast and when they took over the running of Holby prison, he reckoned he'd be in line for a top position. Then they'd see how he exercised authority.

There were still a few cans in the fridge and he cracked one, tipping it back so the icy lager ran down over his chin, soaking into his T-shirt. It tasted good, like metal in his mouth.

It was time to settle up with Martin. Tonight. Tonight would see it finished. He dropped the can and walked to the kitchen door. Reaching up he hooked the pads of his fingers over the top of the frame and slowly pulled himself up, feeling the swell and pain of his muscles burn inside him.

'Ash. Martin. Wait.'

Sara hurried after him. Like everyone in the department she was casting slightly nervous looks at the ceiling, heating vents, dark corners and anywhere else a large and, presumably by now, hungry arachnid might lurk.

'I was just going for a coffee,' he said.

'I'm on break too. Can I er . . .'

'You don't have to ask, Sara. It's your break too.'

'Well, you know what I mean.'

'I suppose I do.' There was no trace of her earlier upset and as they walked along to the canteen she was more relaxed than he'd known her to be since her arrival in the department.

'Coffee, tea?' he asked.

'Orange juice for me. It's too hot for anything else.'

'Why don't you find a table, near the window if possible. D'you want a cake?'

'With these hips?' She mimed her shape, exaggerating the size of what were, Ash decided, very attractive curves. 'I'll have a yoghurt. Any flavour.'

A table emptied by the windows and she hurried off. Ash joined the queue and found himself behind a familiar pair of shoulders.

'Julian?'

'Ash? Hey, good to see you.'

'You too.'

The long-serving Casualty consultant shook his hand warmly.

'What are you doing back in Holby, Julian? Not signing up for another stint?'

'I don't think I'd be welcome. Anyway, it's always a mistake to go backwards. Keep your eye on the next signpost, not the last one.'

'Where are you now?'

'Birmingham Royal. I'm taking over Neurosurgical. It's all infarctions and subarachnoid haemorrhages. Speaking of which, Charlie Fairhead was telling me you have an arachnid problem of your own. He was suggesting I might apply my specialist knowledge of the subject.'

'I wish you would. They're going absolutely bananas up top. You'd think we had the plague loose.'

'It'll all work out in time. But what about you, Martin?'

'Well, I'm still here.'

'You haven't thought of taking promotion?' He turned to the counter, 'I'll have a tea, please,' then back to Ash. 'I don't suppose things have improved since my time.'

'Two per cent cuts across the board, Julian. It's got worse. I'll have a coffee, an orange juice and a strawberry yoghurt, please.' He took his stuff and continued: 'I don't know what I feel about moving, which is what I'd have to do.'

'Why not? It's a wrench at first, I know that, but a new perspective can make all the difference. Anyway, you've got a lot of talent so don't waste it. Nice to see you.'

'You too.'

Ash carried his tray across to the window seat. It wasn't cool but it wasn't quite so hot. A couple of HCAs went past spidering their fingers at him. He ignored them.

'So who was that?' Sara asked.

'Julian. Used to be the Casualty consultant.'

'He looked nice.'

'He could be, but he could also be a real toughie at times. Which I don't suppose is such a bad thing. Is strawberry all right?'

'Hmmm?'

'Strawberry yoghurt?'

'Yes, of course. I can eat any yoghurt at all, any flavour, any time. How much was it?'

'No,' he said, 'it's OK.'

'Are you sure? Is this a sort of meal out, the one we didn't have at your place last night?' She was smiling.

'You know how it is – things get mixed up. And I do have—'

'It's something that's really bothering you, isn't it? I can see that, Ash.'

'It's a problem, that's for sure, and I don't know how to deal with it.'

'Can you talk about it?' She tore the lid off her yoghurt and began to eat. 'I don't want to poke my nose in or anything but sometimes it helps to share it.'

'It's something I have to do. I owe someone. I think I owe them. But someone else told me that perhaps I should say no, even if it does seem wrong. That sounds mad at first. She said I shouldn't be afraid to be selfish.'

'Is she a friend of yours?'

Was Sara's concern just about his problem or was she wondering if there was someone else in the background? 'She's a patient here,' he explained. 'In the children's cancer ward. She's in a sterile environment at the moment. I go and talk through an intercom. She's a science fiction freak. Used to sit out at night, she told me, and look for UFOs. She's pretty bright, too. You'd like her.'

'What's her name? Maybe I could go and say hello.'

'It would be great if you could, they get terribly bored in isolation. It's Lisa Benjamin. There's a Macmillan nurse over there, Angela Read. She'll introduce you.'

'But that doesn't help you.' Sara was scraping round the edge of her tub, spooning up every scrap of yoghurt. 'See, I am an addict.' The spoon vanished between her lips, then her tongue flicked out to remove just a speck of strawberry caught at the edge of her mouth.

'Look, Sara, about this morning . . .'

Her face fell. 'Don't apologise. Please, don't do that.'

'I wasn't going to. I was going to say I hope you weren't embarrassed.'

'By Dr Lowell? No, not much, anyway. She is a bit high-powered. Anyway, I was grateful, I really needed a hug and a kiss and, I have to say, I, um, did quite enjoy it.'

'Well, me too. But I . . . I was out of order. I mean we shouldn't, not on duty.'

'What about off duty?'

'Well that would be different.'

'And when are you off duty, Mr Ashford?'

'I've got a problem tonight. The same thing as yesterday, but I reckon, one way or the other, it'll be over by tomorrow.'

'One day at a time, right?'

'It's often the best way, in this place.' They stood up together and took their trays to the waste bins. 'So perhaps we could make a date for . . . What do you think about roller skates, Sara?'

'When I was a child my mother couldn't keep me off them. My brother said girls couldn't skateboard so I got into roller skates instead. Demon queen of the rinks, that's me. If they had an Olympic event I'd be a gold medallist. Why?'

'Street hockey. I mean I play, I love it. Fast, furious and full of fractures, they say, but it certainly takes your mind off work. The team is playing this weekend. Do you fancy coming along to watch?'

'Is this another thing girls don't do?'

'No way. The girls' team is hot to trot at the moment. We could use you.'

'What about you, Ash?' She asked. 'How do you feel?'

'I feel . . . OK. I mean I had a relationship. Nikki. We were close. It was pretty deep and when it broke up, then things inside me got broken too. What I'm trying to say, Sara, is that I'd like to go out with you. I think we could have a good time together but I don't feel ready for—'

'Anything deeper?' she cut in.

'Yeah. I'm sorry, does that sound arrogant? Saying what I'm ready for. It's about you as well as me and maybe you don't feel . . .'

She took his hand. 'I can look after myself, Ash. I'm a big girl. Let's play some street hockey.'

'Ash.' It was Adele. 'Can you go down to the department? There's a policeman talking to your mother. I think you should be there.'

17

His mother was looking flustered. A couple of uniformed police officers, a man and woman, were sitting facing her in the interview room. The WPC had her notebook open and was taking notes while her colleague asked the questions. Unfortunately he didn't seem to be getting very far. He gave Ash a questioning glance when he came in. 'Yes, sir?'

Ash and his mum spoke at the same moment: 'This is my son . . . mother.' Then they both laughed. The WPC joined in and the atmosphere lightened appreciably.

'They keep asking me these questions, Martin, and I keep telling them I can't remember a thing.'

'I know it seems like we're just going over and over the same events, Mrs Ashford,' said the WPC, 'but actually we've found out quite a lot you didn't think you'd remembered.' She checked her notebook, 'For instance, that the car was an old one, that it was "a sort of gold colour" and had something hanging in the back window. And there was a long scratch down the near side.'

'Well it's true, I didn't know I'd seen all that but now my memory is scraped clean as a sweet potato skin.'

'Are you absolutely sure, Mum?' Ash asked. 'If the police think it was . . .' he looked at the constable. 'What *do* you think it was? Drink or kids stealing cars and joy-riding? We've had quite a bit of that around Holby. There was a terrible train crash.'

'I remember it, sir, don't worry. In this case, though, we don't think it's kids. More likely someone who'd had too much to drink. Mrs Ashford and Mr Kent both feel the car was driven straight at the crossing without any regard for those who might be using it. Other than the possibility that some lunatic was actually trying to run them both down, that's the only explanation.'

'And you haven't got any other witnesses?'

'There was someone else at the kerb and they got a glimpse of the number plate, but I'm afraid it was too filthy to read properly. And to be honest, sir, most people don't take note of things like numbers in these kinds of situations.'

The WPC said: 'I think we've probably got everything Mrs Ashford is likely to remember for now. But if anything else does come to mind, anything at all, will you give us a call? Here's a number and this is my name. Constable Carswell here will be available if I'm not there.' She snapped the notebook shut.

'I'll ring you if I do, though I'm sure I won't. Like I told Martin, it was all so quick.'

'Well, just in case.' She handed over the paper and both officers left.

'You've been at the centre of attention, Mum,' Ash said. 'Maybe you'll be in the local paper. Perhaps they'll send a reporter round.'

'I hope not. Mrs Marwell was in the paper over her daughter's triplets and two days later someone broke into her flat. I don't want any of that, thank you very much.'

'We'll keep it quiet then, shall we?'

'I think that's the best thing. Did you find out how Mr Kent is coming on?'

'He's doing all right, don't you worry. They're going to keep him in for a while.'

'What about Barabbas?'

'What about him?' Ash was puzzled. Who was this addition to the scene? Some kind of pet, presumably.

'Mr Kent's old cat. Eighteen years old this month. Mr Kent is going to make him a fish-food birthday cake with those Super Gourmet Luxury Chunkies.' Her expression softened and Ash knew she was remembering. 'Do you recall, Martin, on *Blue Peter*, when they made a cake like that for their cat's birthday. You were so excited, you wanted to rush out and make a cake for our little Puddles.'

'Oh come on, Mum, that can't be true. Excited over a cat-food cake? How old was I?'

'You must've been all of five. 'Cos poor Puddles was run over when you were six, wasn't she?'

To be honest he could hardly remember the cat and certainly couldn't dredge up the least hint of a cat-food birthday cake, but that might well have been the mind's defence system refusing to accept such an embarrassing view of himself. 'Perhaps you could see if Mr Kent has his flat keys with him, Mum.'

'Of course he has his flat keys. What kind of fool would go out without them?' she snapped. 'Really, Martin, sometimes I can't see how you did so well considering you're sometimes so silly.'

'I can see you're getting the old sparkle back, Mum. I was just trying to say that maybe you could look after, um?'

'Barabbas. The thief who was saved instead of Our Lord. Don't tell me you've forgotten all your Sunday School? Oh, I remember how sweet you looked in that little white—'

'Mum, I'll ask a nurse to take you to see Mr Kent. There will probably be someone from the Social Services with him. You speak to them, arrange to look after his flat and . . . the cat. You may have to arrange something about his pension. Does he have a family?'

'His boy used to play cricket for Hampshire. A wicked slow left arm, so they said, and a fierce cutter of the ball. He once took twelve runs in an over off Michael Holding.'

She certainly was on better form than he'd known her for a couple of months. 'Mum, all this excitement seems to have done you good.'

'I'm not so slow and old as you seem to think, Martin. Besides, I had a little word with the doctor, didn't I?'

'Oh. Did you?'

' "Oh, did you?",' she mimicked in an innocent voice. 'As if you had nothing to do with it. I can remember you now, standing there telling me you hadn't eaten any cocktail sausages and there they were, every single one on that tray with the end bitten off. Oh, you were a handful.'

'All right, there's nothing wrong with your memory, I grant you that. But I didn't—'

'You can't lie to your mother. You never could and you never will be able to.'

'So what did he say, this doctor?'

With immense dignity, she answered: 'That is a matter between me and my physician. Now, when can I see Mr Kent?'

'I'll get on to it straight away, Mum. Why don't you come through to Reception, you can wait there. They might need the interview room for someone else.'

Going back into the kitchen, Janice couldn't hear any splashing from the pool. Maybe Carly had got fed up and gone to her room. She'd been out there a long time. Checking the clock, Janice saw it was almost four hours and she felt a twinge of concern.

'Carly?' She went out on to the patio and was unable, at first, to see her daughter.

'Mummy . . .' She was lying beside the pool peering down at something, Janice went over.

'What is it, love?'

'Look, ants. It must be an ant-house down here because they're all running in and out.'

Janice squatted to have a look. Carly's back was red and peeling in places and hot to the touch. Her forehead and the back of her head were burning too. 'I think you'd better come inside now. It's a bit too hot to stay out for long,' she said.

Carly didn't protest. She took her mother's hand and followed her into the shady kitchen.

'Orange juice?'

'Mmm, yes, please.' Her voice was curiously listless, as if she couldn't really care one way or the other, which was most unlike her.

After pouring the juice and adding a couple of ice cubes, Janice felt Carly's forehead again. It was still hot. Not surprising, perhaps, but she asked Carly how she felt.

'I've got a bit of a headache, Mum. I feel a bit – sort of tired and yukky.'

'Well, I'm not surprised you're hot, poppet. You've been out there roasting all afternoon. I think we'll have you for dinner, shall we, served up on a bed of rice with a salad?'

Carly could only manage a tired smile. 'Can I have a rest, Mum?'

Carly never asked to have a rest.

'Are you sure?'

'I feel a bit sick. A bit whirry.'

'Whirry?'

'Mmm. Sort of whirry.'

'Well, let's just put some calamine on and then you can have a little nap if you want.'

'Oooooh, it's cold.' Carly shivered as Janice slopped on the lotion. Once her swimsuit was off the contrast between white and red skin showed just how much she had caught the sun. Janice felt a real concern growing in her. Should she call the doctor? No, surely not for a bit of sunburn. And anyway, she'd been to the surgery only yesterday. 'I think you might have an uncomfortable night, young lady.'

'Like Sir Friday Knight with an itch in his armour?' They'd been reading stories about the Round Table and Carly had invented an extra group of knights who had the kind of problems with rusty armour and a hasty need for the loo that King Arthur's men never seemed to experience. Normally she delighted in the tales of the Kitchen Table, as they called them, but this time her remark was no more than a stock response.

Janice picked her up and carried her through to her room, lying her on the sheet. 'Don't pull up the quilt cover, will you?'

'Of course not, Mummy.'

Janice felt her head again. It was dry and hot. The room was humid and she opened the window, but it didn't make any difference; there wasn't a breeze to blow and the curtains hung without a movement. 'I'll bring you some more orange juice.'

As she left the room, Carly mumbled, 'Don't want . . .'

Just walking downstairs brought Janice out in a sweat and she wondered why Carly had been so dry. Perhaps she should just call the doctor and have a word, to reassure herself. She stopped in the hall and picked up the phone. Then put it back again. She couldn't call, not today. But at the same time what if Carly was ill? She knew from so many talks with the people at the health centre that children were always vulnerable and goodness knows, Carly had her fair share of lumps and bumps. No, she'd wait a while and see how Carly went. A cool drink would probably do the trick, and a little rest. She'd soon be up and about.

They were getting low on orange juice. Not surprising in this heat. The supermarkets were probably running out of soft drinks. There was just one carton left; she pulled up the waxed cardboard wings and pinched them, then poured a glass for Carly and one for herself. The fridge was making more noise than usual – it was having to work extra hard. As she went back upstairs, Janice thought that if they didn't get rain soon they'd all melt. It was so oppressive, the atmosphere getting heavier and hotter by the minute. Maybe that meant they were going to have a thunderstorm. She hoped so, they needed something to clear the atmosphere. 'Here we are, love.'

Carly was asleep. She went over and knelt by the bed. The child's face was flushed deep pink and her breathing was heavy. Her skin was hotter and drier than ever.

'Carly, wake up, love. I've got something for you to drink. Carly, wake up, it's Mummy.'

The child didn't stir. Janice touched her forehead again. It really was burning. She shook her. 'Carly!'

There was no response. For a moment the room swam in front of her eyes, then she jumped to her feet and rushed downstairs to ring the surgery.

'So?'

'Yes, so what?' Mike grinned.

'Come on, Mike, what did you say to my mother?'

'We both agreed that you're a bit of a devious sod, Ash. You set her up. Come to think of it, you set me up, too.'

They were in Admin, sorting through duty rosters. As usual they were being asked to use too many HCAs, who were cheaper than trained nurses in salary terms but could not accept the same patient responsibility.

'I didn't mean to, to, er . . .' Ash said, 'I just knew she'd never go to the doctor. It's this thing she's got about my father. She thinks every hospital and doctor in the country is waiting to kidnap her and hold her forever.'

'She should be so lucky. Have you seen this memo from Jane Scott? Why aren't we moving patients through faster? Our contract states that a nurse should be seeing patients within half an hour and a doctor within two to three hours. What does she think we are down here, a production line?'

'Perhaps you should ask Josette Lowell, Mike. She seems to be in the know.'

'She's just doing a job, that's all. Statistics. I don't somehow think she's got any personal axe to grind.'

Ash felt like saying, well you wouldn't, would you, but he kept his mouth shut and asked instead: 'What about my mother, anyway?'

'Gastritis. Plain and simple. Almost certainly, anyway. Did you know she takes aspirin almost every day?'

'No.'

'For her phlebitis. Someone told her it was a good idea. She can't remember who. Pity they didn't tell her that aspirin can irritate the stomach lining and cause some of the symptoms that I guess you both thought might be stomach cancer.'

'That's about the size of it. She doesn't eat a lot of meat and her fibre is OK but you never know, or at least you don't until it's too late. Still, I'm relieved.'

'I told her to see her GP. I think she will now she knows it's nothing too bad. She's a nice lady, she thinks a lot of you.'

'As well as thinking I'm a devious sod?'

'Oh yeah, she told me all about you and the cocktail sausages. Did you really eat the end off each one?'

Ash blushed. 'It was some meeting of the Caribbean Society. She was doing the cooking and there were these trays of little sausages, each one with a cocktail stick in it. And I was hungry. You know what kids are like. And I knew that I couldn't steal one, Mum would've gone wild if I'd done that. But if I had a little bit off each, then nobody would notice and it wouldn't really be stealing. I thought she'd explode when she found out. Luckily everyone else thought it was a great hoot so I got away with it.'

'And some would say you've been getting away with it ever—'

The red phone shrilled. Ash reached across and picked it up. The voice came sharp and tinny. Mike lifted an eyebrow. Ash listened and put the phone down.

'GP referral. A child with suspected heatstroke. The mother called through. He asked us to – well, I'm not quite sure what he did ask, but it sounded to me like he wasn't too sure about the mother. There seem to have been too many problems for this child. He asked if we could keep our eyes open.'

'Great, make it our problem, not his. Who is it, anyone we know?'

'Cowling?'

'Oh yeah, Tom Cowling is OK. I know him. He's not normally one to panic. We'd better do as he says.'

The doors to Crash were open and a couple of paramedics were carrying a child through. The mother, youngish, well-dressed, her hair expensively done, followed. She was talking to one of the paramedics but as soon as she caught sight of Mike and Ash she rushed across. 'It's my daughter, Carly. She's been in the sun. She won't wake up. She was having a rest and then she wouldn't, couldn't wake up so I called Dr Cowling and he said I should—'

'It's all right, Mrs Parker, I'm sure there's nothing to worry about. Does Carly have any allergies, any medication she's taking?'

Ash hurried into cubicle two with the paramedics. 'OK, Carly, can you hear me?' There was no response but he went on talking anyway. 'We're going to slip you off the stretcher in just a moment. That's a good girl, we'll just lift you up and there you are. You'll be a lot more comfortable in a moment.'

Adele came through with a saline solution. 'Mike said you'd be wanting this. Put a line in and bring up the salt. Ooh, what a poor little mite. As red as a lobster, isn't she? Hold on there, love, and we'll have you right as rain in no more than a blink.'

'We'll want some solution to cool her down, I should think,' Ash said while he put the line in. They'd had a number of heatstroke cases and there was no real danger as long as the patient's temperature could be brought down and the salt replaced. Sometimes, in weather as humid as today's, the body found it difficult to sweat but cooling would redress that balance too. There shouldn't be any long-term danger here at all.

Adele began to swab and the child's eyelids began to flicker. 'She's coming out of it. You want to tell the mother? She should be here when the little one wakes up.'

'Will do,' he replied. Adele had a way with kids. They were comfortable around her and she could handle even the most difficult cases with no trouble at all. Come to think of it, she could handle just about everybody without any trouble at all. Ash wondered if he should suggest she took over Mark Calder's job.

'Mrs Parker?'

Janice was waiting in Reception. As soon as Ash arrived she started talking, explaining how it was that Carly had been in the garden, how she blamed herself but she didn't want to smother the child with too much attention. That was what had happened when she'd been young but, of course, she could understand the problem. Only it did mean that sometimes Carly had accidents and really she was embarrassed about the number of times they went to the doctor, although Tom Cowling was so good about it and he and Carly really got on well and so on and so on, until he was able to hand her over to Adele.

'Hello, Mummy,' the child beamed, and from the way she held out her hands to her mother, and from Janice's response, there was no doubting at all the love and affection between mother and daughter. So what had the GP been on about? Some kind of generalised anxiety? Over what?

Outside, with Adele, while she filled in the notes, he asked if she'd done any kind of check on the child. He didn't need to explain any further.

'She's perfect, Ash. Nothing wrong there at all. You saw them together.'

'I agree. It's probably nothing at all. The GP just mentioned that Carly had a more than usually high accident rate. And the mother did seem rather apologetic, as if she was trying to head off criticism with her whole life history.'

'Some kids are always falling over. If you like, I could mention something to children's ward. I suppose we'll keep her in for observation overnight?

'Yes, I think Mike would want to do that. We'll see. It's just that . . .'

'What?'

'I dunno. I've got a feeling. Something I can't quite put my finger on. Maybe from college. A lecture. You know how it is, you can see the place, the time, everything, but can't quite grab the words. Crazy.'

'That's how it is sometimes. Crazy!'

18

Iceman spun the top off the Thunderbird and drank. He passed the bottle on to Petey, who passed it on to Gary, who was back in for the time being at least. Iceman wasn't fooled, though, and didn't have any intention of turning *his* back on the guy.

The rest of the gang were drifting into the playground where they usually gathered when it wasn't raining. Built when the estate was new, it was a sunken area that could be used for football or netball without fear of damaging windows. Then it was found to be a great place to trap victims, where they couldn't get away and their cries went unheard. Later still, it became something of a dump and some of the local drunks had settled there. Until Iceman and the guys had got a can of petrol and torched the rubbish. The place had burned for days – the fire brigade were too scared to come into the estate to put it out. After that the drunks left it empty.

Speeder, a tall skinny kid, arrived with a ball he'd stolen and they started kicking it against the wall until Gary got pissed off and stabbed it.

Iceman laughed. 'Hey, Gary, you really killed that ball. That's one dead ball.'

Petey laughed. 'He's a ball-killer.'

Gary didn't even smile. 'One day they're going to be yours, Petey.'

'Hey, hey,' Speeder held up the deflated sphere. 'Is this fair, guys? I mean, some kid probably loves this ball. Takes it to bed with him. It's his friend.'

Speeder was weird, everyone said so. Iceman said: 'Outstanding. Get Gary to buy a new one.'

'Looks like my old man's head,' Speeder said, regarding the wrinkled rubbery surface. 'Maybe we should kick that against the wall.' Speeder's old man was even weirder than his son.

'Maybe we should kick your head against the wall,' said Gary. 'Hey, Ice, what d'you think, or have you got something better to do?'

'Like what've you got in mind, Gary?'

'Like did you do anything about Benny? Your mouth was big enough yesterday, talking all that stuff about dope and things.'

'Things?'

'Yeah, that's right. Things. Money things, like we could maybe move in and make some money because I'm getting really pissed off hanging round with sod all to do except do without.'

A few of the guys were nodding at that. Gary had three or four of them behind him. Iceman still had most of the gang and that included Big Jo, who could tear Gary into pieces if he ever had a mind to do it. Course, they'd need to find a spare mind he could borrow first.

'You OK, Jo?'

Jo thought about that for a while, finished the Thunderbird, holding the bottle above his mouth to let the last drops fall from the glass lip, then said, 'Sure, Ice,' and threw the empty bottle straight up into the sun. Everyone scattered as it came down and shattered on the tarmac.

'You're a mad sod,' Petey said. Big Jo grinned, as if it

was the sort of thing he did every day. Which was about right in his case. How he'd stayed out of prison or some kind of secure home for so long was a miracle.

'Well, yeah,' said Ice. 'As it happens I have been thinking about Benny. I've also been thinking about Vernon.'

'Go on. I'm listening.' Gary leaned against the wall, arms folded, his head on one side so that you could see the tattooed web across his throat.

'Petey's been doing some watching, right?'

'Stayed up most of the night,' Petey said. 'I mean I hung around my mum's 'cos she's got this back window in the lav. You can see out over Benny's flat. They had the lights on all night. After that black guy went away, Vernon went out a couple more times. He also went out this morning to get some food. Only he doesn't come out the front like he should.'

'What does he do, fly?' Gary and some of the others laughed.

'No, they've got this fire escape at the other end of the balcony. The steps go down the outside of the block. I mean they're concrete an' all, proper stairs, but I bet most people don't know anything about them 'cos they've blocked off the old balcony, you remember, because it wasn't safe.'

'You mean we could get up there without anyone knowing?' Gary said.

'You're beginning to get the picture, Holmes,' Iceman drawled. 'What it also means is that the kid won't reckon on anyone being there when he comes down next time.'

'Only somebody will?'

'Outstanding again, Gary. You really are showing an improvement. We should hang you over the balcony more often. OK, so next time Vernon comes out, we'll be there and we'll ask him to tell us how old Benny is doing, on account of we're so worried about him our little hearts are aching.'

'You reckon,' Big Jo rumbled, 'he's got a stash in there for real?'

'You've seen the man. Look at him. He don't dress that way on income support. And he keeps that girl of his and the baby in pretty good style.'

'Hold on,' Jo said. 'If he's got the baby, why don't we grab it, sort of like for ransom. He'd have to pay us to get it back.'

'Where is the baby?' Iceman asked.

'In the flat.'

'Fine. So how do we get it? Go and knock at the door and say, "Excuse me, can we have your baby to hold for ransom?" Not very bright, Big Jo, not even for you.'

Speeder asked: 'Doesn't she come out? Take it for a walk or something? My mum's always taking the baby out.'

'That's 'cos it's your stupid sister's baby,' Gary said, 'and she's gotta go to school so she can't look after it and your mum hates its guts. She'd probably give it away if anyone was dumb enough to want it.'

'Will you both shut up,' Iceman shouted. 'What we have to do is find out what's going on in that flat. Petey reckons that Benny is sick. The kid has been bringing in bandages, going down the chemist for pills. Stuff like that. If he is out of it, then we can walk in there and clean up. And I don't mean do the dusting.'

'He knows some heavy guys,' Speeder said. 'I seen him talking to fellers who look like something out of *New Jack City*. They've got gold, they've probably got shooters as well. I don't want to get shot.'

'Nobody's gonna get hurt except Benny and the kid.'

'You sure about that?'

'No Speeder, I'm not, because I'm not a sodding fortune-teller. Look, why don't we just get over to Benny's place and see if we can't have a chat with Vernon next time he pokes his head out? Is that all right with you?'

'Sure, I'm on.'

Iceman took a run at the wall and jumped, getting a purchase on a ledge to push himself all the way up to ground level. He stood looking down at the others. 'Come on, then.' He turned and walked off, not waiting to see them follow him. It was hotter than ever now, and muggy with it. Tonight was going to be a real bitch, like a steam bath. Maybe it was also going to be his first move into the real world.

He walked into the shadow of a block but it wasn't any cooler. His T-shirt was wet. He took it off and shoved it in the back pocket of his jeans. He reckoned he could've done one of those jeans ads they had on TV, he was just as tough as the blokes they used. Anyway, they were all actors and probably benders as well. Petey fell in beside him, offering a fag. He took one and lit up, drawing the smoke in deep, blowing it out in a thin stream.

'We can cut through behind the car park, Ice.'

Half the flats above them were empty, the windows boarded up, some with the boards ripped off by squatters or the drunks who'd moved out of the play area. In a strange kind of way Iceman actually liked this place. It was the end of the line and if you could hack this, you could hack anything. All it needed was the guts to go all the way and, at last, he was going to find out if he had it in him.

Benny's block was in the newer half of the estate. Repairs had been carried out here, the rubbish was still emptied, most of the flats were lived in. This was where the Horn of Plenty and the betting shop were situated and where most of the kids came from. The pub had its usual crowd spilling out of the doors across the pavement. Speeder's dad was there, Gary's mum, a few other people Iceman knew. His own mum seldom left her flat, preferring to sit in front of the TV and dream about what might have been.

The gang followed the same tortuous route that Ash had taken the night before, though for them it was as familiar as the local High Street. It gave Iceman a good feeling to see people get out of the way as they approached and stand back, watching them pass with fear and admiration. He was someone on this estate; he'd earned his position and he wasn't about to let a prat like Gary take it away from him.

'Round the back.' Petey pulled his arm. 'You can get through the hallway.' They went into Benny's block but kept going, through the stairwell and out to the back. Here the building caught the full force of the afternoon sun and the shadows were as deep and dark as keyholes. Over their heads the condemned balconies stuck out from the face of the block, bits of bracing-rod emerging bent and rusting from the crumbling concrete. At the far end of the building a spiral concrete stairway wound right up the side to the topmost balcony. The bottom of the stairs was blocked by a metal barred door, secured with a large lock and wound around with barbed wire.

'Keeps the animals in,' Petey whispered.

'What?' Gary called. 'Come on, bleedin' James Bond, we're not on a mission here. We don't have to whisper. Anyway, the bloody thing's locked.'

Petey was bouncing, hardly able to contain himself. When they got to the door, which looked pretty well sealed, he reached round to the side where the hinges were and pulled the metal free. At some time or another the bottom set of hinges had been cut and the whole thing moved just enough to let someone crawl through. 'Smart, right?' He let the door fall back and even from this close you couldn't see that the hinges were loose.

Built on to the end of the block, just behind the steps but out of sight of the gate, was a series of concrete bunkers, originally intended for dustbins. Now they were mostly empty or piled high with rubbish. The stink was indescribable and the flies were something else. You could be eaten alive by that many flies.

'OK, Gary, you 'n' me, we'll wait in here. When the kid comes out, we'll take him. The rest of you, clear off back to Petey's place. Your mum's at work, isn't she?'

'Yeah, till eight.'

'You wait there. You'll be able to see when we pick up the kid. Get over here fast.'

Gary was poking round the rubbish. 'Bloody hell, Ice, they've got rats in here.' He shoved a body with the toe of his trainer.

'What're you worried about, mate? It's dead, isn't it? I mean if you can't take it, then that's fine. Crawl out of here any time you want.'

For a moment it looked as though Gary would take him up on the offer and go. The rest of the guys waited. Gary shrugged. 'Sure, no problem. I mean it's a sodding sight cleaner than some places I've hung out. Yours, for a start, Speeder.' He slipped into the lean-to and was lost to sight.

'OK, clear off, the rest of you, but stay sharp. Hasta la vista, muchachos.'

They ran off across the baked earth. Iceman joined Gary in the stinking dark rubbish hole. He pulled out a pack of fags. 'Smoke?'

Ash knew he really ought to go and see Lisa before he went home, to clear up any unpleasantness left over from their meeting. There was little enough room left in her life for anything but the huge, brute fact of the cancer and he didn't want there to be sourness between them. Maybe if he waited until tomorrow he could pick up another book – that should put her into a better mood.

He'd seen his mum to a taxi after she'd spent some

time with Mr Kent and agreed to look after Barabbas. She'd also forgiven him for setting her up with Mike, who she seemed to like. 'Nice boy you're working with, Martin.' He'd told her that Mike was hardly a boy, but she hadn't listened. Still, she'd gone home happy.

Karen was coming out of Charlie's office, her face set in annoyance. Charlie followed her. 'Don't complain to me, Karen. I agree with you, if they want pregnancy tests done in Surgery they should do it themselves, not send patients down to us so it comes out of our budget.'

'It's the sneakiness of the whole thing that gets me. They must know that A and E can't make cuts like other departments.'

'It's what we keep telling them. Even Mark Calder agrees with that but he's—'

'Don't even mention Mark Calder or bloody Jane bloody Scott.' She marched past without noticing Ash.

'Karen seems her normal calm self.'

'She'll get used to it. Aren't you off yet?'

'Aren't you?' he asked.

Charlie indicated a pile of papers a couple of inches tall on his desk. 'I've got to go through that lot tonight. I'd rather do them here than take them back to the flat. Oh, by the way, there was something I wanted to ask you, Ash.' He sifted through the papers and came up with a pharmacy form. Once, the department drugs were all drawn from a central store and charged to the overall hospital budget. Now, under the new system, A and E had to account and pay for everything it used. 'Two hundred milligrams of nubane you took yesterday. What was that for?'

It had been for Benny but he could hardly say that. 'God, Charlie, I don't know. I was so frantic I can't remember. Wasn't there that building site accident? I think it must've been that.'

'I can't find the forms for that either.'

Of course he couldn't. Ash had 'lost' them. He felt thoroughly miserable. He knew Charlie would believe him and would cover up his 'mistake', but he was abusing a friendship and that scalded like acid.

Charlie was speaking as he put the sheets back into order. 'OK, but let's make sure things don't go walkabout in future, Ash, it just makes it that much harder to run the system.'

Ash grinned sourly: 'What makes you think they want you to run it, Charlie. I thought the idea was to wind it down. Anyway, I'm off.'

'D'you want a lift tomorrow?'

'Only if it's really no trouble.'

'It's really no trouble. I enjoy having someone to talk to. I get . . . ' He shook his head sadly.

'You were cut up over Ken Hodges, weren't you?'

'Yes, I was. I know you and Duffy had your difficulties with him.'

'In the end it turned out OK.'

'And then Ken left. God, it's a funny world, the way things get turned around just when you think you've got them sussed. Now get out of here or I'll put you down for an extra shift.'

'Any time, Charlie. And don't bother to pay me for it – you know how much I care about this place.'

'You and me both.'

He grabbed his jacket and went out through Reception. Mrs Parker was still there, waiting. He stopped by her chair. 'Hello. How is Carly?'

'Oh, she's much better, thank you. It looked a lot worse than it was. I was so worried, as you can imagine. Do you have any children of your own?'

'Not married. No children.' He thought of Nikki and the baby she might have had. What would he be feeling now if he was going home to a wife and a child of his own?

'Well I'm sure you will have one day. I can tell you, they take up so much of your time. Well, I'm always busy but I try to make sure there's time for Carly and I to spend together. We read, you know, because I feel you can't give your child too much help at home. It makes all the difference in school. I've always believed . . . '

She stopped and got to her feet, looking at a man who had just come in. 'It's my husband. I called him, you see.'

'Yes, well you would do.'

Ash moved away as the man, a good few years older than Mrs Parker, walked across the room and took his wife's hands in his. A look that was almost one of despair passed over her face. Not at all the kind of expression Ash would have expected to see on an occasion like this. He heard the man say, in quiet, careful tones: 'I came as soon as I could get away, Janice. Now, you'd better tell me exactly what has been going on here.'

Janice watched the young man leaving. He seemed so sympathetic, someone she could talk to. Frank took her arm.

'Now come along, Janice, I know it's been upsetting but you simply must pull yourself together. After all, it's Carly we should be thinking about, poor little mite. I expect you were somewhat worried.'

'Don't you want to see her?'

'Of course I do,' he said. 'Can we go through now? Hadn't we better check with a doctor? And what exactly did you mean when you called me? You said they'd want to keep her in overnight?'

'Yes, Frank. To be sure there aren't any problems.'

'We certainly don't want any of those, do we. No, I'm sure they're quite right. After all, they are the experts.'

She wondered what would happen if she started

screaming at him or just leaned over and bit his ear. No point really, it would hardly be the most responsible of actions and she had Carly to think about. As always.

The black sister who had been so good with Carly came through. 'Mrs Parker. Mr Parker, here you are at last. Carly is asking where Daddy has got to and I told her I wouldn't come back without him. Would you like to come through now?'

'Excuse me, I've been waiting over an hour. Can you tell me when someone is going to see me?'

The speaker was a large young man with an angry voice and red hair that seemed to be growing in small clumps over his otherwise shiny scalp. His lips were flecked with foam and he was obviously working himself into a fury.

The sister sat beside him and took his hand. 'Now you know what I told you. We're being as quick as we can but if someone comes in who needs help more than you do—'

'I need help, don't tell me I don't need help. Look at this.' He slapped his head and a few ginger hairs drifted away in a sunbeam. Tears sprang to his eyes.

'I know you need help,' the voice was so calm and yet so full of authority. 'But there's a little boy through there who's swallowed half a bottle of bleach. He's very sick indeed. Now you wouldn't want to come before him, would you?'

'Well, no, I s'pose . . .'

'But as soon as we have a space, then you'll be in it. I promise you that. I can't say how long and won't lie to you about it. We'll do our very best, that's all I can say.'

'All right. I s'pose I can . . . well, I haven't got anywhere else to go. Not looking like this.'

'Thank you,' she said and Janice thought it really sounded as if she meant it. 'Now, Mr and Mrs Parker, will you come with me.' She took them through the double doors. The department was busy, nurses moving purposefully about their work, a porter pushing a woman through on a trolley, calling out, 'Who's doing the ICON' then grinning down at the woman, 'don't worry, love, it may look like chaos but believe me, it's worse.' Then laughing so infectiously that the patient joined in too.

'Here we are, Carly, here's your daddy.'

Frank went through and enfolded Carly. He might have his boring points but he did love her in his own slow, grey way. Janice stood by the door of the cubicle where she could look through into the department. There was an area where people seemed to come and go, bringing paperwork and x-rays, which they looked at in just the way people did on TV. An older man, the doctor who had attended Carly on her arrival, was talking to a young woman who was waving a sheet at him and almost shouting. 'I know a femoral hernia from an inguinal hernia, Mike. And for you to say otherwise is a load of—'

The older doctor said: 'Balls?'

For a moment the young woman stared at him, then she burst out laughing and waved the sheet in his face. 'Exactly. Testes. And this one is strangulated, I'd guarantee it.'

'So you want to send him off to Surgery?'

'What do you think?'

'No, you tell me, Karen.'

'OK, then yes, if we don't do something here then the intestine is going to get pinched.'

The man nodded. 'I'll get on to the surgical reg at once. It's Norman McQuaid. Nice guy. You'll like him.'

'Great. I'll tell my patient. Oh, my God though, you should've seen his face when I palpated the scrotum and said, "This'll have to come out." Poor guy thought he was going to lose the crown jewels.'

'Don't tell me you didn't enjoy it.'

The young woman hurried away. The man picked up the phone and began to punch out a number. As he did so a beautiful black woman in an exquisitely cut business suit passed. 'I'm going now, Mike. I'll meet you at the hotel . . . ?'

'Seven,' he said. 'We can have a drink. Then I'll show you the bridge at dusk. It's very impressive.'

A nurse came hurrying by with a big green laundry bag and then a man leading someone in a hospital robe and two doctors with stethoscopes.

Janice thought it was the most exciting place she'd ever been. It beat the health centre by a mile. All these people so busy, doing work that was so important. If only she hadn't got married and given up her life then perhaps she could have been like the young doctor, hardly out of her twenties and making life and death decisions half a dozen times a day.

'Mummy . . .'

She sighed and turned back to the cubicle. 'Mummy's here, Carly.'

19

The cupboard wasn't exactly bare but it wasn't over-flowing either. Ash felt he'd like something decent to eat, there had been too many meals grabbed on the run recently and he'd always believed that food deserved to have trouble taken over it. That was something his mum had taught him with all those wonderful meals.

There were some pasta shells in a jar and, after checking in the fridge, he found he still had some soft mascarpone cheese.

'Conchiglie al mascarpone e noce,' he said in a terrible attempt at an Italian accent. It meant pasta shells with cream cheese and walnuts but sounded better in the original language and tasted brilliant in any language. It was also quick to prepare and a little went a long way. Nikki had been amazed when he'd produced it. She'd never imagined him as a cook but, as he'd said, when you've got to look after yourself, you soon learn to handle a saucepan and a cheese-grater.

Within twenty minutes he was sitting in front of the video, his supper on his lap. He sprinkled some parmesan, freshly grated, not the stuff in the tubs that smelt like sick, and dug in. The film was one of his favourites: *Adventures of Baron Munchausen*, directed by Terry Gilliam. It was wild, crazy and about as far as you could get from the nitty-gritty of life at Holby General. It also made him laugh, and that was something else he needed tonight.

The food made him feel a lot better but he didn't dare relax too much. There were decisions he had to make tonight and he was going to need all his wits about him. Charlie wouldn't follow up the loss of a few painkillers. It happened in any busy department. But it underlined his intention not to attempt any medical treatment of his cousin. He knew this was the right thing to do, he couldn't compromise everything he believed in as a nurse. On the other hand, Benny was out there waiting for him, needing his help to get away from the estate, probably even the town.

He tried to shut his mind to the whole question: he'd think about it later, when he'd seen Benny and had the facts, whatever the facts were at that moment. Things seemed to be changing all the time. On the screen Baron Munchausen was riding a huge cannonball, his coat-tails flying around him. A soldier from the besieging army goggled as the amazing sight flashed past. In the hall, the phone began to ring. Ash pressed the pause button on the video and walked through. 'Hello?'

'Hello, Martin.'

He didn't know the voice. 'Yes, hello?'

'Heard your mum nearly had an accident. I was so sad to hear that.'

'Sorry, who is this?' There was something about the accent that seemed familiar.

'Oh, come on, Martin, you remember me.' The voice suddenly became hard as slate. 'Because I remember you, you little bastard. Oh yes.'

'What the hell is this? Who are you?'

The voice went back to its snake-like calm. 'We met, oh, somewhere around. Seem to recall, Martin, that you had a few things to say at that time. A few ugly things that I didn't like.' The voice went back up. 'After what you'd done, you murderous sod. Well, you're going to pay. Just like your mother and that stupid old prat she was with.' There was a laugh and to Ash it sounded totally insane. 'Well, everything has to be paid for, Martiiiiin, and I'm coming to collect. That's right. X marks the spot!'

'Look, just what are you talking about? Are you in trouble? Do you need help of some kind?' It was always best to try and get confused, disturbed or violent people to talk. Ash didn't know who this nut was but if he had been something to do with Mum's accident, then he shouldn't be out on the streets. 'If you've got a problem, maybe we could get together, talk it through. Maybe I could help.'

The laugh came again. It didn't sound like it found anything funny in the situation. The voice said: 'No, *you've* got trouble, Martin, not me. I'll be seeing you around.' Then the line went dead.

Ash noticed his hand shaking from the strain of squeezing the receiver. He put it down, breathing in and out slowly. Relax, he told himself, calm down, keep it cool. Occasionally they all came up against disturbed patients. Sometimes the patients followed them out of the hospital into their personal lives. It was an occupational hazard. People identified with doctors and nurses. In a shifting, often frightening world, the figure in the white coat provided reassurance. Yet his caller hadn't sounded like he needed any reassuring words.

He sat back down in front of the video. The last of his pasta was cold so he didn't bother to eat it. He didn't restart the film, either. The Baron would have to wait – Ash had got his own fantasy right on the other end of his phone. Only this guy sounded more like something out of Stephen King than one of Terry Gilliam's creations.

He tried to think. That tickle of memory the voice had

aroused – could it bring anything back from the hundreds of cases he'd handled over the past few months? The voice had an angry whining sound, like a child who's done something wrong but blames everyone else for it. And there was more than a hint of violence there, as if the bloke might explode in your face without warning.

He got up and went through to the kitchen to make some coffee. As he turned on the tap something in his memory turned too and he saw the department. It was a night shift about two months ago. He remembered the face, shiny, as though it was covered with thin plastic, a narrow face with lots of small teeth. Yeah, the guy had too many teeth, like a shark. And a wife, that's right, it all came flooding back now. The wife had been burned by hot fat. Badly burned. Full thickness on the chest and face. And she'd died. Not from the burns, though they were bad enough, but from a heart problem.

The kettle clicked off and he poured the water. As he stirred in the skimmed milk he remembered how he'd been sure that this was no accident. The woman had other bruises, old ones that were consistent with battering. He'd tried to talk to her but she was unable to respond. So he'd talked to the husband. He couldn't remember the name, just the face and the insistent demands that they save his wife's life.

Mike had taken the case and Ash had mentioned his suspicions. Mike said there was nothing to go on, the bruising could have come from any number of causes; the fat accident could well have been just that, an accident. As for the woman's heart, she had a congenital weakness, and her body was under massive assault. Death wasn't surprising in the circumstances.

As usual Ash had felt angry. Looking at the woman, at what had been done to her, he'd felt that once more someone was going to walk away from the consequences of their actions. He didn't want to use the word evil but he remembered now, as he drank the coffee, that he had felt the husband to be evil. He'd questioned him in the interview room, pushing and probing far beyond anything that would have been acceptable with a truly grieving relative. This man had been swinging from mood to mood, weeping for his lovely wife one moment, almost laughing at Ash the next, then angry at the hospital for letting her die. He'd talked about suing the Authority, getting millions in damages. In the end Ash had decided the guy was totally off the wall and had left it. He was just too crazy to get mixed up with. But maybe he'd left it too late and the man had fixated on him as the cause of all his troubles.

What had he said about X-ing Ash out? Did that mean that the X scrawled into his phone pad had been put there by this guy? The idea made him shiver, despite the sultry heat. He ran through to the hall. The top sheet had been torn off and thrown away but the marks left by the pencil still showed clearly through the next five or six layers. He tore them all off, until the paper was unmarked.

Should he contact the police about the call? The WPC had given his mum her number. He reached out for the phone and as he did so it rang. He snatched it up, his heart beating at twice the normal rate.

A huge blue fly wobbled through the thick air and settled on the edge of an oil can. Iceman picked up a length of wood and brought it down carefully, trapping the fly so they could hear its angry buzzing. Then he flicked his wrist and the fly splattered across the green tin. Gary blew out a stream of smoke from pursed lips. 'Radical!' He shoved a black plastic sack to one side. 'Ought to torch this place. Only thing for it.'

'Wait.' Iceman was at the door, listening. 'I think he's coming.'

211

Trainers padded down the concrete steps, paused, and there was the squeak of metal being moved. Ice and Gary were out and round in seconds, taking Vernon before he even saw them.

'Hey, Iceman, lemme go, hey, OK, you lemme go or you be in big trouble.'

Ice hit him in the mouth with the wood he'd used on the fly.

Gary chortled. 'Hey, now that really is radical.'

Before Vernon could shout through his smashed lips, they were dragging him away from the block, towards Petey's place. The others met them as they reached the hall.

'Through and out the back,' Iceman snapped. 'There's an empty garage, second along.'

None of the others had thought this far ahead. He saw that Gary was really pissed off at himself. If it had been up to him, they'd still be standing round outside the spiral stairs. Planning, that was what leadership was all about.

Vernon was thrown into a corner where he bounced off a pile of old tyres. Big Jo shut the door – it was bent but he forced it and stood guard. The others gathered around Iceman.

'You are in some deep do here,' Vernon mumbled. 'Messing with Benny is a bad move.'

Iceman hit him again, once round the side of his head, knocking his glasses off, then a jab in the gut and a cross-hit over the nose. Vernon started to cry.

'Listen, kid. Nothing personal, see.' Ice rapped him over the knuckles. 'This is just about money.'

'Gimme my glasses, I can't see.' Vernon suddenly sounded his age: a frightened fourteen-year-old.

'You don't have to see,' Gary said, stepping on the glasses and grinding the lenses into the concrete, 'you only gotta listen.'

'What you have,' Iceman said, 'is one very bad movie

and you can't get out of it. We want to ask you a few things about Benny.'

'I dunno,' Vernon said. He was trying to regain his cool but it was beyond him. They'd hurt him a lot and he didn't want any more.

'Come on, your sister lives with the guy.'

'Only sometimes. He just visits.'

'Like now. He's visiting now.'

'Yes.'

'So why doesn't he come out and drive that big car of his? Who was that bloke you brought in last night? You said he was someone for Benny, you gave us some good blow to keep out of the action. Why? Nobody *gives* blow away.'

'I don't know. I swear I don't know.'

Iceman only had to raise the club and Vernon started to talk. They were all behaving as though they were in the kind of films they watched on video. This was where they learned their lines but sometimes, as it had now for Vernon, real life, real fear surfaced and blew all the dreams into dust.

'There was some deal that went wrong,' he babbled, 'Benny got hurt. He's hurt pretty bad, that's why he called in this guy. It's somebody he knows from being kids together. Sort of a doctor, who isn't going to tell the cops.'

'How did he get hurt?'

'He got shot.'

There was a whistle from Big Jo. The others were impressed too, though a couple also looked like they might want to wet themselves.

'This is the real thing,' Gary breathed. 'He got shot?'

'Yeah, in the guts, it was bleeding.'

'Hardcore!'

In spite of his fear and pain, Vernon could appreciate the effect he was having. Style was the currency the

213

gangs used on the estate and getting shot in a drugs deal certainly had all the style you could ask for.

'So if he's shot,' Petey said, 'I mean, what good does that do us?'

'I dunno yet,' Iceman said. 'Just shut up and let me think. Kid, how come he's still hiding out?'

'Someone else got hurt, one of the other crew. They're looking for him 'cos he's still got the—' If Vernon hadn't been carried away with his own story, he'd wouldn't have got that far. As it was, he shut his mouth as soon as he realised.

Iceman didn't bother to hit him. 'He's still got the stuff from the deal. Right?'

Vernon didn't answer but his expression said it all: he'd let Benny down, he'd blurted everything out.

'What is it, how much?'

'I dunno, he doesn't tell me that. I just deliver sometimes.' No point in keeping quiet now. 'He's got a lotta places he uses. It isn't just our flat.'

'Yeah, but at yours he's got his babymama and that makes a difference to these guys.' Nobody disagreed with Ice; he had their total attention. 'We can get in the same way Vernon got out. Old Benny there isn't going to be any trouble, not if he's as bad as the kid says.'

'What if he isn't,' Speeder said. 'What if he's got an Ingram or something up there? You know what these people are like.'

'We'll send you in first,' Gary said, 'You can weird him to death.'

It broke the tension, everybody relaxed.

'So, OK,' Iceman said. 'Is this it, is everybody in?'

'Sure,' Big Jo grinned, 'this is our movie, Ice.'

'That's right, it's ours. We are going to make some money. Fast money. That's the best thing in the world.'

'What about the kid?' Petey asked. 'We can't just let him go.'

Iceman slipped an arm round Vernon's narrow shoulders. 'Hey, no way. I like this kid. He's my friend. He can share my Kiaora.'

'You gonna let me go, Iceman?'

'Sure. Only I like you so much, kid, that I want to treat you to a kebab and a cold drink. I mean it's pretty hot, right?'

In the garage it was almost unbearable. 'You reckon we might have a storm tonight?' Big Jo asked.

'We are gonna have the mother of all storms. Which is fine for us. Jo, let us out of here and then keep hold of Vernon. Don't hurt him. He's not going anywhere without his glasses, right, kid?'

'Right.'

Big Jo lifted the sliding door with a screech of tortured metal. Evening sun glared in. A sheet of plastic fluttered in a breeze, the first for weeks. Over on the horizon there were clouds, rolling like a dark, angry border to the clear skies. Iceman sniffed. 'Yeah, you can smell it, there's gonna be some rain tonight.'

'Who is this?'

He was waiting for the whining, threatening voice. Instead it was a woman.

'Is that Marty?'

'Yes.'

'This is Susie.'

'What is it, what's happening?'

'It's Benny, he's getting worse. And my brother went out and he hasn't come back.'

He could hear the baby crying. 'How bad is Benny?'

'He's finding it hard to move around. He says it hurts all the way down his side.'

'Does it smell at all?'

'No, I don't think so. It just hurts, that's all.'

'He needs a doctor, Susie.'

215

'Well he's got you, Marty.'

'It's not that simple any more.'

'He says you're the only one who can help him.'

'I don't think so.'

'You have to come tonight.'

'I'll come but I can't promise anything.'

'I didn't tell him about my brother not coming back. I haven't told him yet.'

'I don't understand. Susie?'

'I'm scared that someone has got Vernon, maybe they're keeping him, 'cos of Benny, you understand. There's the baby too. I don't want no trouble.'

She was getting hysterical, losing control.

'Try and calm down, Susie. I'll come, but you have to stay calm. OK?'

'OK.'

'If your brother isn't there, how am I going to get to you?'

'I'll meet you. Don't worry.'

'Where? Outside the pub?'

'I don't think so. Too many things are going on here. I don't want to take no more chances.'

'So where?'

'The stop after the pub. The bus goes round the corner. I'll wait there for you.'

'What about the baby, are you going to leave her?'

'Nobody is going to hurt her. I'll take the dog off the leash. He'll protect the place while I'm out. Can you be there by half past ten?'

He looked at the clock. There was a clear hour to go. 'I'll be there.'

She put the phone down.

There was no point in calling the police about Mum's accident now. He'd do it in the morning. Benny came first.

He had a first-aid box in the bathroom and he shoved it complete into a shoulder bag. He also put in a couple of old towels. He kept fifty quid for emergencies buried in a sugar tin he never used at the back of the kitchen units and he took that too. It was almost like he was on the run. He just hoped to hell it wouldn't end up coming true.

20

Hot, damn hot. That was the trouble with Korea. Froze you one day, boiled you the next. Scrubbs decided the only thing to do was get rid of the jacket. No camouflage value in it, not being yellow like that.

Sam Smith agreed. 'Best dump it, mucker. Travel light. Reckon this'd be our best chance to go for a break.'

'You reckon, Sam?'

'I do, Scrubbsy. And it's up to us. No officers around. So, as usual in this man's army, it's all down to the NCOs. We've got to set an example to the lads. Still kids, some of 'em. They look up to you and me and we can't let 'em down.'

Scrubbs folded the yellow plastic coat and shoved it down behind a phone box which hadn't worked for years. If he needed it, he could pick it up afterwards. After what? Well, best let old Sam sort out the details. Scrubbs' thinking hadn't been so clear lately. Probably a reaction to the lack of vitamins and the marching. On and on and on. And seeing the poor buggers who couldn't make it any more. 'Reckon it's time for a snifter, then, Sam? Little bit of something to set us up?'

'Sounds all right to me. Lead on, Sar'nt-Major.'

He was a good lad, was Sam Smith. Never minded stopping for a quick one. Course, they had to be quick with all them communists ready to take you out of the line and give you a good clubbing.

The NAAFI was crowded. Briefly it did occur to Scrubbs to wonder what exactly it was doing out here somewhere beyond the Ky-Loh Pass, but not for long. The blokes seemed to know him. There were shouts and greetings, people were slapping him on the back as he pushed through. Sam had got lost somewhere but he'd turn up, he always did. Old Sam Smith.

Mehmet pulled out another box of pitta bread. Things were going well tonight. The heat hadn't stopped people buying; of course, kebabs were designed for a hot climate but his customers didn't know that. They just needed something to soak up the beer.

As he served a customer, he noticed a disturbance over at the Horn of Plenty. 'Go on, shove off, Scrubbsy, and don't come back until you've got the money to buy your own booze. I won't have no one begging in my pub.'

The landlady was a thin northerner but tough as old nails; no one messed with her, if there was going to be any trouble, and there generally was, it had better happen outside. Mr Sergeant-Major had probably been trying to get someone to buy him a drink. Right now he was cowering away from the woman as if she were going to beat him to death. She gave him a final shove and he went rolling into a crowd of drinkers.

Shouts of disgust, anger, laughter, went up and the old man found himself pushed and pulled and spun around until he could no longer keep to his feet and fell sprawling over a bin. There was more laughter as he tried to get to his feet and smiled along with the others as if he'd enjoyed the joke, too.

Mehmet felt helpless anger. Back in Turkey, in the village where he'd spent his first six years, he could

219

remember how the elderly, even the crazy, had been respected and cared for. Here, in this country, all the traditional ways had broken down and it seemed to be everyone for himself.

Someone had emptied a packet of crisps over Sergeant-Major who was trying to brush them off like they were insects. Then, as if to prove Mehmet wrong, someone else sat the old man down and stuck a pint in front of him. The group settled to their own conversation, occasionally checking up on Sergeant-Major or refilling his glass. One or two obviously asked him where he'd got his amazing orange overalls – a question Mehmet would have liked to have put as well – but Scrubbs didn't seem to know.

After a couple of pints he began to talk earnestly to himself and sketch out maps in the spilt beer on his table. He was obviously planning something because even when extra pints were placed in front of him he hardly paused in his earnest discussions with himself.

At half past nine there was a sudden rush and Mehmet was working non-stop filling orders. One day, he reflected, as he cut, sliced, diced and packed the pittas, his son would be here beside him working. No, not here, but in a better van or maybe even a shop with a flat over the top where the family lived. It gave him the energy he needed to work at top speed and keep a smiling face for his customers.

When at last he had time to stop and look, Sergeant-Major had vanished. Unfortunately, Iceman and the gang had taken his place.

'Hi there, Peeps!'

'How many times I got to tell you, my name is not Peeps.'

For some reason this made the gang howl. Iceman came right up to the counter and grabbed a cleaning rag. He sniffed it and gagged. 'Arrrggghhh, it's revolting.'

He threw it over his shoulder and one of his gang caught it, threw it on, then grabbed his throat and started to collapse with bloodcurdling howls of agony.

'Why you don't stop, mate. This is my work. I make my living for my family with this van. You go away, you stop my customers.'

'I'd say I was doing them a favour,' Ice said.

'You go, I give you kebab, huh?' Mehmet felt disgust at his own weakness. He'd sworn he wouldn't surrender again but here he was, crawling to these bullies.

'Frankly, Peeps, I'd rather have cholera.'

The gang howled. Mehmet noticed the little black kid was with them, the one with the big glasses, only he wasn't wearing his glasses tonight. That was unusual, Iceman's gang didn't like blacks. 'You just go away then, you don't bother me.'

Iceman shoved the counter. The van rocked, the gas grill behind the slowly turning meat rattled.

'Sure, we're going, Peeps, but we'll be back some time to collect the rent.'

'I don't pay you rent.' He lifted the meat knife. For just a moment he saw fear in Iceman's eyes before the youth jumped clear of the van and his face set in sharp, ugly lines. 'Nobody threatens me. You're really in trouble.'

'Ice, pack it in.' It was one of the others, Mehmet didn't know his name. A skinny kid with weird eyes. 'We got business.'

'Yeah. That's true. Peeps here ain't going nowhere. Like I said, we'll be back, mate.'

They strolled away, looking at him over their shoulders, all except the big one, who was struggling to keep hold of the little black kid.

He came out fast, a black bag over his shoulder, looking hot and bothered.

Deevers slid down behind the wheel. Maybe his phone call had caught Martin where it hurt. He wondered where he was going tonight? To see his girlfriend? Or maybe to the cops? That wouldn't do him any good, they'd listen but what the hell, he was just another jumpy nigger. Deevers giggled, he liked the sound of that and hummed the words to himself as he watched Martin walk along to the bus stop and wait. When was the guy going to get his car mended?

He began to whistle tunelessly through his teeth. Maybe he should slip up to the flat while Martin was out and add a few personal decorative touches. But no, they'd got beyond that. The feeling in his chest, the metal band slowly tightening round his head, told him it was time to hand out some punishment.

He ripped open the glove compartment and pulled out the snapshot. God, it was at times like this he really missed Sherry. What a woman she was, what a loss to any man. What a mistake Martin had made, picking on him back at the hospital. It was always the same, officials in their white coats, they thought they could treat ordinary people with utter contempt.

'Well, let me tell you, mister, ordinary people have had enough, we're beginning to fight back. You want trouble, we've got trouble.'

Some prat walking his dog stopped and looked in the open window. 'Sorry, did you say something?'

Deevers looked at him and smiled. 'You got a problem, Grandad?'

'I was just asking, there's no need to be rude.'

Deevers looked at him some more. The prat went white and hurried off. He was laughing so much he almost missed seeing Martin hop on to the bus.

He let it pull away before following. No point in pushing your luck. It was just a cruise, that's all, following the double decker through town and out towards the

222

Golden Road estate. 'Now you tell me, Martin,' Deevers murmured, 'just what the hell you are doing in this neck of the woods? Not your kind of scene at all. Good works, Martin? A bit of rough? Well, we'll see, won't we.'

One day he'd get his car fixed, Ash promised himself that. If he got out of this mess in one piece, he'd take the car into the garage and tell them to make it like new. He'd be able to afford it on the savings from bus tickets alone. Which reminded him, by some strange route, of his bounced mortgage cheque. He still had to do something about that. His pay wasn't due for another week. Well, maybe they'd wait and maybe they wouldn't. It was in the hands of fate. He didn't want to borrow from friends or his mum. Perhaps he should get Benny to organise a bank raid. But then considering what had just happened to his cousin, maybe that wasn't such a good idea.

The bus was passing through the estate. He could see the lights strung up outside the Horn of Plenty. It was darker than normal now that the clouds were rolling in from the east, following the sun down, catching its last coppery tints, and the air was so thick and hot that it seemed as if you could reach out and grab a handful and squeeze moisture from it like a sponge.

He reached up and pressed the red button. 'Bus Stopping' appeared on the illuminated panel behind the driver and he got up and swung round on to the platform. A hot wind blew against him, ruffling his hair. The bus squeaked to a halt and he jumped off.

There was no one at the stop. He waited, walked a few paces into the dark but realised he'd get lost in a moment. The only thing to do was wait. He shifted the weight of his bag and leaned against the vandalised shelter. The glass panels had been knocked out long since and someone had even tried to bend down the metal roof. It must have been such an amazing effort.

Why do it? Ash thought. Why not put half the energy into climbing Everest or taking over ICI? But then the answer was all around him.

A car slid past, the driver's arm visible out of the window. Music spilled from the speakers: 'Your Cheatin' Heart'.

'Marty?' She came out of the dark, looking smaller and younger, more vulnerable on her own.

'Susie, hi. Where were you, I was —'

'It's OK, c'mon, this way.' She grabbed his hand and pulled him from the road. 'We're going a different way. Benny thinks the others know where he is. He's getting ready to go.'

She was still running, still holding his hand. He had to bend to stay with her. They scooted round blind corners, up and down alleyways, between blank walls, once they went through a fence across some kind of allotment, then arrived at the hallway he'd seen last night.

'Benny's going to leave?' Ash caught his breath. He thought he was in good condition but Susie wasn't even breathing heavily. Perhaps fear was lending wings to her feet.

'Tonight, I told him, he has to go, because of the baby. I won't have her put in danger.'

'Good.'

'But I won't have you selling him out. You understand?' Her face was taut with strain. She looked capable of anything if he disagreed. 'I can't promise. I have to see him first.'

'You'll do what you can. Come on.' She began to run up the stairs. He followed.

Deevers stood behind a garage wall. The chase through the estate had been exhilarating. He'd felt like a hunter, a panther on the trail of its prey, knowing that one misstep or hesitation would be fatal and that he would have lost Martin and the girl in the concrete maze. At the same time he hadn't been able to make any noise. His training had really paid off, his whole body was buzzing with energy and expectation.

The only problem was, what the hell was Martin up to? Surely he wasn't at it with the girl? Maybe she was family? But there was no point speculating. He watched them vanish into the hallway. There was no way he could get close enough to follow them into the flats and find out which number they were going to. He'd have to wait until Martin came out and take him then.

Perhaps he should have a weapon for the first attack. He decided to wait round a corner and crack Martin across both knees as he passed. That would bring him down and Deevers would have time to work. Unless, of course, the girl came too. Well, he could handle that without too many problems. It had been a while since he'd spent time with a woman. And doing it to Martin's girl would make it all the sweeter.

He looked around to see if he could find anything useful. After a few minutes' searching he settled on a length of steel barrel, about four foot long, with a nasty jagged tear on one end. That would mess up Mr Pretty Boy Martin's good looks. Yeah, that would do nicely.

He undid a couple of shirt buttons but it didn't make any difference. It was too damned hot, if the weather didn't break soon, the steel in his hand would go limp. The thought made him smile, then he stiffened and shrank back into the darkness.

A group of kids passed him. Eight or nine of them, with one really big bugger holding this little one. The guy in front looked up at the block where Martin had gone.

'OK, there we go. She's in. Everybody ready?'

'Are we really gonna do this?' a tall kid asked.

'We really are.'

Somebody else said, 'Radical. All riiiight!' and the kids went across, not to the door but along the building and round the corner.

He waited a few moments before following them over the dry grass. Once he got to the block wall, he began to ease himself along, keeping close and low. It was very dark tonight. Not a star, not a glint of moonlight; the clouds had the whole town locked up so tightly you couldn't see a . . .

It was a noise that alerted him, the tiny mechanical sound of a car door being opened, the squeak of springs as weight was being taken off them. His eyes were used to the dark but even so it took him a while to locate the long, low shape of the car parked against the opposite block. In fact it was only a gleam reflected off the deep shine of the car body that gave it away.

Then there was movement. Men this time, not kids, silhouetted against the storm clouds as they moved from the deeper shadow of the block behind them. They were following the kids. And he was sure he caught another reflection, light on a blade, a blade long enough to stretch from wrist to ankle height. He swallowed, his throat suddenly dry. What was this, Blackbeard the pirate?

They crossed in front of him and went round the end of the building after the kids. Deevers couldn't work it out. Just how many people were after a piece of Martin? Was there going to be a queue or something?

He hefted the pipe, feeling it slap cold, hard and very unyielding into his sweaty palm. 'C'mon, c'mon,' he hissed, and began to whistle between his teeth.

It was the worst moment of Iceman's life. So far. Things were going to get a lot worse, they were going to get about as bad as they could be, but that was later and the moment when these three niggers just materialised out of the dark and one of them held up this sword and said, 'Freeze, boy,' was bad enough to be going on with.

'What is this?' he croaked.

'This is the wrong direction home,' one of the shadows said in a voice that moved like liquid granite. 'You kids are out way past your bedtime. Go back to Mama.'

No more than that. No argument, no pushing for a fight. The bottom had just dropped out of Iceman's world.

Big Jo moved up beside him, the only one of them too stupid to be scared. 'Hey, Ice, you want me to—'

'Shut it, Jo. We're out of here right now.'

'Right, boy. It's too heavy for you. Go get yourself a milkshake or whatever. And forget about us.'

The gang backed away, walking at first, then breaking into a run, pounding the pavement until they were back under the streetlights in front of the pub. Iceman didn't know who'd broken first but he had an uneasy feeling it was him. He felt sick to his stomach. He leaned over a concrete waste bin and spat the sour taste out of his mouth.

'Oh, wow, that was really cool, Ice,' Gary taunted. 'I really admire the way you handled those guys. Yes, sir, yes, sir, and would you like your bottom wiped while I'm still available? Outstanding.'

'Shut up, Gary.'

'This is about big money, fast money. That's what you said. Well, I don't see any money, maaaaaan. Anyway, where's Vernon?'

They looked around. He wasn't with them.

'I must've let go when I come up to you,' Big Jo said.

'He won't go far without his glasses,' Speeder said. 'But I s'pose he was almost home anyway. Probably find his way by feel.'

'What d'you think they wanted?' Petey asked.

Gary laughed. 'Just to make Iceman fill his pants. Which they pretty nearly did. Right, guys?'

At least four of the others joined in the cackling laughter.

'I didn't see you doing any better,' Iceman said. 'I mean you're so brilliant, Gary, why didn't you tell them to sod off?'

'Because it wasn't my idea, I wasn't going to make any easy money. I wasn't the masterbrain, you were. And I don't see any money.'

'No?' Iceman pushed himself upright. 'You don't? I mean I don't know about you people, but I'm getting really pissed off with being pushed around by niggers and wogs and scum like that in my own country right here in my own housing estate. This is our territory.' He looked at them: he had their attention. They were with him again, waiting for the Iceman to deliver. 'So let's go and collect the rent. All the rent.'

Two hundred yards away was the lighted serving hatch of Mehmet Ali's kebab van. The young Turk was standing, resting both hands on the counter. His face was white and tense as he caught sight of the gang.

'Cooee,' Iceman called in a high-pitched voice, 'we're baaaaack!'

21

She had been wrong about the smell. Ash noticed it as soon as they got through the door: corruption. Perhaps in the heat and general smell of the flat, Susie hadn't picked it up, but coming in from outside, it was as obvious as the pit bull.

'Come on, Steel, come on.' Susie calmed the dog, which was bristling as it faced Ash, and snapped the leash back on to its collar. She gave its massive head a scratch and, after a few moments, it settled down, still keeping an eye on the visitor.

'He's nervous,' she said. 'Missing Vernon.'

'You don't know where he is?'

'I just hope to God he's all right. You'd better come through.' She called out, 'Benny?'

There was no answer and she hurried to the bedroom door pushing through it in a panic. Benny was lying on the bed, bathed in the light of a silent TV screen. 'You're here?'

'Where the hell else would I be?' Is Marty with you?'

Ash followed her into the room. The smell was stronger here, almost enough to make him gag. He looked at Susie and she looked away, smelling it too but unable to accept what it might mean.

'Marty, good to see you, pal. You hear. The kid ain't back. That's bad news.'

'What'll they do to him?'

'Hey, not a lot. It's what they're gonna do to me, cousin. We have to think about moving.'

Ash went to the window and opened it. The wind was warm but at least it cleared the stench a little. A walkway ran outside, along the face of the building to stairs at the end.

'That's the way we'll go, Marty, out the back.' Benny coughed, a wet, unpleasant sound and when Ash turned, there was a speck of red on the sheet. Benny hastily rearranged the bedding to hide it.

'You've been coughing blood?'

'Not a lot.'

Ash sat on the bed. 'Lean back, that's it.' He took a pair of rubber gloves from the first-aid box and began to remove the dressing over Benny's wound.

'Heeey, take it easy, man, that hurts.' Sweat sprang up on Benny's forehead and began to run in rivulets down his cheeks. The smell was worse and when the last layers of bandage came away Ash's fears were confirmed. His face must have betrayed him because Benny's voice was loaded with fear as he gasped, 'What the hell is wrong, Marty? You gotta tell me.'

'Gangrene. It's what they call gas gangrene. When you have a wound like this tissue gets torn . . .' he shook his head. The stench was like a coating of grease on the inside of his mouth.

'Come on Marty, don't flake out on me now.'

'I – it's the bacteria, Benny. They breed in damaged tissue. They spread.'

'You mean I'm being invaded?'

'I mean you're in bad trouble.'

He went back to the window to take a few deep breaths and think about the situation. Benny was absolutely right, he was being invaded. The bacteria in his wound would spread from the damaged to the healthy tissue and would produce a gas which would cause decomposition, and it wouldn't stop. In effect, Benny was rotting alive and the only cure was surgery, cutting out the affected area.

Benny was moving the dressing back in place. Ash took a deep breath, hurried back to the bed and stopped him. 'Leave it open. Oxygen helps slow down the spread of the bacteria.'

'Come on, I can't run with half my guts hanging out.'

Ash almost laughed. 'Benny, you still think you're in the game, don't you?'

'Man, they are not going to get me. I'm gonna be free and send for Susie and the baby, Vernon too. We're gonna live high and wide on what I got stashed here.'

'Benny, they got you as soon as that wound started turning bad. You need surgery.'

'Later. They got surgeons in Jamaica, I'll buy a whole hospital full when I get there.'

'How?'

Benny squeezed the pillow he was lying across. 'This is my support, Marty.'

'It's a pillow.' Ash went to pick it up and rearrange it. Benny's left hand, which had been hidden under the covers, came out with a thin-bladed knife.

'Leave it, Marty. This stays with me.'

Ash stepped back. Susie was in the doorway, holding the baby. Her eyes were wide with shock.

'Benny, you never said. You told me it was a set-up. That they – that you were sold rubbish. That it wasn't your fault.' She screamed the words: 'You said it wasn't your fault!'

'It's for you, Susie. And Vernon and the baby.'

'Benny,' Ash said, 'just hold on a minute. Are you saying that you . . . I'm sorry I can't get my head around this.'

'It's simple Marty. I told you, I'm a middle man. I get

231

the stuff, I pass it on and I take my cut. I see a lotta money pass through my hands. Well, this time, I took my cut – and I kept the stuff. There's a lot of money here. Money for life. For all of us. You too, Marty.'

Susie's voice was hardly audible: 'What about Vernon? What about the baby, the risk, Benny?'

'No pain, no gain, Susie.'

Ash knew, in that moment, what he must do. Benny was using him, using the girl, using all of them. There *was* no obligation. He didn't have to hold the rope. 'Benny, I'm going to call for an ambulance.'

'No way, man. I'm not going into no hospital.'

Susie was there too. 'I told you, you don't harm my man.'

'He's using you, Susie. Can't you see that? You don't owe him a damn thing.'

She held up the baby. 'I owe him this. I don't care if he lied, he's the man I've got and you ain't hurting him, you ain't sending him away.'

He looked at the two of them, both trapped, both unable to change. He said, slow and clear: 'Susie, he will die if he doesn't go to hospital.'

In the silence that followed he could hear the rush and crash of his own heartbeat, like waves in his head.

Out in the kitchen the pit bull began to growl, a sound unlike anything Ash had ever heard before. It was pure aggression and made every hair on his body stand up.

'Jesus!' Benny began to scrabble at his bandage. 'Help me, Marty. Get this back on.' He started to tie it round his chest. Ash plunged into his bag and pulled out a clean dressing. 'At least use this.' He looped it round and began to secure it.

'Tighter,' Benny yelled. 'If I gotta run . . .' he bellowed as Ash pulled the dressing then tied it on. The growling was getting louder.

'Maybe it's Vernon,' Susie whimpered.

'It ain't Vernon, and you know it,' Benny spat at her. 'C'mon, we gotta go, girl.'

The dog began to bark, ugly sounds like saw-cuts tearing flesh. Benny pulled himself off the bed and stood swaying, one hand against the wall, the other holding knife and pillow. Figures moved outside the window.

'They used the fire escape!' Benny screamed. 'Susie, get the dog!'

The window exploded into glass shards that scythed across the room.

Karen flicked through the channels. There was nothing on. But then, there never was when you actually wanted to watch the TV. She wandered over to the bookcase, rejected a pile of *Hospital Doctors* and the latest *Lancet* and finally settled on *Vogue*.

As she flicked through the fashion spread she thought how strange it was that, in a few years, if her career went in the right direction, she'd be able to afford these kinds of clothes anytime she wanted. It was a long way from her upbringing. Of course, she might well have better use for her money, though a few additions to the wardrobe wouldn't go amiss.

The doorbell rang. Not Andy, he had a key, and besides, his ward meeting was going to run on tonight. She checked the time. Ten fifty. Late for a caller. She attached the safety chain before unlocking and opening the door a few inches.

'Dr Goodliffe?'

An elderly man in a sports jacket that was far too heavy for this heat, a striped shirt, grey slacks and polished brogues, stood on the landing. He carried a briefcase and looked harmless enough.

'Yes.'

'My name is Taylor. I'm sorry to bother you so late. I was working, I thought I might drop by on my way home. I wonder if I might come in. There are one or two things I would like to talk about.'

'I'm sorry, I don't know you, do I?'

'I'm a chemist, Dr Goodliffe. I believe there were some problems over a prescription of mine?'

Should she even be talking to this man if there was going to be a case made out of it? But then there probably wasn't, the way things were going. There was only her complaint about Ash's interference.

'All right, wait a minute.' She shut the door, unhooked the chain and let him in. 'Do you want a cup of tea or anything?'

'No, thank you, I am not a tea drinker.' He sat down on the sofa without being invited. There was something precise about him, as if he'd go on in his own way no matter what anyone else said. Opening his case, he began to take out various papers. 'Now, Dr Goodliffe, I won't waste your very valuable time, I'll come straight to the point.'

'Are you sure we should be talking about this? I mean, in view of what happened. Isn't it unprofessional?'

'In view of what happened?'

'Well, Mr Bryant's accident. The, um, prescription. The whole thing. Isn't that what we're talking about?'

His lips pursed, Mr Taylor shook his head. 'My dear young lady, I have already talked to your Mr Calder, is it?'

'Mark Calder. Yes.'

'And he assures me that the governing board of Holby General have no interest in pursuing what was obviously a totally peripheral component of the incident in question.'

'Does that mean they're not taking any action?'

'There is no action to take, Miss Goodliffe. There is no case, ergo there can be no action. Yes?'

Karen began to feel a certain shortness of breath, like

she needed a good shout. 'Mrs Bryant may not agree with you.'

'The poor lady has more than enough to worry about with the recent tragic death, through cardiac arrest, of her husband.'

Taylor was obviously a man who could wrap anything up in so many words that you lost sight of it. 'Could you get to the point please, Mr Taylor. It is getting late and I'm on duty early.'

'Of course. Now, as you can see' – he handed her a couple of typed sheets with details of an incident in his shop involving Ash – 'this is a record, duly attested and signed by myself and my shop assistant, of a visit by a Mr Martin Ashford. The gentleman is, I believe, a nurse.'

'Yes. He's a senior staff nurse.'

'Quite. Now he came into my shop and used threatening language, accused me of malpractice and virtually threatened to close me down by any means at his disposal. Now I know that our Caribbean brothers are somewhat excitable . . .' Karen's eyes popped. She couldn't believe what she was hearing. *Caribbean brothers*? '. . . But to be so insulted, and on my own premises too – well, I am an Englishman and I don't take kindly to bullying.' He smiled thinly. 'I'm sure you understand.'

He took her shocked silence for agreement and went on: 'I am considering issuing a writ against your Mr Ashford. I mentioned as much to Mr Calder and he – well, he told me that you and Mr Ashford were, how might one put it, at loggerheads.'

Loggerheads? she asked herself. What the hell were loggerheads?

'And that I should speak to you while preparing my documentation in the case against Ashford.'

'Oh, now I see, Mr Taylor. You want me to dish the dirt on this "Ashford".'

'If you have any legitimate grievances that you might wish to share with me, I'm sure that they could buttress our case in a most satisfactory manner.' he leaned forward. 'Miss Goodliffe, I intend to teach that young man a lesson he will not readily forget.'

'And you'd like my help?'

'I would appreciate your, how do they say it nowadays, input.'

'Is this how I come across to Mark Calder? Is this what he thinks I'm like?'

'Mr Calder appears to think very highly of you. Now, I believe that you yourself have instigated complaints procedures against this Ashford. Is that correct?'

There was a tearing sound. She looked down and saw that the *Vogue* was still in her hands, twisted and half ripped through. She didn't know she had the strength. She put it aside. Her voice was calm, though a slight tremble betrayed the rage waiting just under the veneer of politeness. 'Mr Taylor, there are a couple of things I have done recently that I have regretted. The first was starting that procedure against a senior staff nurse whom I respect highly and value as a friend. I shall withdraw it tomorrow.'

'You may not find that so easy, my dear girl.'

'I am not your dear girl, I am Dr Goodliffe. The second is allowing you into my flat. Now, as you put it so succinctly, Mr Taylor, I may have a little difficulty in withdrawing the complaint, however I will not have the least difficulty in throwing you out of here.' She got up and strode to the door, opening it wide. 'Now get out.' She bit her lip and smiled at him while he packed his case and came to the door.

'I have to say, Miss, that I find your attitude most unfortunate.'

'Goodnight, Mr Taylor. I won't say it's been a pleasure.' She slammed the door on his reply, waited till she could hear his footsteps descending the stairs and sighed: 'Well!'

Ash threw himself flat as the glass crashed around him. In the silence that followed a voice said, 'What is this, a hospital?'

Somebody else laughed. 'That's what Benny's gonna need.'

'Oh no, man, you got that wrong, Benny's gonna need a morgue.'

After that, everything started happening at once.

Susie had made it to the kitchen and released the dog. Ash looked up to see it pounding along the corridor towards him. He looked down again, burying his face in his arms as it leaped over him.

'What the hell—' One of the newcomers bellowed before he was cut off and began to shriek.

When Ash looked up next time, he saw Benny slumped back across the bed, being held by a tall guy in a black tracksuit and beret, gold glinting at the neck. The guy had a knife, the blade pressed under the jawbone. He was looking back at the struggle taking place on the floor, where the dog had the fallen man's face in its jaws. A third man was pulling at the collar, bellowing, while down the corridor both Susie and the baby were screaming.

'Call it off, Benny, or I cut you now.'

Benny looked up at the man holding him. 'I can't, Maxie. It won't stop now. It's a crazy animal.'

The man on the floor had stopped squealing and begun to whimper through what was left of his mouth. 'Use the effing cutlass, man.'

A blade swung, once, twice, a third time before the growls finally stopped. Ash got to his feet. Blood dripped from the ceiling.

'Who the hell are you?' the cutlass man said, lifting

the blade as though he intended to use it again.

'I'm a nurse, I can help your friend.' He went straight to the fallen man who was writhing, holding hands to his face.

The man on the bed looked over. 'Whoooooa, man, looked like old Hannibal Lecter had a piece of Zeek.'

'Throw me the bag,' Ash said. He was running on automatic, doing what his training told him to do, because he knew that once he started thinking about this situation everything was going to fall apart. He pulled out some dressings. 'Water, I'm going to need water.'

The cutlass man took his shoulder in a grip that could crush bone. 'You don't need nothing, pal. Just tie his face in place and we are out of here. Benny has to come, he has something that belongs to us, some people want to see him.'

'Look, please don't, OK? I won't give you any trouble,' Benny was pleading to the one who still held him. 'Maxie, listen to me. I'm hurt, I have to get help. Let me go with my cousin here.'

Oh, thank you, Ash thought, that is really going to help.

'Just lemme get to hospital, then I'll give you the stuff, the money you can have it all. Look, look, you don't trust me? Take the girl, hold the girl, she's got a kid. OK, it's my kid. You hold them, right? That'll prove I'll come back. Marty, hey Marty, you tell them I'm the guy who'll hold the rope. When I say something, I'll do it for sure. Huh?'

'Go get the woman,' Maxie said. Cutlass went out and came back a moment later with Susie and the baby. Maxie beckoned her to the bed. 'You ain't much. I don't think he'd come back for you.' He took his knife from Benny's jaw and held it between him and Susie. 'I don't think he'd care if I cut you up. No, I surely don't. What d'you say Benny. You or her?'

Benny shook his head but he didn't answer.

'Is there a key to the bathroom? Lock her in with the baby.'

Cutlass took them away.

'OK, cousin, how's the nursing going? You got his face in one place yet?'

'It'll do but he needs a transfusion fast. And surgery. They might be able to save something.'

'We'll see. OK, get him on his feet.'

Cutlass returned and helped Ash lift the whimpering man to his feet.

'Zeek,' Cutlass said, 'we be out of here any time now. You be fine to walk it?'

'I can't see nothing, man.'

'We'll be hanging on to you. Cousin Doctor, you take Zeek.'

Cutlass and Maxie held Benny between them. He began to moan in pain as they moved him and Cutlass wrinkled his nose. 'Wouldn't want to get too close to you, Benny.'

'He needs hospital too,' Ash said.

'He don't need a thing except to realise the error of his ways and indulge in some good confession. Come on, pilgrim.'

They went out the front way, passing the bathroom from which there was no sound. Benny looked back and caught Ash's eye, giving him a wink as if there was still something they could do. Maxie held them back on the landing. It was dark, no lightbulbs had worked here for years. They listened. Beyond the sound of TV sets there was nothing to hear. 'Let's go!'

Benny began to curse as they bumped him down the stairs. Zeek tried to speak but managed only bubbling sounds. As they reached the foot of the stairs and struggled outside, Ash could see that the whole of the front of his shirt was black with blood.

The wind was increasing, it was hard to catch your breath, as if a vacuum was sucking all the air off the surface of the earth.

'I gotta stop, I need a rest,' Benny was sobbing.

'Shut up. You'll have all the rest you need.'

The shape of a car loomed up out of the darkness. Locks bleeped, doors opened without an interior light coming on. They fell into the back, plush and smelling of new leather. The doors shut with a whoosh of air.

'OK, let's go,' Maxie said. 'And you people back there, try not to get blood on the seats.'

The car began to move. With a shock, Ash realised the pillow full of drugs was back at the flat. Benny was still playing his game and would go on doing so right up until the end.

Mehmet saw the gang gathering like wolves around his van. Iceman held up both arms in salutation. 'Hey there, Peeps. This is our patch. You're trespassing.' He was shouting, and one or two heads turned in momentary curiosity outside the pub but nobody was going to interfere.

Mehmet knew that he was on his own. 'Go away, this is my place, I'm staying here. You got no right to clear me off,' he shouted back. His voice cracked halfway through and he had to start again. He was frightened, he realised, so scared he could hardly move.

The gang circled closer. They weren't in any hurry. They had all night and they were going to enjoy it. 'Peeps, you had your warning, you didn't listen. That's a pity.'

The words echoed off the buildings: 'You didn't listen . . . You didn't listen . . .' Mehmet scrambled through into the driving seat of the van and switched on the engine, praying it would start first time for once. It did, coughing smoothly into life. He looked up at the mirror half covered with a photo of Ayse and the boy. Until that moment he hadn't known what he was going to do: run or fight. But the sight of his family did something to him. He stamped on the accelerator, wrenched the gear stick into reverse and swung back.

'He's gonna run,' Big Jo bellowed.

Speeder picked up a stone and flung it at the van. It went in through the serving hatch and smashed something.

'Head him off,' Iceman called. 'He's gonna go for the main road.'

Nobody had worked out what they were going to use to stop the van, they just ran, laughing and shouting, throwing whatever was to hand. Bricks, bottles, pieces of road sign all smashed into the back of the van, knocking the gas burner loose, so it fell against the cooking meat. The fat began to burn immediately and drip bluish flames down on to the rust-pitted floor.

Mehmet spun the wheel. The pub flashed past his windscreen. Then he jammed his foot on the brake, changed up and, spinning the back wheels, launched the van at the gang. As he drove, the rising wind funnelled in through the open cab windows, feeding the flames as they took hold of the painted wood interior.

'Oh, wow, will you look at that!' Big Jo was transfixed as the van headed for him, flames bursting out of the serving hatch with painful brightness. Speeder grabbed his jacket.

'Jo, he's crazy, it's on fire, get out of here.'

Mehmet saw the big kid looming out of the dark. At the last moment he spun the wheel, missing him by inches. However the trail of fire he was pulling behind him wrapped round both Big Jo and Speeder, igniting their hair like torches, leaving them bald and scorched but otherwise unharmed.

'Oh, maaan,' Speeder put his hands up to his head, then slumped to his knees.

Big Jo sniffed. 'Hey Speeder, what's that crazy smell? Stinks like the cat got burned.'

Heat seared Mehmet's back. He didn't have to turn, the roar of flames and the brightness around the van told him all he needed to know. He pushed at the door but it had warped and wouldn't budge. On the mirror the photo of Ayse and his son bubbled in the intense heat. He felt his shirt begin to smoulder and tiny pin-pricks of fire started burning all over his back. He threw himself through the cab window, falling as the flames caught his clothes and candled around him. Screaming, he began to roll over and over as the van careered away, now an unguided inferno, lighting the tower blocks with a flickering lurid brightness.

Iceman watched the van with total disbelief. They'd been rolling over Peeps for months, the little creep didn't have it in him to fight back. 'Tonight is turning out to be a real bummer,' he said. Petey arrived beside him, wild and out of breath.

'Hey, just like a video, Iceman. Look at it burn.' He darted away as the van clipped the kerb and headed across the road, straight for them. 'Iceman, come on, let's get out of here!'

Petey tugged at him but he didn't move. He was hyp-notised by the burning monster bearing down upon him. By now the whole rear section was burning, flames shooting up twenty feet into the air, blowing like feath-ers of fire in the wind. It was beautiful and crazy at the same time and he couldn't stop watching as it got nearer, and he could feel the heat on his face, blistering his skin.

'Iceman!' Petey bellowed. 'Move!'

At last he shook himself out of his trance and turned to run. As he did so a car came round the corner, cutting it too close. He was caught in the headlamps. He would have been knocked down had not the driver instinc-tively swung round him, straight into the path of the burning van. The two met with a shriek of metal. The car doors sprang open and forms rolled out, then the car and van exploded, sending out searching fingers of flame in every direction.

Iceman felt an unimaginable power lift him up and squeeze until there was no breath left in his lungs. He looked at his hands, at his fingers. They were on fire, each one of them burning, the nails blackened and turning back. His mind, his ability to understand what was happening to him, broke down seconds before the pain started and he began to scream.

22

'C'mon, Marty, stay with me. You can make it.'

'What – where?' His head was splitting. He tried to shake it but the pain was too bad. He shut his eyes. He wanted to rest, to lie still, to sleep.

'Marty, wake up. I need you. C'mon. We have to get back.'

'Back? Back where? He sucked in a breath and tasted burned petrol in the air. His head began to clear and he remembered. 'What the hell happened, Benny?'

'There was this thing, I dunno. Like a fireball. We hit it then everything just went to hell. I grabbed you and got out of there fast.'

'What happened to the people, the guy who was hurt?'

Benny shook him, not very hard but enough to bring a twinge to his head. 'Stop being a damned nurse for five minutes, will you? We've got to get the stuff and collect Susie and the baby and then get the hell out of here.'

They were heading back across the estate. Ash could hear shouts and screams and a series of small explosions. Light flickered above the block behind them as if someone had a huge bonfire.

'Help me, Marty. I helped you back there. I could've left you to burn.'

Ash took Benny's arm over his shoulder and, half supporting him, began to walk. 'Which way?'

'I told you, back to the flat. We'll use the fire escape.' He snorted. 'Sort of appropriate, right?'

'What if some of those people, Maxie or the other ones, got away? Won't they come back?'

'Course they will, that's why we have to move. So shut up and walk, Marty.'

In silence they limped and shambled back past the residents who were beginning to emerge from their flats, drawn by the noise and the flames. There was something of a carnival atmosphere about the crowds, with people losing their normal suspicion of each other and talking and laughing together.

Ray Deevers wasn't talking or laughing with anyone but he was beginning to feel that things were turning his way at last. A few minutes before, he'd been seriously pissed off. He thought he'd got everything settled: he'd wait for Martin to come out and jump him when he did. Except he arrived with an escort of black pirates and a couple of wounded guys. What were they doing up there, he wondered, playing small wars or something?

He'd given up for the evening after the spades had taken off in the limo. Then he'd heard the explosion and joined the crowds drifting round to the pub, where it seemed it had all happened. And who should he see heading back towards the flat but Martin and one of the wounded guys, who was hanging off his shoulder and looking like he wouldn't last the night.

He still had the length of pipe and he tightened his grip, turning and walking against the flow of the crowd, after Martin and his mate. He'd have to wait until they were out of sight, he'd need some peace and quiet for his work, but then nobody ever said he wasn't a patient man.

The shrapnel had been bad all evening. They'd been using the big 88s to shell the Allied lines and the casualties had been high. Scrubbs had heard a lot of screaming earlier; some poor sod whose number was up. Luckily Sam Smith hadn't copped anything, they were both still fighting fit. 'Over there, at two o'clock, Sam. See them?

'Wait, wait. Yup, got them. A platoon at least. Looks like they've been using flame-throwers. Place stinks of petrol.'

Easing his head above the trench Scrubbs made out the advancing communist troops. They were well provisioned, moving forward silently, no need for commands. He'd give them that, they were trained to perfection and their morale was high. Well, it was about time they saw what the British fighting man could do when the chips were down. 'Sam, I reckon we should execute a flanking movement. Leave the platoon here for covering fire, then you and me can get round behind 'em. It's the element of surprise.'

'We'll surprise 'em, mate, right up the arse with a Bren. Five hundred rounds!'

Scrubbs summoned the lance corporal and explained what they were going to do. All around, the hills were picked out with lights where the communists were dug in. They were using the loudspeakers as well, blasting out noise to stop the Allied troops sleeping. He told the corporal, a good, steady lad from Blackpool, to hold the position until daylight and then, if Scrubbs and Smith hadn't returned, to head back to base. 'All right, Mucker, ready to go?'

'Any time, Scrubbsy.'

'Good luck, lads,' he said, and slipped out of the trench, keeping close to the bare earth. Sam was right behind him. He knew he could trust his old mate to guard his back, whatever happened. They were a team. Mates. That was what the army was about.

*

'Wait, wait.' Benny was in a lot of pain. Even in the dark Ash could see that his wound had started to bleed again. It wasn't surprising with all the movement, but it wasn't a good sign either.

'Why don't you wait here, Benny. I'll go back to the flat and let Susie out of the bathroom. She can come back with me.'

Slumped against a low wall, Benny took some time to catch his breath. When he did, his voice was sharp: 'No way, Marty. This is my stuff, I ain't leaving it.'

'What about Susie?'

Benny lurched forward. 'What about Susie? Come on, help me here. It's not far now.'

They could hear the sound of fire engine sirens behind them and it seemed to give Benny the energy he needed. Ash thought he must be moving on sheer willpower by now, his gaze fixed on the flats in front of them.

As they staggered round the end of the building a shape detached itself from the darkness. Both men froze.

'Benny? That you?'

It was Vernon. He was speaking in a funny way, as if he'd got something wrong with his mouth and he didn't have his glasses on.

'Yeah, it's me. Where the hell've you been, kid?'

'Iceman, this guy, he —'

Benny shut him up. He was already struggling with the gate at the foot of the fire steps. 'Never mind. You been up to the flat?'

'I was scared, man.'

'OK, gimme a hand.'

With Ash and Vernon helping, they managed to make a gap wide enough for the injured Benny to get through. Above them the stairs spiralled round into a dangerous and unknown darkness.

'I don't know if you're going to make it up there,' Ash said. 'And I don't think I can carry you.'

'We go. If you don't want to help I'll go on my own.'

As they went, step by step, Ash realised that Benny was doing exactly the same now as he had all those years ago at the ghost house. He was dragging Ash after him by the sheer force of his character.

When they reached the first balcony, they stopped to rest. From this height they could see the flames from the accident and the flickering blue lights of the fire engines.

'C'mon.'

'No, Benny. That's it. It's got to stop.'

Benny grabbed Ash's shoulders, holding himself up, his fingers digging into the flesh. He opened his mouth but no sound came out, his lips were frozen in a silent, shocked O. Ash felt something behind him, that's all he could say, it wasn't a sound, or a smell, just a feeling, and he turned as a length of steel pipe slashed past his face and hit Benny before bouncing off the edge of the balcony.

Vernon shouted, 'Yardies!'

Benny howled and staggered back, falling with a cry.

'Hello, Martin. Time to pay.'

Ash looked at the face. It smiled and showed a lot of little teeth. 'Remember me?'

The pipe rose, knuckles gleaming white with strain, and came crashing down again, ripping Ash's shirt. He leaped back, away from this madman and caught his feet in Benny's legs, crashing down beside his cousin. He could hear Vernon whimpering somewhere in the dark.

Deevers stepped forward. 'Oh, you've been so lucky tonight, Martin. Such a pity it isn't going to last.'

They'd ordered chicken cooked in cream and Mike, feeling relaxed, had suggested that Josette might like to choose the wine. She picked a Condrieu, and Mike was a little miffed, since he rather prided himself on his knowledge of wine and didn't know this one. She told him it was grown on less than forty acres in the village of Condrieu on the Rhone, and that Monsieur Robert, who produced this particular vintage, was the best grower.

As they drank, she praised its spicy apricot taste. Mike thought it was more like overdone sausages, and having seen the price he wondered why he'd just spent nearly forty pounds on something he could've got from the hospital canteen for forty pence.

'It's lovely,' he said. 'A real discovery.'

Josette looked at him over a forkful of chicken, her eyes huge and so beautiful, and it came to Mike exactly why he was paying for the wine and the meal. Because you don't usually get the chance to eat with a star. There was another reason, of course, but that was a question he wasn't even prepared to ask himself yet, let alone answer.

'We discovered the village two years ago when we were on holiday. At that time they didn't export their wine.'

The hovering waiter refilled her glass. It was that kind of restaurant, the kind at which she was evidently used to eating. He wondered who usually picked up the tab, then dismissed the thought as being sexist. She was quite capable of paying for herself. 'So,' he asked, 'how did you get into statistics?'

'Like a lot of people. I fell into it.'

'I can't believe you'd just fall into anything, Josette.'

'Do I seem like a designing woman, Mike?'

'I don't mean that, not exactly,' he said. 'I suppose I find it difficult to see how you can apply numbers to medicine.'

'It's easy enough to do it. Don't you mean that you can't see *why*? What would you say, that medicine is a mixture of art and science? That there is no way to calculate patient flow, so why are we trying to do it?'

'You took the words right out of my mouth.'

There was the faintest hint of a smile on her lips and he had the impression she was way ahead of him. He went on: 'I don't know that I really want to talk about work. Spoils the pleasure of the meal, doesn't it?'

'Well, tell me about you, Mike.'

'What's to tell? I went to school, did some sports, failed my A-levels.'

'There you are, that's interesting. A doctor who failed his A-levels. Go on.'

He felt uncomfortable, as he always did when talking about himself. 'Well, after I messed them up, things were pretty difficult at home.'

'Your parents were disappointed?'

'They wanted me to succeed. That's reasonable, isn't it? Maybe they wanted too much. Anyway, I cut and ran. I went round the world. It was easier then, fewer civil wars, less disruption. Europe, Israel, Iran. This was before the Shah left. Russia, now that was fascinating. Hard to get visas and travel permits, but once I was in the country, people were so kind. I was in Georgia where they still thought Stalin was a hero. It was a whole country, a different culture, which nobody had seen for years.'

He talked on, telling Josette about his adventures and his return and eventual decision to go for medicine. She was a good listener, able to draw people out, encourage them, ask exactly the right question to bring out a funny or sad story. In fact she had the ability to make him feel that he was sharper, brighter, funnier than in fact he was; and as the meal went on he began to see her not only as a beautiful woman but as someone who understood him in a way that no one else, not even his wife Frances, ever had. That this was because she was flattering him outrageously didn't actually penetrate his mind.

'So there I was, faced with a choice. Should I go to Norwich General or come to Holby?' He looked down at the tablecloth, strewn with crumbs, and missed the yawn that Josette tactfully hid behind her hand.

The waiter placed the bill beside him and murmured, 'Would you care for any more coffee, sir, madam?'

Checking the price, without service charge, he thought of asking for a brandy – a double. Instead he shook his head. 'Josette?'

'Not for me, thank you, Mike.'

He added a tip to the bill and handed over his credit card. He wondered what he'd say to Frances if she happened to check the statement. 'What's this one, Mickey? A dinner for £175? Were you taking the department out?' Well, better not to think about that.

'OK?' Josette stood, smoothing her skirt over her hips. As he followed her out Mike felt a surge of pure desire and realised that in the most basic way, he wanted this woman and had drunk enough tonight to try and get her, whatever the consequences.

In the taxi they kissed, a long electric moment which brought every nerve in his body alive. He ran his hand down her back, feeling her heat through the thin silk of her dress. 'Josette.' His lips moved against her face. She put her fingers against them, stopping his words. He began to kiss them working down to her palm.

She said, 'Here will be fine, thank you.'

The taxi stopped. Mike saw that they were in front of her hotel.

'Thank you for a lovely evening, Mike.' She opened the door.

'Josette . . .' He went to follow her.

'Better not, Mike. You're not quite in a fit state for public consumption.'

'I thought . . .'

'Mike, you're married, remember? You told me all about Frances.'

Had he?

'I'm not in the business of coming between husbands and wives.' She laughed, a delicious sound that almost made him throw himself out of the cab, at her feet, consequences be damned.

'Whooa, boy. Goodnight.' She shut the door and walked inside.

'Where to, guv?' the cabby asked. 'I don't reckon the cold showers are open this time of night.'

He couldn't go home. He'd never sleep. Might as well go back to the department and catch up on some of his admin. 'Holby General, Casualty entrance,' he snapped out.

'Blimey, mate, not that bad, is it?'

'Just drive!'

23

Ash rolled frantically to one side. The pipe came hissing past his face and Benny screamed. The sound was lost in an immeasurably greater noise as thunder crashed across the sky and rain began to lance down. In seconds the balcony was awash, the concrete slippery underfoot, the rain so hard it was splashing back to waist height, creating a mist of water that made it impossible to see anything clearly.

A boot jammed against Ash's back, trapping him against the wall. 'Now, Martin.'

He wanted to shout, NO!

Instead he heard another voice, not his own, not Benny's or Deevers'. A harsh, bellowing 'Aaaaarrrrgh!' As lightning slashed across the darkness he made out an orange shape rushing through the curtain of rain, arms flailing wildly. It hit Deevers full tilt, crushing him against the crumbling balcony wall. Ash felt the whole thing shudder.

'What the hell?' Deevers was shouting too, trying to free himself from the arms that had been locked round him.

'Come on, lads! We'll show these bastards how the British army fights. Take 'em, Sam. Back up, lads, back up.'

His own arms trapped, Deevers began to kick and headbutt, making no impression at all. Ash clambered to his knees and grabbed Benny under the arms. Vernon appeared beside him and they began to pull the wounded man away from the struggle.

'It's my mind, it's my mind, you bastards. Leave it alone!'

'I don't want your bloody mind,' Deevers snarled, biting down on Scrubbs' ear with all the strength of his jaw. There was a roar of agony and the smaller man was shaken like a rat in a dog's mouth then lifted bodily off his feet and swung against the wall. Glass smashed and tinkled as it fell. Scrubbs began to sing wildly: 'Three German officers crossed the line, Parlez Voo.'

'You're crushing my bloody ribs!' Deevers bellowed as the grip round his waist tightened.

'Three German officers crossed the line, Parlez Voo.' Thunder crashed again and Scrubbs froze, his huge white face peering up into the rain.

Deevers managed to get a hand free and began pounding Scrubbs' skull. 'No, my head, my head!' Scrubbs let go of the wildly struggling figure and, grasping his head, began to spin round where he stood, his feet skidding on the slippery surface. Deevers scrambled to his feet, took a step back and, two-handed, slammed the staggering orange giant in the guts with the steel pipe.

Scrubbs stood there a moment, the blood and rain washing down his face. 'Well, me old mucker,' he said, and fell sideways, hitting the balcony wall. It shuddered and gave way and he plunged into the darkness.

'Christ!' Ash crawled to the edge and looked down. A siren sounded and powerful headlamp beams scythed through the rain, coming to rest on the figure sprawled there below.

Vernon craned over and shouted against the crash of the storm.

'It's the cops, man.' They were all soaked to the skin by now and the balcony was inches deep in running water. Deevers was nowhere to be seen.

Benny was only half conscious. A blow from the pipe had done something bad to the wound. 'Why cops? What happened?'

Ash tried to make out how serious the damage was; lights had been switched on in the flats but the rain was still too heavy to see through. 'Benny, it had to happen. A small army smashed into your place. Somebody was going to call the police. Vernon.' The kid looked at him, his face streaked with blood. 'Can you get upstairs and let your sister out of the bathroom?'

'I can handle that.'

'Then do it. And get the pillow from Benny's bed and bring it down here.'

'Yeah, you're my man,' Benny groaned. 'We'll leave 'em all. Just you and me, Marty. The old team.'

Feet sounded on the fire escape.

'No, Benny, that's all over now. It's time to face up to what you've done.'

'You can't do this to me, Marty. I held the rope for you.'

'And I held it for you – for too long,' Ash said. 'Now I'm cutting it loose.'

He stood up, blinking in the light of the policeman's torch. 'Over here. This man is sick, he needs a hospital.'

'So does half this estate, mate,' the officer answered. 'And who are you, anyway?'

'I'm a nurse. I need an ambulance now!'

The officer called down. 'Terry, get on to the medics. We need another ambulance.'

Helen Chatsworth enjoyed night duty in Casualty. It gave her time to catch up on her work since patient demand was generally low, except on Friday and Saturday nights. Her first few weeks in the department as a Project 2000 had been pretty hairy at times and she knew that Sara Eeles, who was doing days, was finding the whole thing something of a struggle.

By now, however, and after a lot of help from Adele, she was beginning to feel she could cope with most of what A and E was likely to throw at her. Helen had just finished putting a dressing on a sprained foot and seen the patient back to Reception when Aruna Sharma, the night SHO, grabbed her.

'Helen, there's been some kind of problem on the Golden Road estate. We've got at least six serious casualties arriving any moment and God knows how many minor injuries. If there's anyone in the rest-room buzz them down immediately.'

'I think I saw Dr Barratt popping in earlier.'

'Where?' The SHO's relief was obvious.

'He said he was going up to his office.'

'Great, thanks.' She flew off, leaving Helen with a half-rolled bandage, muttering, 'Quiet night? Some chance!' as she picked up the internal phone and called through to the rest-room. They were using a couple of agency nurses this shift, which wasn't usually a problem, although working alongside strangers could bog you down if things got frantic.

Mike was deep in a column of figures, all thoughts of Josette mercifully forgotten, when Dr Sharma tapped at the door.

'Come in, Aruna, how's things? I would've popped down but I didn't want to disturb you.'

'Disturb me, Mike,' she said. 'We've got six at least coming in. Serious burns, a bullet wound, concussion. I don't know what else but I need you.'

He shoved the papers back in the drawer and slammed it thankfully. 'You've got me. What's the ETA?'

They hurried down the corridor, hearing the sound of sirens as they went. 'Don't bother with that ETA!'

'Should we alert the burns unit?'

'At this time of night, I don't know. Let's see what we've got first.'

They arrived in Crash just as the first paramedic team burst through the doors. 'Name not known. Mid-twenties. Extensive burns to face and chest as a result of vehicle explosion. He was unconscious when we found him. We gave him twenty milligrams of nubane.'

The figure on the stretcher flung out an arm and shouted: 'My beautiful van,' before lapsing into another language.

'Cubicle three. Helen, please,' said Dr Sharma. 'We'll probably want some fluids. One hundred milligrams of pethidine and some moxoline.' To the paramedics she went on: 'Let's get him through.'

The night sister had appeared beside Mike, acknowledging his presence with a nod as the second stretcher arrived. The stench of burned meat was overpowering; the terribly burned figure hardly resembled a human being at all. There didn't seem to be an inch of flesh that hadn't been charred into blackness.

The paramedic was plainly shocked as he stuttered out his report. Even as he spoke Mike rapped out: 'Twenty milligrams IV omnopon, and I'm going to want the anaesthetist. We won't move him, no point right now.'

The door burst open and more casualties arrived, including a huge figure in an orange suit, another burns victim, an injured boy and a serious face wound.

'Bloody dog,' the paramedic said. 'Chewed his face to hell. No name, though, but about thirty, I'd say. We gave—'

'We're going to need more help on this,' Mike said. 'Give Charlie Fairhead a call and get on to Dr Goodliffe, will you, nurse?'

The agency nurse looked at him blankly.

'Go to Reception, they'll know. Now move it!'

She went. Mike turned all his attention to the burns victim, leaving the sister to take the face. When he saw Ash coming through with yet another stretcher, he said, 'I don't know how you knew but I'm bloody glad you're here.'

'I came from the estate. Golden Road.'

'What happened down there tonight? No, tell me later. Just get stuck in for now.'

In Reception the agency nurse found a crowd from the Horn of Plenty, most of them well on the way to being aggressively drunk (not that there were many other ways to do it on the Golden Road estate), all of them demanding immediate treatment for injuries sustained from fragments of the exploding kebab van. There was also a gang of kids, two of them totally bald with slight burns, and all of them almost out of their minds with excitement. The crush and the noise was indescribable and it took the receptionist, an older woman in the mould of the late lamented Norma, almost ten minutes before she had them sitting reasonably quietly waiting for the treatment that would arrive in its own good time.

'Hmm, think they can walk in here without a by-your-leave. Well, not while I'm on duty. Yes, dear? Call Mr Fairhead and Dr Goodliffe? Well, they won't like it but . . . Oh, I see, Dr Barratt said so. Well, in that case . . .'

She picked up the phone and dialled while the nurse plunged back into the department, ignoring the wolf whistles from the heaving crowd.

'I'm concerned about his airway, Christine,' Mike told the anaesthetist. 'I'd like you to put a tube down for us.'

'Sure thing. Let's do it. I don't know if you have any

258

long-term prognosis. Are you going to refer him to the burns unit?'

'No, I don't think there's any point,' Mike whispered, 'with seventy per cent full thickness burns – well, he's dying, Chris. I don't think we can do more than make him as comfortable as possible. I've got IV omnopon and I'm thinking of an escherotomy.'

'That would make sense.' The anaesthetist was already working, intubating to clear the throat and lungs, though it was obvious to both of them that the interior damage was almost as severe as the exterior. The flesh had been cooked crisp, like an overdone joint, and was restricting the movements of the chest, and thus the breathing, as well as shrinking and crushing the tissue beneath.

Mike knew that an escherotomy could relieve this pressure, so, taking a scalpel, he began to make deep cuts in the crisp, blackened flesh, opening it up like the crackling on roast pork. He cut across the forehead, the chest and flanks and down the arms and legs, allowing the less cooked tissue the freedom to move.

'OK, the tube's in, Mike. Anything else?'

'Relatives. We'll need them. Have we got any kind of identity?' he asked the agency nurse, who had been watching her first escherotomy with horrified fascination.

'I think he's something to do with those boys in Reception.'

'See if he is, will you? And try and get an address.'

In cubicle three Dr Sharma and Helen were working with Mehmet Ali. His burns were, on examination, less serious than had at first been thought. Painkilling injections had been administered and they were irrigating the burned area with a saline solution to cool it down.

The patient was still unconscious, occasionally moaning

or murmuring in a language they couldn't understand. There were services available for translation but first they had to work out which language he was speaking. They decided to leave this problem for later.

Helen had ascertained that the patient had a collar-bone injury and had sustained a fracture in the ulna, the small bone in the lower arm, but these could be treated with comparative ease. Dr Sharma left Helen to deal with these while she saw to the facial injuries, which were a good deal more urgent.

'I'll want blood tests and cross-matching, and we'll have some anti-toxin in case of tetanus,' she murmured to the CNS assisting her, and then got to work trying to clean up the ruined face and see what might still be usable for the eventual rebuilding that the plastic surgeon would carry out. She knew that prompt action now could save hours of work later.

Charlie Fairhead had arrived just before Karen and both of them had slipped into the routine without complaint. Charlie was working with the third burns case, while Karen had checked with Mike and then gone to the gunshot and gangrene, where she found Ash.

The two of them worked quietly and efficiently together. Ash told her the history of the case as far as he knew it.

'You shouldn't really be attending a relative,' she said, clearing debris from the wound. 'This is going to need surgery, you realise that?'

'As soon as I noticed the smell.'

'It's incredible, it shouldn't happen in this day and age. But then, I s'pose, people shouldn't get shot. We'll want his blood group, I don't s'pose you know it off-hand?'

'Do you know your cousin's blood group?'

'I don't know my cousin. Look, swabs here and here. I

wonder if some of this might be infarction rather than gangrene? The colouration doesn't seem to indicate . . .' She shook her head, 'I'm still not properly awake. It doesn't matter, we can check later for that. Ash.'

He was inserting a cannula, concentrating so he didn't see her face. 'Yeah?'

'Your man Taylor came round tonight. To my flat. He wanted me to support some kind of writ he's issuing because you went to his shop. He says you were aggressive, that you threatened him.'

'I was angry. I should think anyone would be. Mr Bryant had died. He didn't have to. It was Taylor's fault.'

'I just wanted to say that I told him to go to hell. I was thinking about it, about how I behaved with you. I was wrong. I should've listened, and if I'd been more open to suggestion you wouldn't have needed to go to see Mike.'

'Can I have that in writing?' he laughed. 'It must be the first time you've ever admitted it.'

'Don't push your luck, Ash, take it while it's on offer.'

He looked up from the cannula and saw that her expression was earnest and serious. 'I do. Thanks, Karen.'

'I'll tell Mark tomorrow that I want to withdraw the complaint. Anyway, I don't think it would actually have gone against you. Taylor obviously issued the wrong prescription.'

'How do you prove that, though?'

Benny groaned and flicked his eyes open. He focused on Karen. 'Hey, what happened? Some guy was going crazy. Everything sort of fell.' He tried to move and groaned in pain. Karen held him down.

'You must stay still. We're going to move you to the surgical ward as soon as we can, they'll be able to make you more comfortable.'

He shut his eyes. 'I don't want to be comfortable, I want to be rich. You still here, Marty?'

'I'm here.'

'The stuff, what happened to it?'

'The police have got it, Benny. I gave it to them.'

'Why, man, why?'

'There'll be no reason for the others to go after Susie and Vernon.'

Karen cut in. 'You shouldn't be talking.'

'I shouldn't be here, sister. I reallyyyyy . . .' His eyes glazed over and he slipped into unconsciousness as the IV analgesic kicked in.

'They'll have to do an exploratory to check on the bullet. It doesn't seem to have touched anything vital but we'll need to see. You got him to us just in time, I'd say, Ash. I think he owes you a lot.'

'I think he'll owe me about five years with remission for good behaviour, if he's lucky.'

Dr Sharma looked into the cubicle. 'Karen, can you give Charlie a moment with the burns case in cubicle four?'

'On my way.'

'Aruna,' Ash grabbed her before she went. 'The old man, Scrubbs.'

'Scrubbs?'

'The concussion. Where is he?'

'Six, I think. I don't know if anyone's had time to fill in the board yet.'

He went through to Admin and checked. The department was crowded with lumps and bumps being ferried in and out of cubicles or treated anywhere there was space. Nurses, HCAs, even the night porter, a man who made Frankie seem shy and retiring, were rushing between cases, trying to sort them according to the system. Against the general bedlam, the sound of the rain was no longer so loud. The storm was beginning to pass and the atmosphere didn't have that oppressive feel which had been so uncomfortable over the last few days.

The board was full but Scrubbs hadn't been written up yet so Ash went and looked in number six. The sister was with him. She was an old friend. Many a night Scrubbs had wandered into A and E, been given a tea or a coffee and sent on his way with a kind word or two.

'How is he?' Ash asked.

She shrugged. 'Concussion. We'll have to watch for compression, that's if he'll stay around. I don't know. But then I never knew how he managed to keep going as long as he has. These overalls, they're paramedic issue. Where did he get them?'

'He must've taken them when he went off yesterday. He left his own clothes and grabbed these, I suppose. Probably a bit of an improvement.'

'Do you know what happened?'

'I think Mr Scrubbs saved my life this evening.'

On the cot the ungainly figure stirred. 'Reporting for duty, sir. Sar'nt-Major Scrubbs, discharged by the MO fit and ready for active service. Sah!' Then he began to snore.

'He fell from what, twenty feet on to hard earth?' the sister asked. 'It's a miracle he didn't break everything, never mind something.'

'Probably the drink, relaxes the muscles, he would have fallen like a rag doll.'

'Cue for Tina Turner. I think we can leave Mr Scrubbs for the moment.' She hurried out.

Ash waited a while then, sure he was alone, gave a quick salute. 'Thank you, Sergeant-Major.'

The ventilator was barely moving. The vital signs were no more than a glimmer. Mike stood by the head of the bed.

'He's slipping away, Chris.'

The anaesthetist flicked a glance at the instruments. 'That's the best thing. He was never coming through it.'

The agency nurse came in. 'Mr Fairhead has been checking with the boys. There's a mother, apparently. We tried to get her but there was no phone. We asked the police to call but she was drunk and didn't want to know. The boys in Reception told me his name was Iceman. That's all. No other name. Nothing.' The woman was trying to keep her emotions under control.

'Thank you, nurse. That's all.'

She left. The two doctors looked at the shape on the bed. Mike noted the time and wrote it on the notes. 'Three am. I think that's it now, if you agree, Christine?'

'Yeah, that's it. I'll call the mortuary porter on my way out. Do you want to grab lunch some time this week? There's some BMA business we ought to discuss.'

Mike pulled the sheet up. 'Yup, fine. As long as I don't have to pay for the meal.'

'Why, you're not usually a tight-wad.'

'Let's say I spent a lot of money tonight and had a close escape.'

'The famous Barratt charm get you into trouble?'

'Just the famous Barratt credit card.' They went through to Admin. Charlie cornered them as they entered. 'The other burns are both stabilised. We should be able to do a chart and send them up to burns ward first thing.'

'Great, thank you, Charlie.' The crush around them was slightly less now. Mike went on: 'Things seem to be calming down a bit. I think the night shift can handle it now. We'd better be heading home for a couple of hours' sleep before we start again. Thanks for coming in. Tell Karen thanks too, and Ash. Or was he here anyway?'

'Better not ask right now.'

Aruna Sharma went past with a big grin on her face. She aimed a pistol finger at Mike. 'It's Turkish!'

'What is?'

'Mr Mehmet Ali's language. Except he speaks English

too, so we don't need a translator. His wife is coming in with, from what I could work out, about a hundred relatives in tow.'

'I'm off, anyway.'

'OK, thanks. Should I tell the police about the dog attack? Ash said the animal had been put down already.'

'What has that man been up to?' Charlie said.

'What has who been up to?' Ash asked as he came in with more Hartmanns.

'You, Mr Ashford,' Charlie said. 'It sounds like you've been mixed up in a gangster film.'

'I'll tell you tomorrow.' He put the bottle in the fridge. 'I'm heading home.'

'You want a lift?'

'I promise, Charlie, one day I will get my car working again.'

'Get out of here, you two,' Mike said, 'before we get a train crash or a couple of jumbo jets falling out of the sky.'

'Yeah, well if they do,' Charlie said, 'they'll do it on us.'

24

Driving back through the empty town, Ash was cocooned in a bubble of weariness. The rain had stopped, streetlamps cast an unearthly orange glow over the slick tarmac and puddled concrete pavements and the late-night music playing on the car radio was smooth, like a glass surface you couldn't get a hold on.

'OK, sleeping ugly . . .'

'What?' He came awake with his heart in his mouth.

'Home. You want to sleep in the car, that's fine, but I think you'd find your bed more comfortable, even for the few measly minutes you've got before I see you again.'

'Yeah. Great, thanks, Charlie. I promise—'

'You'll get your car working soon. I know. Night, Ash.'

'Night.'

He slammed the car door, let himself into the communal hall and began to climb the stairs to his room. His body ached all over, it ached on the aches, he felt like taking a hot bath for a month. Then sleeping for a year.

He let himself in and reached for the light switch. A hand took his and squeezed. 'Hello Martin. Remember me?'

A fist slammed into his stomach. He doubled over, the breath driven from his body, then felt himself lifted and flung across the room on to the settee. It skidded back across the floor and cannoned into the hi-fi stack. The light went on, painfully bright after the darkness, and there was the man with the small teeth. 'Thought I'd gone away, eh?'

Ash shook his head and tried to clear it. 'What do you want?'

'I want you, Martin, I want you to beg me, I want you to plead: please, Mr Deevers, let me go. I want to hear you hurting, Martin, like Sherry hurt. I want to hear you scream like she screamed.'

He pulled himself up against the back of the settee. His stomach ached like hell but he had to think. 'You phoned me up, didn't you?'

Deevers grinned and shut the door quietly, flipping the snib on the lock. 'That's right. It was me.'

'You were here before, in this flat?'

Deevers stepped across the room until he was halfway between Ash and the door. 'That's right, it was me.'

'Why?' He was beginning to get his breath back but looking at Deevers, it was plain that in a fight the other man would win. His muscles stood out from his squat body like steel wire; he was literally humming with tension.

'I wanted to get to know you, Martin, get inside your life. Find out where it would hurt the most.'

'Is that why you tried to run my mother down?'

'I would've got the old bat too, if that stupid guy hadn't been there.'

'Why?' It was uncanny. The man was talking about murder like missing a train. 'You're crazy.'

'No, Martin, I'm just very angry about what you did to my Sherry. And I'm afraid you're going to have to pay for it.'

He was across the room in an eye-blink, grabbing Ash almost carefully by the shirt-front to pull him up so they

267

were standing face to face. Being this close, Ash could smell him and he stank of electricity, a sharp ozone smell that oozed out of his pores.

'Stop it.' Ash spoke as calmly as he could. 'There's no need to do this; once you've done it, you can't go back. Nothing is going to be the same.'

'You killed Sherry.'

'No. You killed Sherry.'

He was lifted and thrown back on the settee. Deevers stood there in the middle of the floor, his fists clenched, his brows clamped down over shut eyes, but Ash knew that if he tried to take advantage, the man would be on him in a second.

'No, Martin, you killed her, with your questions. Your dirty, sneaky little questions.'

'Why were they sneaky? Why were they dirty?'

'You know why.'

'I don't.' He could hear his voice trembling with effort and tension and maybe with fear, too. 'Why don't you tell me?'

'I don't know anything. It was you, Martin, all of you in your uniforms and your white coats, thinking you're so marvellous.'

'What questions didn't you like?'

'Your questions, Martin.'

'What didn't you like about them?'

'You had no call to ask them. No right. She was mine, not yours. Oh, she knew, yes she did, she kept her mouth shut. She always kept her mouth shut until you started asking questions.'

'It had happened before, hadn't it? Sherry ending up in hospital, being hurt. And she never told.'

'Never. She knew what was right.'

'That you could hit her any time you wanted?'

'It was punishment. She deserved it. She knew she did. Oh yes, even when she went away, she knew she had to come back. She needed what I gave her. And you, putting ideas in her head, spoiling it all.'

He wasn't going to get through with rational argument, that was clear. Deevers was crazy, probably certifiable. Ash had noticed that smell before, rising off paranoid schizophrenics, and he had no doubt that this man was living in a world in which his behaviour was perfectly rational and sensible.

'I think we've talked enough.' Deevers opened his eyes. There didn't seem to be any whites to them at all, they were like red holes in his face. 'I've given you the chance to explain. Now it's time to beg, Martin. I want you on your knees. I WANT YOU ON YOUR KNEES!' He screamed. 'NOW.'

Ash would never have said he was a violent man. Sure he could get angry about injustice, he could fight a union case through a tribunal, he could give and take with the best of them in a tough game of street hockey, but sudden, overwhelming violence was not, he would have maintained, his scene.

Deevers grabbed him by the shoulders and forced him to his knees in front of the sofa. 'Now beg her forgiveness. Say it: Sherry, please forgive me. SAY IT. Mr Deevers, please don't hurt me.'

'Mr Deevers,' Ash began, 'I've had one hell of a day and this just about tops it.' He came up off his knees like a rocket, his head catching Deevers under the chin, shutting his sharp little teeth like a trap on his tongue.

'You bastard. You hurt me!' Deevers whined through bloodied lips.

Ash stood back. 'That's right, I hurt you.' He bunched his fist and launched it into Deevers' face.

'Now I want you to think of this as purely therapeutic,' Ash said, hitting him again, this time in the solar plexus. Deevers looked puzzled. No one had ever done this to him before. Then he began to crumble, slipping slowly to the floor. Ash caught him as he went down and lowered him gently the last few inches.

He went through to the kitchen and found a newspaper which he put under Deevers' head to stop the blood staining the carpet, then picked up the phone and dialled.

'Hello, Holby Casualty? I need an ambulance.'

It was mid-morning before the police had finished with him. The inspector who had taken the interview had said: 'Mr Ashford, what are you, a one-man crime wave?'

'Look, I didn't do anything,' he protested. 'OK, I should have reported my cousin earlier, but I didn't know about the drugs until the last moment. Once I knew he had them, then my mind was clear. I was going to report it.'

'I accept that. And I can understand that your primary duty was medical, but why didn't you get him into hospital earlier?'

'Because we're not the police, Inspector. We can't make people go to hospital. It's their choice, just like they can walk out whenever they want, unless two psychiatrists and a social worker get them committed by a court.'

'Like your man Deevers?'

'Not my man.'

'You certainly taught him a lesson he won't forget in a hurry.'

'I think I was going hypo. You know, I'm diabetic and if I don't take my medication at the proper times, things can go a bit wild. And it had been a long day.'

'It had.'

'Will you be arresting Benny?'

'Yes. To tell the truth, we're more interested in the Yardies. The other gang. If your cousin co-operates, he could find the courts going a little easier on him.'

'I think he'd do anything to get out of trouble. What about Mr Deevers?'

'He won't be going anywhere for a while.'

'I think he's insane. Really, I mean, he should be in a hospital, not out on the streets or in a prison.'

'That'll be for the court to decide. You'll be wanted, obviously, to give evidence. In both cases. I'd say you're going to be something of a legal star, Mr Ashford.'

'Thank you, but I could do without it, Inspector.'

He got back to Holby in time to grab a snack in the canteen. Mike was there eating overdone sausages on his own. Ash joined him at the table.

'Get everything settled with the police?'

'For the time being. Ah, not lunching with Josette? I didn't have time last night to ask how the dinner went.'

Mike examined the burned end of a sausage closely, severed it with a transverse slash of his knife and positioned it firmly on the tines of his fork. 'Fine, it was fine. Just colleagues, Ash, that's all. I thought we owed it to her.' He popped the sausage into his mouth and began to chew.

Ash bit into his cheese and pickle sandwich. 'Good. I thought she was leaning a little too far towards the management view of the department. I'm glad you were putting our case to her.'

'Yes, I think I did a pretty good job.' He stopped chewing. 'This sausage is gristly,' he said through a full mouth. 'Still, at least it's cheap. Now, Ash, this business of Karen's.'

'The complaint? She spoke to me last night. Old man Taylor called on her. I think he rubbed her up the wrong way and she's dropping it.'

'That's good, but you know Taylor has been in touch with Mark Calder and Mrs Kingston.'

'No, I didn't know that.' He put the half-eaten sand-wich back on his plate. Suddenly he didn't feel hungry.

'I'm afraid so. Now, I don't think the man has a leg to stand on but Mark is running round in ever-decreasing circles squawking about Holby being sued for massive damages etcetera, etcetera.'

'That sounds like Mark.'

'Anyway, he and Mrs Kingston want to see us, that's you and me, at three pm. I told them we'd all been up most of the night and it might be thoughtful if they let us go home as soon as our shift is over but you know what they're like.'

'All too well, Mike.' One more problem he could do without. Still, now that Karen had come round to his side, they might actually be able to do something about Taylor, before he mixed up another prescription. He pulled himself to his feet, yawning. 'I'd better get back down there, anyway, Mike. Enjoy your sausages.'

There were a couple of lumps and bumps in Reception, both of whom had been diagnosed by Frankie as malignant tumours. Ash told the porter that he was certainly malignant and probably a tumour, too.

'Nah, me old mate. I've been on a course.'

They were standing at the reception desk. Frankie went on: 'Bin telling Mie about it.'

The receptionist nodded. 'It's quite amazing how he knows these things. Just like that, he can look and right away he understands.'

'What kind of course, Frankie?'

'St John Ambulance. First aid. That's right. Passed first time an' all.' He tapped his head: 'Up here for thinking,' and did a little dance. 'Down there for dancing.'

'Well, maybe I'd better have a peek at the patients any-way. Just to be sure.'

'Be my guest.'

After seeing them he checked on Scrubbs, who had

been moved back upstairs to his old ward. It seemed he was quite popular and at least one elderly lady had immediately started delivering cups of tea to his bedside.

Benny had been moved to Surgical and was being operated on that afternoon. The surgical team saw no particular problems in his case. Ash knew he'd have to go and see his cousin and he felt that the meeting would be anything but easy. Still, he had cut himself free from that rope at long last and wasn't about to get re-attached.

Wiping the lumps and bumps off the board he saw Karen talking earnestly with the young mother who had brought in the child suffering from heatstroke yesterday. Looking out now at the grey lowering skies, it was hard to imagine that they'd been sweltering under a heatwave only hours before.

'A bit cooler, and that's an improvement.' Adele arrived with a green laundry sack which she dumped in the corner. 'I shouldn't be carrying this. It's a waste.'

'Absolutely, Adele.'

'I hear you had a busy night.'

'A few ups and down. Nothing out of the ordinary.'

'I'll believe that when I see it. Nothing is ordinary in this place! Ah well. Carry dat sack, tote dat bale.' She hefted the laundry bag and staggered off. For a moment she reminded Ash of the elephants in the Munchausen movie, each carrying a towering mobile fort. Then it struck him.

'Karen.'

She turned from her conversation. 'Can it wait a moment, Ash, I'm talking to someone.'

'No, no it can't. Look, just one moment.' To the mother he said, 'I'm terribly sorry, but something has come up and I must talk to Dr Goodliffe for a second.'

'Please, that's all right. I'll wait in Reception, Doctor.'

Karen didn't look pleased at being interrupted. 'I hope it's a good one, Ash.'

'Yeah, I know, you don't want to have to report me again.'

She had the grace to blush at that. 'I'm sorry. I hear that you and Mike are seeing the all powerful two this afternoon?'

'Yes. It should be interesting. But not very. There's not a lot to worry about, I hope. Anyway, that isn't why I cut in. The child, the heatstroke case.'

'Hmm, she's in children's ward at the moment. We'll discharge her later today.'

'What about Social Services?'

'I've been thinking about that. I called the GP yesterday and he says that the child, Carly, is always in and out of the surgery with something or other. Not that he can find any evidence of abuse. He knows the family, there don't seem to be any problems. He's spent time with the girl, I've spent time with the girl. Everything is fine.'

'Except she keeps having accidents?'

'Some people are clumsy. Why? Do you know something I don't?' she asked.

'Last night I was running a video.'

'Well that's great, Ash. I'm glad you have at least some time for relaxing.'

He grinned. '*Adventures of Baron Munchausen.*'

'Fine. I've seen it, it's OK, yeah.' She was, frankly, puzzled.

'Munchausen's syndrome by proxy!'

'OK, Ash, I'll bite. What is it?' she said. 'Tell me, though I've got a feeling I'm going to regret it.'

'No way,' he said. 'It's going to make your name in the department. In the hospital. The diagnostic coup of the year.'

'Don't keep me in suspense, Dr Schweitzer. What is it?'

'A syndrome in which the parent creates illness or

accident in the child and, through them, seeks attention and treatment.'

'Hold on, that was the Beverley Allitt case. Oh, come on, Ash, that was serious stuff. Murder, the whole can of worms.'

'Yeah, I know, but it's not always so spectacular. What if your patient's mother has the beginnings of the syndrome? If you can catch it now, before it becomes pathological, you could save mother and child a lot of problems in future.'

'Well, I don't know.'

Would she, he wondered, accept his suggestion? Had she really changed in the two days since the Bryant case, or was all the old resentment of the junior doctor faced with an experienced nurse about to flare up again? Her face betrayed nothing.

Then she laughed. 'Thanks, Ash. I can use that. I really think it might help in this case.'

25

Mark Calder's desk was clear. He sat behind it rather like Napoleon surveying his empire. Mrs Kingston sat to one side, almost as an observer. Ash and Mike were both given straight-backed chairs facing the desk, like naughty kids.

Mike, for one, was in no mood for play-acting. 'Well, here we are, Mark, Mrs Kingston. Can we start this meeting now?'

'I'd like to establish one or two guidelines before we actually begin,' Mark said. He looked across to Mrs Kingston and she nodded.

'Yes, we don't want to appear unsupportive of our own staff.'

'I'm sure you don't,' Ash said.

'But at the same time we must give proper weight to a complaint by a member of the public who is also a member of a professional body with which we, as doctors, must deal.'

Mike said, sharply, 'Neither of you are doctors. I am and I feel that, professional body or not, Taylor is an incompetent old fool.'

Mark raised his eyebrows and went smoothly on: 'And that is exactly why this is an informal meeting. No minutes will be taken.'

'You're worried that Taylor will sue us,' Ash cut in. 'It's that simple.'

'Nothing is ever that simple,' Mark said. 'What we have is an elderly man who should retire. He can't face the thought and so he keeps on working. It's irrational. It's understandable, but it is also potentially dangerous. I agree. What we have to do is diffuse the situation and then apply subtle pressure behind the scenes.'

Mrs Kingston stood up and leaned one arm on the bookshelf that ran behind the desk. Her manner was exaggeratedly casual, as if none of this was actually happening and if anyone ever said it had, she would deny it all. 'I've had some contact with colleagues of Mr Taylor's. They agree to, as it were, encourage him to retire at once. They think they can manage this and also persuade Taylor to withdraw his threat to issue a writ against the hospital and personally, against you, Mr Ashford.'

'He really will withdraw?' Mike asked.

'He will,' Mrs Kingston said, 'as long as he receives a letter of apology from Mr Ashford.'

'Oh come on!' Ash was on his feet, furious. 'Are you serious about this? You want me to write . . . a . . . lett . . . errrr . . .?'

His voice tailed off. Mrs Kingston peered at him.

'What is it, are you all right?'

Ash swallowed. It was the loudest sound in the room.

'Don't move,' he whispered.

'What?' Mrs Kingston turned and found herself in an eye-to-eye confrontation with the bird-eating spider, which had just emerged from a heating duct and was squatting on the bookshelf.

'Oh!' she said very quietly, and slid to the floor, cracking her head on the edge of Mark's desk.

Nobody moved.

Except Isabella, who began to flow along the shelf

with that fluid motion that only eight legs can give.

Ash emptied the waste bin, stepped across the room and placed it over the spider. On top if it he piled five thick volumes of the *Medical Directory*. Furious scratching came from under the bin.

'Call the Holby Zoological Society, will you, Mark?'

Mark's fingers seemed strangely rubbery but eventually he managed to press the right buttons, get through and arrange for someone to collect the wandering Isabella.

Meanwhile Ash and Mike checked Mrs Kingston.

'Nasty laceration on the right temple, Ash.'

'Absolutely, Mike. I think we ought to get her to Casualty right away. Do you think we should call for the paramedics?'

Mark interrupted. 'I'm sure we can manage by ourselves. Three grown men and she's not that big.'

'I thought you were staying to keep watch on the spider.'

'Are you kidding, Mike? C'mon, let's get out of here!'

Reception was crowded with Turks – Mehmet Ali's extended family, who had come to support him in his time of trial. Charlie told Ash that the kebab seller had been moved up to the burns unit, although his relatives seemed to have taken root in Casualty. Apparently they were there to 'protect' him from some gang of youths who had been attacking his van. It seemed that they had been the cause of the vehicle fire the night before.

'Still,' Charlie said, 'that's somebody else's problem. I'm off for a long night's sleep. Want a lift?'

'No thanks. I'm meeting Sara Eeles over at cancer ward, then we're going out for a pizza.'

'Good for you. Have fun.' Charlie hurried out.

As Ash made his way through the maze of the hospital, he wondered how things would turn out with Sara.

Better than with Josette Lowell, that was for sure. Mark had been right about that: she was way out of his class.

Sara was waiting outside the sterile area. Her face was pale.

'Ash. Lisa, she . . .'

'What is it?' He pushed past so he could get a glimpse through the protective glass of Lisa's room. It was empty. Just a bed, with the paraphernalia of drips hanging round it. A cleaner was working in there, scrubbing down.

He rested his forehead against the glass, remembering her last angry words to him. Now there would never be a chance to make it up. 'She knew it would happen,' he said. 'She said they were close. The people from the stars. She could hear the mother ship sometimes at night hovering over Holby. Last night, all that lightning, and the thunder, she must've thought they'd really come for her at last.' He couldn't see the room properly, everything was blurred.

'Hey, what's up, Doc?'

He spun round. Lisa was grinning under the Jamaican cap, swathed in a dressing-gown, sitting in a wheelchair behind which Angela, the Macmillan nurse, stood with a big smile on her face. 'They let me out early, Doc. Time off for good behaviour.'

'She's responding so well that Dr Small said she could come out of isolation this morning. I said it's because she's got such an ace team behind her.'

'Hey, Doc,' Lisa said. 'What's up?'

Ash shook his head. He couldn't find the words to answer her. 'C'mon, Doc, you're not gonna get all soppy on me, are you?'

'Who, me?' he growled. 'No way. Tough as nails, kid, that's Ash. Still, I'm glad to see you.'

She held up a paperback, the one he'd lent her, with the brightly coloured painting of dragons on its cover.

'You said there were another fifteen in the series. So just keep 'em coming.' She yawned hugely. 'Oh yeah, I got another one for you. What's the difference between . . .' she yawned again and her eyes began to shut. 'Um . . . what's the diff . . .' she smiled, her eyelids flickered closed and she was asleep.

'It's been an exciting day,' Angela whispered. 'She needs to catch up on her rest. Come back tomorrow.' She wheeled the tiny figure away. Ash looked at the book he'd taken from her and shoved it into his pocket.

Sara said: 'You really thought she was . . .'

'I suppose I did for a moment.'

'You were crying?'

'Ironman Ashford never cries. Except when the bank bounces his mortgage. or his car breaks down. Or he runs out of clean shirts. Still, what the hell, lose a few, win a few. C'mon, I'll buy you a pizza.'

'What topping?'

'Everything topping,' he laughed, and slipped his arm through hers. 'We'll celebrate for Lisa and then we'll go and play street hockey.'

Epilogue

Benny came through his operation well and decided to co-operate fully with the police. He received a three-year sentence and is a model prisoner. He is currently studying financial management and hopes to take a full-time course on his release.

Susie took her baby back to her parents in Liverpool. She doesn't visit Benny and sent back his letters unopened. Eventually he stopped writing. Vernon went back with her and is still at school.

Mrs Bryant decided not to take out an action against Mr Taylor. She sold up and moved to a bungalow in Devon.

Mr Taylor received his apology from Ash and took the retirement that was pressed upon him. His fellow chemists celebrated the event with a dinner at which Mr Taylor's long and unstinting service to the community was praised.

Ray Deevers was sentenced to be held at Her Majesty's Pleasure and transferred to a secure hospital. Here he got into an argument with a fellow inmate over some trivial dispute and was stabbed with a sharpened spoon.

He was rushed to his local A and E unit (not Holby), where he died.

Sergeant-Major Scrubbs was discharged from hospital after a month. He used his accumulated benefit to go on a bender of heroic proportions. He has not returned to the hospital since, nor has he been seen locally.

Janice Parker discussed her problems with Dr Goodliffe and decided to undergo psychotherapy. After a few months she felt that what she really needed was a job that made her feel useful. She returned to college to study Arts Administration and is doing well. Carly's accident rate has fallen to that of a normal seven-year-old. Frank is puzzled by the whole thing and has recently been seeing more of his secretary, a woman as boring as he is himself.

Mehmet Ali recovered and with the insurance pay-out on his old van was able to put down a deposit on a new vehicle. He no longer sells his kebabs on the Golden Road estate.

Gary, Big Jo, Petey, Speeder and the rest still live on the estate and it doesn't look like they'll have much of a chance to move away. Gary now leads the gang. They are still looking for a way to make some fast money.

Josette Lowell completed her survey and returned to her company. She was subsequently offered a directorship which she took up. Occasionally she still remembers that dinner with Mike Barratt and wonders what might have happened if she hadn't sent the ardent doctor off in his taxi.

Dr Brian Rommleson recovered from his ordeal with no ill effects.

Isabella is the proud mother of 121 babies. There were originally 200 but she ate the others before Dr Rommleson could move them to a place of safety.

Lisa Benjamin continued to respond well to her treatment and is now back at school, where her teachers regard her as a very promising pupil. She still sees Ash and hopes to play street hockey when she is fully recovered. She hasn't yet decided if she wants to be a science fiction writer or a doctor, but as Ash said, now she's got the time to decide.

| ☐ Casualty: The Early Years | Laura Waring | £4.50 |
| ☐ Casualty: Swings and Roundabouts | Lynda Del Sasso | £4.50 |

Warner Books now offers an exciting range of quality titles by both established and new authors. All of the books in this series are available from:

   Little, Brown and Company (UK) Limited,
   P.O. Box 11,
   Falmouth,
   Cornwall TR10 9EN.

Alternatively you may fax your order to the above address. Fax No. 0326 376423.

Payments can be made as follows: cheque, postal order (payable to Little, Brown and Company) or by credit cards, Visa/Access. Do not send cash or currency. UK customers and B.F.P.O. please allow £1.00 for postage and packing for the first book, plus 50p for the second book, plus 30p for each additional book up to a maximum charge of £3.00 (7 books plus).

Overseas customers including Ireland, please allow £2.00 for the first book plus £1.00 for the second book, plus 50p for each additional book.

NAME (Block Letters) ....

....

ADDRESS ....

....

....

☐ I enclose my remittance for _____

☐ I wish to pay by Access/Visa Card

Number ☐☐☐☐☐☐☐☐☐☐☐☐☐☐☐☐

Card Expiry Date ☐☐☐☐